She ***stepped out into the encroaching darkness and saw the tall figure that stood nearby.***

Her heart both flutt e. He was the last pers v with her heart so br specter of her past li

"Mark, what are you voice filled with weariness.

"I figured you might like the company on the walk home." He stood in shadows, making it impossible for her to see his features, to gauge his mood.

"It isn't necessary," she replied, forcing a coolness into her tone.

He stepped out of the shadows and into a stream of moonlight that came from the near-full moon overhead. His features were expressionless.

"Actually, it is rather necessary," he replied. "I have some questions to ask you, and I'd much rather do it at your place instead of dragging you down to the courthouse."

Vengeance in Texas: Where heroes are made.

Dear Reader,

It's always exciting to be part of a series of books that involve smart heroines, sexy heroes and danger. I especially love a book where the heroine has a juicy secret in her past…maybe because I've never had a juicy secret!

In *A Profiler's Case for Seduction* you get it all: a woman trying to move away from her shameful past, a hero determined to solve three murders—and when their worlds collide there is danger and passion.

Nothing is what it seems in the small town of Vengeance, Texas, and the twists and turns provide a wild ride.

I loved writing this story and I hope you love reading it.

Happy reading!

Carla Cassidy

CARLA CASSIDY

A Profiler's Case for Seduction

HARLEQUIN® ROMANTIC SUSPENSE

Special thanks and acknowledgment to Carla Cassidy for her contribution to the Vengeance in Texas miniseries.

Recycling programs
for this product may
not exist in your area.

ISBN-13: 978-0-373-27818-3

A PROFILER'S CASE FOR SEDUCTION

Printed in U.S.A.

www.Harlequin.com

Books by Carla Cassidy

Harlequin Romantic Suspense

CARLA CASSIDY

is an award-winning author who has written more than one hundred books for Harlequin Books. In 1995 she won Best Silhouette Romance from *RT Book Reviews* for *Anything for Danny*. In 1998 she also won a Career Achievement Award for Best Innovative Series from *RT Book Reviews*.

Carla believes the only thing better than curling up with a good book to read is sitting down at the computer with a good story to write. She's looking forward to writing many more books and bringing hours of pleasure to readers.

To my brother-in-law,
Michael…just in case he wins the lotto.

Chapter 1

He'd gone rogue.

At least that's what his fellow FBI agents would think if they could see him now, entering one of the college theaters where a lecture was about to begin.

It had been years since FBI agent Mark Flynn had been in such a setting. As he opened the door to the room, heard the chattering of students eager to learn, saw the polished wooden lectern in the center of the stage, he remembered how much he'd loved college and soaking in the knowledge offered by each teacher and every class.

Brainiac, that's what his fellow students had called him when he'd been at university, but it had been his high IQ and his thirst for knowledge that had made him not a trust-fund baby, but rather a think-tank subject for the FBI.

The seating was theater-style and most of the seats

were already taken. Knowing he wasn't going to sit through the entire lecture, he spied an empty spot in one of the last rows and slid into the chair.

He focused intently on the lectern where within minutes sociology professor Melinda Grayson would begin a lecture. He had no idea what the topic of the day might be, although he knew this course was about sociopaths. Still, he wasn't here to listen to what she had to say. He was here to observe, to form impressions and follow through on a gut instinct that had him at odds with most of the other members of his team.

Darby College and the small town of Vengeance, Texas, located forty miles outside Dallas, had been lucky to get a professor as renowned as Melinda Grayson. With her stellar credentials she could have found employment at any college or university in the country.

He found it slightly odd that she had chosen Darby and the small town as her home, but he found most people rather odd in the choices they made and the forces that drove them through life. Certainly he recognized that he was considered more than a little bit odd by many of his friends and coworkers.

The room began to quiet and expectancy shimmered in the air as a young man and woman took two seats that had been left empty in the center of the front row. He instantly identified them as Amanda Burns and Ben Craig, graduate assistants to Melinda.

For a brief instant it was as if everyone in the room had stepped into a vacuum, so great was the silence that stole over the group of students. And then Melinda appeared. She walked with measured strides toward the lectern and began the lesson for the day.

Mark leaned forward, his gaze focused intently on the beautiful woman who commanded the room. Her long black hair flowed across her shoulders and he knew from her photos that her eyes were an intense green. She appeared slightly fragile, tall and almost too thin. The white cast on her left arm only emphasized the appearance of frailty and was a reminder that she was a victim of an alleged crime.

However, there was nothing weak or vulnerable in her strong, low voice or in the way she owned not just the lectern but every space of the stage. Clad in a pencil-thin black skirt, high heels and a red jacket, she was dressed for power, and she had it.

Innocent victim or wildly dangerous?

That was what he needed to figure out about the lovely professor. Right now all he knew was that on September 5, Melinda had been kidnapped. She'd resurfaced almost two and a half weeks later. During her captivity, she'd been beaten and videotaped then released by some unknown perpetrators and, during the time she'd been supposedly held in captivity, three men had been murdered.

To Mark, it all seemed so obvious. She had been "kidnapped" three days before the murders were discovered and all three men had been dead for twenty-four hours when they'd been found. Somehow he believed that she was intrinsically tied to the murders, but there was absolutely no evidence to prove or disprove his theory that she was involved.

She'd taught her first class since her ordeal on Friday, but Mark had been tied up and hadn't been able to attend.

That was why he was here now, watching her, assessing her in an attempt to do what he did best…crawl into the dark mind of a killer. It was this unique ability that had made him a respected name in the bureau, and it was also this ability that had destroyed his marriage two years before and kept him from actively parenting his three-year-old daughter, Grace.

His heart clenched tight at thoughts of his daughter, with her mop of dark curly hair and bright blue eyes. Of all the things good that he'd done in his life, Grace was at the top of the list. The last thing he wanted to do was in any way taint her with the darkness that sometimes gripped his soul.

He jumped as a hand touched his arm. He blinked, tearing his thoughts from his daughter to the woman seated next to him. Long brown hair framed a pretty face with large gray eyes. She was older than the usual student, perhaps in her late thirties, and as she smiled at him a hint of unexpected warmth whispered through him. She had a beautiful smile.

She had a laptop open and held several pieces of paper and a pen toward him. "For taking notes," she whispered, and then smiled again.

Rather than explain to her that he wasn't here to take notes on the lecture, suddenly aware of the faint scent of wildflowers that drifted from her, he took the pen and paper and whispered a quick thank-you.

As he turned his attention back to Melinda he tried to stay focused on her, but his fellow classmate had definitely broken his concentration.

How long had it been since he'd noticed the beauty of a woman's smile? How many years had it been since he'd paid any attention to the fragrance emanating from a particular female? Far too long.

Probably a wife and mother returning to college with her children in school or half-grown, he thought. But a quick glance showed him an unadorned ring finger on her left hand.

Maybe divorced and trying to find herself, get a career going after a few years of marriage. Mark admired anyone who sought education no matter what their age or their circumstances.

He frowned and tried to stay focused on the reason he was sitting here. He shouldn't be so acutely aware of the woman next to him, frantically typing on her laptop as if attempting to memorize every word of the lecture.

It vaguely irritated him that, suddenly, his concentration was divided between the outrageously gorgeous professor commanding the room and the quiet beauty seated next to him.

There was a small group of students at the front of the theater who appeared to be hanging on to every word that fell out of Melinda's mouth. Groupies, he guessed.

Melinda's power and beauty would automatically draw a band of devout followers, but now with the news of her recent kidnapping and beatings, she had risen in stature to rock-star celebrity.

Victim or killer?

He wouldn't discover the answer to that question just by sitting here, and he felt a sudden need to escape from the scent of wildflowers and the two women who were sparring for attention inside his head.

He slid out of his chair and eased out the door and into the hallway that would take him outside the building and into the fresh September air.

Once outside he drew in a deep breath and sat on a nearby concrete bench beneath a large leafy tree. It was only then that he realized he still held the paper and pen that the woman seated next to him had handed him.

He settled back against the bench. The lecture would only last an hour. He didn't mind waiting until the woman emerged from the building to give her back her pen.

The Darby College campus was a mix of brick-and-glass buildings amid a plethora of trees and meticulous landscaping.

Mondays were busy on the campus, and the students wore colorful clothing that competed with the autumn leaves on the trees popping with shades of orange and red.

September 25. It was hard to believe that it would soon be a month since Melinda's "kidnapping." Rumor had it that she was suffering from post-traumatic stress disorder, but nothing of that condition had been evident in her today. She'd given off the aura of strength and control despite the cast on her arm and her willowy figure.

He twirled the pen between his fingers and fell into thoughts of the case. The news of the kidnapping of the esteemed Melinda Grayson had rocked the small town, but shock had shuddered through Vengeance over the three murdered men who'd been uncovered by a geology class that was exploring a nearby area for minerals.

Lost. He quickly became lost inside his head as he

thought of all the intricacies of the various elements of the murders and Melinda's kidnapping, beating and then inexplicable release from her captors.

A sudden flurry of students leaving the building jerked Mark back to the here and now. He was vaguely surprised that he'd been seated on the bench and zoned out for thirty minutes or so.

He quickly stood and watched the people walking by him, seeking the gray-eyed woman who had lent him the pen and paper and had captured his attention with her lovely smile and sweet fragrance.

Moments later she emerged from the building. Clad in black slacks and a white blouse with a black-and-gray lightweight sweater tossed around her shoulders, she definitely didn't look like the customary jean-clad young kids who swirled around her.

She clutched her laptop case to her chest and her eyes widened in surprise as she saw him approaching her. At six feet four inches Mark was accustomed to towering over people, but this woman was taller than most women. The top of her head would have fit neatly beneath his chin if he'd pulled her into his arms.

This kind of thought was so alien to his brain that when he reached her he merely held out the pen toward her, momentarily speechless.

She took the pen, her eyes filled with surprise. "Oh, goodness, have you been waiting here all this time to give this back to me?" She had a deep, melodic but slightly husky, voice. "You didn't have to do that. It's just a cheap pen."

"You loaned it to me," he said, finally finding his own voice. "I just wanted to return it and thank you."

In truth he wondered if he'd just wanted to see her out here rather than in the dim theater. The overhead sunshine transformed her hair from plain brown to chestnut, with strands of cinnamon and gold sparking bright amid the soft strands.

"You should have stayed for the lecture. Today was really good," she said as she tucked the pen inside her purse. "When it was announced that Professor Grayson was teaching a class on the sociopath in society, the classes filled up the very first day. But I haven't seen you in any of her classes or in the lecture hall before." A faint blush stained her cheeks, as if she suddenly became aware that she was doing all the talking.

"I'm not a student here, but you obviously enjoy Professor Grayson's lectures."

"I think she's brilliant." There was no question of the hero worship that laced her voice as she spoke of Melinda.

Mark's brain once again began to work overtime, weighing possibilities and attempting to separate a personal attraction to the woman from his work. "I'm Mark Flynn," he said. "And you are?"

"Dora. Dora Martin." She pulled her laptop closer against her chest in a defensive gesture and yet her smile remained open and wide.

"It's nice to meet you. Are you a local?"

She nodded. "At least for the last three years. I've been attending school and I work part-time in the bookstore. I'm studying to become a criminologist." She raised her chin a notch as if to defy him to question her career choice.

"Actually, I'm an FBI agent," he replied.

Her eyes widened once again. "So, you're here about the murders."

"I'm part of the team working on the case." He felt his mouth curve into an unaccustomed smile as he realized he'd made up his mind. He needed a source, somebody who was familiar with the campus, somebody who might have inside information on the illustrious professor. Dora Martin might be just what he needed for a little insight into the professor she obviously worshipped.

"I noticed there's a little coffee shop on campus. Can I buy you a cup of coffee, Dora Martin?" he asked.

She gazed at him for a long moment and once again she pulled her laptop tight against her body, as if forming a barrier between herself and the world...between herself and him.

His breath caught in his chest as he waited for her response, telling himself he could always find somebody else to use for information. Still, he was shocked by how much he wanted her to say yes.

"I only have a little while before I have to get to the bookstore," she replied with a touch of hesitation. "But a cup of coffee sounds good."

Mark released his breath and felt a natural smile curl his lips for the first time in a very long time. "Great," he replied. Despite his instant attraction to her his only goal was to use her for information. Maybe he could glean a little more information on the woman at the center of the mystery and the crimes that had plagued this town. And if Dora couldn't give him any insight, all that was lost was a few minutes drinking coffee.

* * *

Dora had found herself half-breathless when the tall, dark-haired man had sat next to her in the theater. Handsome and lean, he'd smelled faintly of minty soap and shaving cream. His dark hair had been slightly mussed, as if he had no idea how attractive he was and didn't much care. Hot. The man was definitely a hottie, but Dora had quickly reminded herself that men were off-limits to her.

When she'd walked outside and seen him, the first thing she'd noticed was how the sun danced in his thick, slightly messy hair and that his brilliant blue eyes held a piercing quality that both drew her in and unsettled her.

He'd shocked her with his offer to buy her a cup of coffee and her initial instinct had been to turn him down, to run as far away from him as possible. No men allowed.

It's just a cup of coffee, a little voice had whispered in the back of her head as she found herself accepting his offer. Now, as they fell into step side by side, her tongue was tied in knots.

He didn't seem to mind the silence, as he didn't offer any conversation to break it as they walked toward the nearby campus coffee shop.

"Nice day," she finally said.

He looked at her, as if startled to see her by his side, then gazed around and looked back at her. "It is, isn't it?" He smiled and a flutter of warmth whispered over her.

"Autumn is my favorite time of the year," she said, hoping to keep the conversation flowing.

"It is nice," he agreed.

It was ridiculous that a faint nervous jitter had played in her veins the moment he'd asked her to get coffee. She was a forty-year-old woman, not a teenager, and yet each time she looked at him she felt an evocative heat in the pit of her stomach, a tingle in her veins that she recognized as full-on attraction.

His facial features were chiseled, with angles and planes that created not only a handsome face but also a face with a slight edge, especially with the hint of dark stubble on his lower jaw.

She breathed a sigh of relief as they entered the busy coffee shop. He pointed toward an empty two-top table. "Grab us that place," he said, "and I'll order the coffees. You like it any special way?"

"Just black is fine," she replied. She hurried to the empty table and sat with her laptop case and purse on the floor at her side.

FBI agent Mark Flynn was easy to spot at the counter since he was taller than the others who stood in line before and after him. Maybe she'd agreed to have coffee with him because he was working in the field that she wanted to make her career. He'd solve the crime and be gone.

Maybe her decision to make an exception to the rule she'd made about men had nothing to do with the depth in his blue eyes or the chiseled features of his handsome face, but rather because she knew he wouldn't be around long enough to threaten her self-improvement drive.

Comforted by this thought, she decided to just enjoy this moment, assured that she wasn't going back down the dark rabbit hole from where she'd been pulled over three years ago.

She smiled as he returned to the table with two steaming cups of coffee. He eased down into the chair across from her. "A criminologist," he said, as if they'd been in the middle of a conversation before he'd retrieved the drinks. "I'd say right now you're in a good place for a little beyond-the-books learning experience with everything that has happened here in the last couple of weeks."

Her smile fell away when she thought of the murders and the kidnapping of Melinda. "It's been a terrible time for everyone. First the kidnapping, and then those poor men strangled and left to be discovered by students. At least Professor Grayson wasn't killed, as well. But you probably don't want to talk about your work while you're enjoying your coffee."

He took a sip from his cup and then leaned forward. "So, tell me about Dora Martin. Married? Divorced? What were you doing before you landed here in Vengeance?"

His gaze seemed to pierce through her, as if he could ferret out secrets by merely looking deep into her eyes. And she had a lifetime of secrets about who she had been, about where she had come from, secrets that she wasn't about to share with anyone ever.

"Divorced a long time ago," she replied. "And before I moved here and began my higher education, I was working as a waitress and going nowhere fast."

"It's admirable that you decided to make a change," he said encouragingly.

"Thanks." She looked down at the tabletop and tried

not to remember that it hadn't really been her who had made the decision that she needed to make a change, but rather two people who cared about her.

She gazed at him once again. "What about you? Married? Single?"

"Single and divorced," he replied with a quicksilver frown that danced across his forehead and then quickly disappeared. "This kind of job isn't conducive to relationships. During my brief marriage I saw more of my team members than my wife, Sarah."

"That's too bad."

He smiled. "Actually, we parted as good friends. I have my work and she has hers as a journalist in Dallas, and we share a three-year-old daughter." His smile faded and the focus in his eyes grew hazy.

"What's her name?" Dora asked.

He didn't reply. It was as if he were lost to the here and now, lost to place and time. "Agent Flynn?"

His eyes regained focus and he straightened in his chair. "Sorry about that. I tend to get lost in my head sometimes, and please, make it Mark."

"I asked about your daughter's name," Dora said.

"Grace. Her name is Grace."

"That's nice. So, you're from Dallas?"

He nodded. "A little apartment in Dallas is my legal address, but I'm not there very much. I'll only be here in Vengeance until we wrap up these murders by getting the guilty in custody."

She'd understood that the moment he'd identified himself as an FBI agent. In town to do a job and then he'd get back to his life in Dallas, a life that had nothing to do with hers here in Vengeance. Once again she recognized that this was safe…he was safe and wouldn't screw her up with a single cup of coffee.

No matter how attracted she was to him, he wouldn't be around to tempt her into old, bad habits that would derail her. She could never allow that to happen.

"So, are you also investigating Professor Grayson's kidnapping?" she asked.

"We're all working to seek answers both in the murders and kidnapping case."

"Why were you at the lecture this morning?" she asked, curious about his presence in the theater.

"The topic of sociopaths always grabs my attention. I just stopped in on a whim, but a phone call vibrated my phone and I had to leave to take the call."

"Would you like my notes from the lecture?"

He smiled at her, the smile that wove heat through her entire body. "I suddenly feel like I'm nineteen again and sharing notes with the sharpest mind in the class."

Dora laughed. "Sharpest mind. Wow, I definitely have you fooled."

"I doubt it," he countered easily. "I saw how diligently you were taking notes and it's not the slackers who take a lecture so seriously."

A blush rose into her cheeks as she saw the approval in his eyes. "I take my education very seriously."

"As you should," he agreed, and took another sip of his coffee.

Dora checked her watch. "I also take my job at the bookstore very seriously since it is part of what pays the tuition, and unfortunately, I've got to go." Although she still had a few minutes to spare she felt the need to escape his disconcerting and gorgeous blue gaze and the sexy curl of his smile.

She stood and grabbed her laptop and her purse and then lifted the foam cup of the remainder of her drink. "Thanks for the coffee."

He also got to his feet. "Thanks for the company," he replied. "This has been a pleasant break from business as usual."

"But it's time to get back to business as usual," Dora said briskly. He followed her outside the coffee shop and they stood for a moment on the sidewalk.

"I'll guess I'll see you around campus," she said. "Thanks again for the coffee."

"You're welcome." He murmured a goodbye as she turned to head in the direction of the bookstore. She could swear she felt his gaze burning in the center of her back until she turned left on the sidewalk that would take her out of his view.

Silly, she told herself, gripping her laptop against her chest. She was just being silly because for over three years she'd scarcely noticed the male population around her. Somehow FBI agent Mark Flynn had managed to sneak beneath her antimale radar.

No harm, no foul, she thought as she stopped beside a trash container. She finished the last of the coffee and then tossed the foam cup into the trash and continued her walk to the bookstore, her thoughts still consumed by the handsome Mark Flynn.

She hoped his team could not only solve the murders but also find out who had kidnapped and beaten Melinda and then had released her. It made no sense, and to date, nobody had come up with a reasonable motive for what had happened to the professor.

So far the investigation into the murders had spilled secrets left and right about the three male victims, tawdry tales of bribery and betrayal. They were ugly secrets that had everyone gossiping about who the victims had presented themselves to be and who, in truth, they had been.

Dora wanted the FBI to get to the bottom of the crimes, but she certainly didn't want anyone digging around into her life, past or present.

Her past was filled with shame and regret, a place she tried not to visit in her dreams or thoughts. Her present was still filled with a secret she didn't want known. Not because it would embarrass her, but rather because it would embarrass one of the two people who had plucked her up from the stinking back alley of her existence and given her a reason to live.

Professor Melinda Grayson was not only her teacher but also her older sister and her salvation. Dora would turn herself inside out to keep people from knowing that she was related to the esteemed, intelligent professor. She would never want Melinda's reputation to be tainted by her own past.

Still, it had been nice for those few minutes to sit across from Mark and feel the stir of chemistry, knowing that it was an attraction that would go nowhere, knowing that she couldn't afford any more mistakes in her lifetime. She was like a cat who had already misspent eight of the nine lives she'd been given. She wasn't going to do anything to mess up this final chance.

Chapter 2

Mark stood at a whiteboard in front of his team in the conference room they had commandeered on the first floor of the county courthouse/city hall. The room was midsize and filled with the requisite long tables and chairs where his fellow agents now sat looking at him expectantly.

The team had changed in the three weeks since the bodies had been discovered. Agents had been pulled off this particular crime when a grave of twenty skeletons of young men had been discovered just outside Oklahoma City. Richard Sinclair was the agent in charge, but he ran a fairly loose ship and rarely yielded his power over the others.

For a moment, as Mark stared at the five agents at the table, his brain blanked on everything except the silky look of Dora Martin's hair sparking in the sunshine the day before and the mysteries he'd sensed in the depths of her dove-gray eyes when she'd been so vague about where she'd come from and what she'd been doing before winding up in Vengeance, Texas.

"Earth to Mark," Agent Lori Delaney said drily, pulling him from thoughts of Dora and to his task at hand.

"Sorry," Mark said, and raked a hand through his hair as if the gesture would banish any further thoughts of Dora. He turned toward the whiteboard where photos of the three dead men were taped. Beneath their photos was information about each man written in Mark's precise handwriting.

"Sheriff Peter Burris," Mark began, intending to go through all the facts they knew about each of the dead men for the hundredth time since they'd been called out on the case. He tapped on the picture of the dead man. It was a crime-scene photo, the burly sheriff barely recognizable after having been strangled and buried in his shallow grave.

"He was found with a note card on his body that read Liar. We now know that Peter Burris was a dirty lawman who was blackmailing Senator John Merris among other illegal activities. At the time of his murder he was married to Suzy Burris, an accountant who has since been cleared of having anything to do with her husband's death."

Mark slid sideways to tap his index finger on the second photograph. "Next victim is David Reed, with a note card that labeled him a cheater. He was a sports writer, known to be a playboy. He had a drug problem and was into the illegal sports betting scene. Although he was married to Eliza Harvey, we know that he was having affairs at the time of his murder."

"I definitely would have killed him if he were my husband," Lori Delaney quipped, making the other agents laugh.

They quickly sobered as Mark continued. "Eliza was our number-one suspect until she was cleared, which brings us to victim number three, Senator John Merris, who was labeled as a thief by the card the killer left on his body. We all know now that the good senator was a nasty piece of work who siphoned millions of dollars from the Dawson Exploration Oil Company and padded his own bank account at the same time he put hundreds of people out of work."

"It's almost like our killer did the world a big favor," Agent Donald Thompson muttered, under his breath but loud enough for everyone in the room to hear.

"They were all dirtbags, but they were still murdered," Lori replied. "And I want this killer brought to justice." She was an intense young agent with dark hair and eyes. Mark knew this was the biggest case she'd worked on in her short career.

"All three men were killed within a twenty-four-hour period of time and each of them had been strangled or suffocated," Mark continued. "As we know, what few leads we've managed to get have led us nowhere. There is no question that these men were all killed by the same person or persons, and strangulation is a particularly intimate form of killing, but we have yet to tie these three victims to any one person to make a connection."

"We're working on it," Agent Larry Albright replied

with a weariness Mark knew the whole team felt. So far this had been one of the most frustrating cases Mark had worked. He couldn't get a handle on the killer, none of them could even agree on a specific motive.

Certainly the three dead men all had their share of unsavory secrets, but murder usually uncovered secrets of one sort or another. Nobody was exactly what they portrayed to the outside world.

So far their investigation had run in all directions, focusing on enemies a state senator might have, and who might hate a playboy cheater and, finally, why somebody would kill a dirty sheriff. Each of these people could have faced the consequences of their crimes in a courtroom, but instead the ultimate judgment had been meted out by an unknown person or persons.

The FBI had no idea specifically where the men had been killed, only that, within a twenty-four-hour period, each of them had been strangled and buried in shallow graves on private land adjoining the college campus.

Mark knew the other men and woman on his team were leaning toward a vigilante scenario...one or two people getting rid of the dishonest, the disloyal and the mendacious in one single twenty-four-hour killing spree.

He finished up going over the particulars of what they already knew and what they needed to know, and the group of agents dispersed and left the room. The only one remaining, as Mark began to set up video equipment, was the senior agent Richard Sinclair.

Agent Sinclair was the oldest on the team, a veteran who had seen all the ugly that the world had to offer in his many years in the bureau. He was also the person Mark felt closest to on the team.

"Going to view them again?" Richard asked as he once again sank down at a chair at the table.

"And again and again," Mark replied. He set the video screen so that both he and Richard could watch the "movies" about to play. After loading the DVD into the recorder, he took a seat next to Richard, the remote control in his hand.

"You know that most of the others think you're crazy about this," Richard said, his voice deep and full yet holding no judgment. "They believe you've become obsessed and refuse to see reality."

"I know, and that's okay. I'm just following my instincts. If I'm wrong then all I've wasted is my own time. There are plenty of others to do the rest of the investigative work. I've got to follow through on my gut, right or wrong." He turned to look at Richard, seeking not approval but rather simple acceptance.

"I've been at this long enough to know that sometimes all we have to go on is our gut instincts, and yours has proven to be right more often than not. Play the movie," he said.

Mark punched the remote and the screen filled first with blackness and then suddenly she was there, Melinda Grayson, tied to a chair with a blindfold across her eyes.

Mark leaned forward, his gaze focused not on the woman in the center of the picture, but rather on the background, seeking anything that might provide a clue as to where the video had been shot.

In this particular scene the backdrop appeared to

be nothing but a black curtain or sheet. Melinda was a stark figure in the straight-back chair, tears shining from beneath the blindfold and trekking down her pale skin. "Please, please help me." Her voice pleaded with some unknown captor. The screen went black and Mark hit the remote to pause.

"What are you looking for? The tech team has been over these a dozen times trying to figure out where the video was made, if there are any sounds that could be amplified that might give us a clue. They've come up with nothing," Richard said.

"I don't know. I'm just looking for..." Mark hesitated and then continued, "For something we all might have missed."

Richard got up from his chair and clapped Mark on the shoulder. "I know you do your best work alone, without somebody telling you what to do. Happy hunting," he said, and then left Mark alone in the room.

Mark played the recording again, this time with his eyes closed, listening intently for any whisper of sound before she spoke. "Please, please help me." Melinda's voice filled his brain, but there was nothing else to hear, no traffic noise, no singing of birds...nothing.

He tried to imagine himself as the victim. He'd been kidnapped, a blindfold over his eyes. He'd been shoved into a chair, a rope tight against his chest, hurting him, making it difficult to breathe. His wrists burned from the rope that tied them to the arms of the chair.

Terror. He felt the simmering, near screaming of terror inside him. He was a prisoner of people unknown, he had no idea why they had him or what they wanted from him. He listened in his head to her voice once again.

"Please, please help me."

It wasn't what was there that caught his attention, but rather what he didn't hear in her plea: a lack of sheer terror in the way she spoke the words. She hadn't pulled at the binding of her wrists to the chair as she'd spoken, and she hadn't desperately strained against the rope across her chest. She hadn't looked or sounded terrified.

Maybe she just wasn't the dramatic type. Maybe she'd somehow managed to remain cool and calm despite her dire circumstances. He picked up the remote and clicked Play to watch the next video that they'd received from the kidnappers.

There were a total of four DVDs sent by the captor or captors. The worst one showed Melinda being beaten by a figure dressed all in black and wearing a ski mask.

Mark didn't know how long he sat watching the videos again and again, trying to figure out the question that had yet to be answered. There had never been a ransom demand—there had never been a demand for anything. So, why kidnap and beat a woman, videotape the crime, send the videos to law enforcement and then simply release her? It didn't make sense and things that didn't make sense bothered Mark.

The consensus among the other agents was that it was probably a student prank that had somehow gotten a bit out of control. The fact that she was missing at the same time the murders had occurred was merely a weird coincidence.

Mark didn't believe in coincidences, weird or otherwise. He still believed the gray-eyed woman had some-thing to do with the murders, that the whole kidnapping thing had been orchestrated for show and nothing else.

He frowned as he realized his mistake. Melinda didn't have gray eyes. Hers were green. Dora had gray eyes, and the whisper of sweet flowers clinging to her.

A glance at his watch let him know it was just after noon. He had no idea what Dora's class schedule was like, but a desire to find her and talk to her rose up inside him. He knew that if her schedule at the book-store was the same as yesterday, she would be heading there around four.

As he walked down the long wide steps of the court-house, he was accosted at the bottom of the stairs by a reporter who had become a familiar irritation to the entire team.

Paula Craddock, ace reporter for KVXT, a Dallas television station, stood ready to shove her microphone in his face. Mark had always tried to be kind to the media, mostly because his ex-wife had been part of that industry. But, after three weeks of media frenzy, it was becoming more and more difficult to keep a smile on his face whenever he encountered a reporter.

"Any break in the murder case, Agent Flynn?" She hurried toward him as he hit the sidewalk.

"No comment," he replied.

She fell into step beside him, her photographer hur-rying to keep up with them as Mark started walking down the sidewalk to where his car was parked. "Surely you have something you can tell the viewers. It's a well-known fact that you're one of the FBI's bright-est profilers."

Mark turned to stare at her and finally gave her a tight smile. "And that's what makes me smart enough to say 'no comment.'"

As he picked up his pace, Paula sighed in frustration. She and her photographer hurried back to the bottom of the courthouse steps, where Mark knew she would take up residency, hoping to get something of substance for the latest on this tawdry, explosive murder case.

Mark got into his car and drove the short distance to the Darby campus. His brain was still engaged with the mystery of Melinda's kidnapping and the murders.

It had always been easy for Mark to lose himself in the head of the killer. Sometimes it scared him a little how good he was at picking up vibes from the insane, the evil that could reside in people. But not this time. The note cards left with each man were calling cards of a sort from the killer they sought, but Mark couldn't get a handle on what had compelled the killer to leave them behind. There had been no prints on the note cards, and that particular kind of card was sold in dozens of stores, including the campus bookstore.

Had the killer simply decided to off men with unsavory secrets...secrets that might not have been uncovered without their murders and the note cards that labeled each victim?

Certainly Mark had worked grave sites where multiple victims had been found before, but usually those burial sites had been created over months or years, not in a single twenty-four-hour period.

He found an empty parking space along a tree-lined street near the campus and got out to walk the rest of the way. He was lucky that his team understood that for the most part he was a lone wolf. His specific job required him to do less of the actual investigation work and more of the mind-game tasks that always came with catching a killer.

This was the first time he was having trouble connecting with the killer or killers. He couldn't help but believe that the mere logistics of murdering three men and dumping their bodies suggested more than one person at work. They just didn't have enough information for him to do his job effectively.

As he walked toward the building that held the lecture hall where Dora had been in class yesterday, his thoughts turned to her. He told himself she was the perfect tool to use to gain some knowledge about Melinda and her friends and colleagues on the campus. But that didn't explain the quick beat of his heart as he thought of basking in the warmth of Dora's smile once again.

He sank down on the same bench he'd sat at the day before. He had no idea if Dora had classes in the same building today, but this particular bench and building was fairly central in the campus. From this viewpoint he could see the comings and goings of students in all directions.

If he didn't catch her between classes, he'd wait until later this evening and meander into the bookstore. He just knew that before the day was done he wanted… he needed to see Dora again. It was an alien emotion that he refused to dwell on because it unsettled him.

He'd like to learn a little bit more about Melinda's graduate assistants, Amanda Burns and Ben Craig. The background checks had shown both of them to be law-abiding, upstanding citizens, not even a speeding ticket between them. They were both from good families and took their positions as Melinda Grayson's assistants very seriously.

Mark knew from casual conversations with several other students and staff that both Amanda and Ben worked hard for Melinda, helping her with research and the mundane tasks that a professor of Melinda's ilk would need done. They were both bright and apparently devoted to their boss.

All thoughts of Melinda Grayson flew from his head as Dora stepped out of the building and into the afternoon sunshine. Her long legs were encased in navy dress slacks, and a feminine long-sleeved white blouse with pearl buttons emphasized her slender waist and the fullness of her breasts.

A knot of heat twisted in Mark's stomach as her eyes indicated surprise, yet her mouth curved in a smile that drove all rational thoughts of murder and mayhem out of his mind.

Dora's heart gave a healthy bounce in her chest. Mark was obviously waiting for her. Like yesterday he was dressed in black slacks and a white shirt and black jacket and his hair looked as if it had never met a comb or brush. Yet the messiness of those rich dark strands only added to his overall attractiveness.

"Fancy meeting you here," she said, and tried to ignore her jitters.

"I was just hanging around wondering if maybe you'd like to catch a cup of coffee with me again," he said.

Two days in a row. Dora couldn't help the fact that

his words caused a little thrill to race up her spine. "Unfortunately, I don't have time today. I've got to get right to the bookstore for work." It was probably for the best, she thought, that this casual meeting for coffee…that *he* didn't become a habit.

"What time do you finish up at the bookstore this evening?" he asked, obviously unwilling to let the topic drop. Once again a small dance of pleasure kicked a jig in the pit of Dora's stomach.

"We close the store at eight on Tuesdays and Thursdays," she said. "We're closed on Sundays and open the rest of the week until ten." She closed her mouth, realizing she'd given way more information than he'd asked for and that's why she didn't trust herself to have relationships at this point in her life.

"So, you'll be off at eight this evening," he said, apparently easily picking through the minutia she'd just offered him. She nodded. "Then why don't I meet you at the bookstore at eight and we can grab a cup of coffee or something then?"

"That sounds great." Dora heard the words falling from her lips and knew they were probably the wrong thing to say, but she didn't seem to have the power to stop them.

"Great!" His blue eyes glowed with obvious pleasure and his sexy smile curved his lips. "Then I'll see you later."

She stood stock-still as he turned and headed down the sidewalk away from her. *You should have said no,* a little voice whispered inside her head.

Turning in the opposite direction to head to the bookstore, she tried to list all the reasons it was wrong to have coffee with Mark again, but she kept coming up with the same defense…it was just a cup of coffee with a man who would soon be gone from town.

It shouldn't feel as frightening, as exciting or as earth-shattering as it did. She chided herself for being so silly, for trying to make it all bigger than it was in her mind. He was an out-of-towner, with only colleagues around him every day for almost a month. Maybe he just found himself a bit lonely for regular conversation and she was convenient.

By the time she walked into the bookstore, she had rationalized it all in her mind. The first thing she always noticed upon coming in to work was the scent of the store…the smell of paper drifting in the air from all the textbooks on the shelves.

Dora loved the smell of books, the weight of one in her hand. The store sold more than textbooks and research tomes. There were T-shirts and other apparel in the school colors of red and gold, glasses and tumblers with the Darby Gladiators logos, candles and key chains and an entire assortment of candies and snacks.

"How's it going?" she asked Kathy Taylor, a young night student who usually worked just before Dora came in.

"Slow. I've only sold one candle all day long. But, on the bright side, I've managed to use the quiet time to write a paper that needed to be done before Thursday," Kathy replied.

"If it stays quiet, then hopefully I can work on studying for a test we're having on Friday in my forensics class." Dora set her laptop on the counter next to the cash register.

"If things go this evening like they have all day then you should have a good five hours of quiet time to study." Kathy grabbed her bright pink backpack and slung it over one shoulder. "I'll see you tomorrow?"

"Not if I can help it," Dora replied with a grin. "Tomorrow is my night off."

"Enjoy," Kathy replied as she breezed out the door.

Dora settled on the chair behind the register and opened her laptop, intent on reviewing the notes she'd taken that day in her classes.

However, forensic science couldn't compete with the brilliant blue of Mark's eyes or those tousled strands of darkness atop his head that begged her fingers to provide some sort of order.

No touching, she told herself. It was bad enough that she'd agreed to have coffee with him a second time. She certainly couldn't fantasize about how his hair would feel beneath her fingertips. That would be going against everything she'd promised herself.

Her education, that was all that was important to her. She'd tried the marriage route…twice, in fact, and with disastrous results. Men weren't good for her. She'd made the decision three years ago to get her degree, get a great job, and that would be enough to fulfill her for the rest of her life.

With a new resolve, she began to read the notes she'd taken in her forensics class that day, trying her best to memorize everything she suspected would be on the next test.

She was interrupted only twice by students coming in to browse, but her concentration was broken many more times as she continued to think about Mark Flynn.

Her attention was divided between trying to study and the clock on the wall opposite where she sat. The minutes crept by with agonizing slowness.

She reminded herself that it hadn't been a man who had gotten Melinda out of the circumstances of their early life...it had been education. Three years ago Melinda and Micah Grayson, a brother she'd only recently learned existed, had given her the same opportunity to make something of herself. As far as Dora knew the two had been estranged since first meeting, but had come together as a united force to save Dora.

When Melinda had been kidnapped, Micah hadn't come forward because he was working an important undercover case. Although Dora had been terrified for her sister, she also hadn't gone to the authorities because she had no information to offer them.

Micah had paid for the little house where she now lived just off campus with the understanding that once she was on her feet and had landed a good job, she'd begin to pay him back for his investment in her. He also gave her a small monthly allowance to help with utilities and groceries. Melinda had helped her with financial support and scholarship grants and awards, and had guided her in her choice of classes, but the two sisters had remained virtual strangers.

The last thing Dora wanted to do was misstep and prove to the two people who had done so much for her that the truth was she was just the same old screwup she'd always been.

For a moment she was mired in her past, and her head filled with the scent of cheap booze and sweaty males, of fried food and the sound of her mother's drunken laughter.

She was back at the Daisy Café on the outskirts of the small town of Horn's Gulf, Wyoming. The Daisy Café, a cheerful name for the most dismal place on the face of the earth.

She remembered every whack of the belt that her father had wielded as a weapon, the drunken shouts of her abusive first ex-husband and the killing words of her second husband, words that rang with an unadorned truth and had spiraled her down and out of control.

With a shake of her head, she shoved aside those distant memories of her hometown and all the despair the thoughts of that place and those times created inside her.

A glance at the clock let her know that there were only two hours left and then she could close up shop. Maybe Mark wouldn't show. Maybe something would come up that would keep him from being here when she closed for the night.

She told herself it didn't matter whether he showed up or not. She had no vested interest in him. He meant absolutely nothing to her. She just liked looking at him, and she hadn't realized, until she'd had coffee with him yesterday, that she'd hungered for the normal conversation between herself and a man.

She'd made no real friends here, hadn't given herself a chance to enjoy any kind of a personal life. She had her studies and her work and she'd told herself that was enough, but she recognized now that she'd been socially starving herself.

Even if Mark didn't show up for a cup of coffee,

Dora made a vow to herself that the next time one of her fellow students invited her to come along for a quick bite to eat in the student lounge she'd go. For three years she'd isolated herself, afraid of making a mistake, afraid that any distraction might throw her off course or that she'd say something that would hint at the secrets she held close to her heart.

But, she was stronger now than she'd been when she'd first started school. All work and no play was noble, but it was also unnatural. A little play didn't hurt as long as she didn't lose control of what was important.

At quarter until eight she went into the bathroom and checked her hair, then sprayed a touch of her favorite perfume on the side of her neck.

She straightened her blouse and tucked it into her waistband, then stared at her reflection and told herself she was once again being silly.

And then he was there…standing at her counter, his gaze going around the room and then landing on her with a smile. "I've always loved bookstores," he said.

She nodded. "All that paper scent and being surrounded by such knowledge," she said.

"Exactly," he said, his blue eyes brightening as if pleased that she apparently felt what he did when in a bookstore. "At work I'm surrounded by technology, have the latest Android phone, all the computer gadgets imaginable, but I still like the weight of a real book in my hands."

At that moment a couple of students came in and as Dora waited on them she kept one eye on Mark, who wandered the store looking at the various offerings. He was a curious man, reading labels and studying contents of the items he perused.

There had been several moments when they were having coffee the day before that his gaze had been so intense on her that she'd felt he was studying the contents of her.

Her breath grew tight inside her chest, making it difficult to breathe. Despite this, she finished ringing up the students. *It's just another cup of coffee,* she told herself, and yet she had the feeling that she was about to make yet another big mistake in her life.

Amanda Burns slammed the door to her tiny apartment and tossed her laptop case and purse on the sofa, which was half-smothered by decorative throw pillows.

She'd like to take one of those pillows and smother Ben, the rotten rat. Melinda had assigned them a research project and they were supposed to get together this evening to work on it. But Ben had done it alone and presented the papers to Melinda that day, making him the official golden boy of the moment.

Amanda fought the impulse to reopen her apartment door and slam it once again, needing a release of the anger that ripped through her.

Ben Craig was a sneaky snake who would undercut Amanda whenever possible to get and to stay in Melinda's good graces. This wasn't the first time he'd done that.

Instead of slamming her apartment door once again, she shoved a couple of the pillows onto the floor and sank down on the sofa, picking at a cuticle until it was bloody.

It was hard to believe that she'd once had a bit of a crush on the handsome grad student. Ben, with his short auburn hair and dark eyes, had an intelligence and a suave unruffled manner that had instantly drawn Amanda to him.

However, it hadn't taken her long to realize there was only one person he adored more than himself, and that was Professor Melinda Grayson.

Amanda stuck her finger in her mouth and realized she'd just managed to ruin a perfectly good manicure. Somehow, that was Ben's fault, as well.

Amanda adored Melinda, too. The beautiful, bright woman was not just Amanda's professional role model, but also her personal heroine. She was so gorgeous, so intelligent, and her strength absolutely amazed Amanda.

She'd been through so much with the kidnapping. They'd beaten her and broken her arm, and yet before she was fully healed from the awful ordeal she was back teaching, unwilling to let her students down.

And that creep Ben had gone behind Amanda's back to make himself look good and make Amanda look like a slug. Amanda could positively wring his neck.

On impulse she jumped up from the sofa and went to the tiny closet in the small bedroom. She opened the door and looked up on the top shelf. Nestled next to a large shoebox containing a pair of red cowboy boots that had been an impulse buy was a tin lockbox, half-covered by a nubby light blue blanket. The locked box was positive proof of Melinda's complete trust in her.

Amanda closed the closet and returned to the sofa,

where she once again sank down and pulled a pink flowered throw pillow against her chest.

Ben could knock himself out sneaking around to complete projects and presenting them to Melinda to garner favor, but that box on Amanda's closet shelf spoke of who among the two grad students Melinda trusted the most.

She still remembered the night Melinda had shown up here clutching the tin box tight against her chest. It had been the evening after the day of her release from her captors and there hadn't been a hint of the confident, strong woman.

Melinda had looked small and frightened, her green eyes huge as she'd handed Amanda the box and explained that it had all of her important papers inside.

"The key is in my desk drawer at the college," she'd said, and then had jumped when a car squealed around the corner outside. She'd wrapped her thin arms around her body, as if to stanch an inward tremble, as if to protect herself from further harm.

"If anything happens to me, then you'll have everything safe here," she'd said.

Amanda's heart had fluttered with fear for her mentor. "Do you expect something else bad to happen to you?"

Melinda had given her a rueful smile and raised the arm with the cast. "I didn't expect this to happen to me," she'd replied. "Would you keep this safe for me here?"

Amanda had assured her she would. What Melinda

didn't seem to understand was that Amanda adored Melinda so much she would do anything for her... anything at all.

Chapter 3

The coffee shop was almost empty when Mark and Dora walked in just after eight. It would be closing its doors in half an hour and there were only a few students seated at a couple of the tables.

Mark motioned her to where they'd sat the day before. "Black, right?" he asked as she sat down.

She nodded, ridiculously pleased that he'd remembered the way she drank her coffee. She remembered that he had used a packet of sugar in his, no cream.

Within moments he returned to the table and sat across from her, a smile lighting his handsome features. "I have to admit, I've been looking forward to this all day. I only have other colleagues here in town, and our conversations tend to be all about the crimes."

"Everyone needs a little downtime," she replied, wrapping her hands around the foam cup he'd delivered.

"Exactly."

"So, tell me about this little girl of yours, your Grace," she said, wanting to know more about him, about his personal life when he wasn't chasing monsters and murderers.

She'd expected his features to soften with fatherly love, with pride, but instead tension straightened his shoulders a notch and no responding smile danced across his lips.

"To be perfectly honest, I don't see her much. My work keeps me so busy."

"You should make time for her," Dora couldn't help but chide him. She'd always wondered how her life might have been different if she'd been raised by a loving, caring father rather than her abusive, alcoholic father.

"I know, that's what my ex-wife keeps telling me." He paused to take a sip of his coffee and then carefully placed the cup back in the exact position it had been in before he'd picked it up. "But Grace is so…perfect." A hint of a smile toyed at the edges of his lips.

An ache swelled up inside Dora as she saw that whisper of a smile touch his lips. It was filled with such awe, with such love, a love she'd never felt from any man before in her entire life.

"She's bright and funny and so innocent it scares me," he continued. "And somehow I always feel as if the darkness of my work clings to me and might taint her, might ruin her."

"Every daughter needs her daddy in her life," Dora replied. "And you're obviously a good man, Mark. I'm sure you'd be a terrific father to her if you'd just let yourself, and you'll never know how important it will be to her as she grows up to have a wonderful relationship with you."

He raised a dark eyebrow. "I'm assuming by what you're saying that you didn't have a terrific father in your life?"

"I had the most miserable man on the face of the earth as a father and then when I was eighteen years old I married a photocopy of him." She tried to keep the bitterness out of her voice. "They say that daughters tend to marry men who are just like their fathers. Needless to say in my case that was a big mistake."

"Do you have other family? Mother? Brothers or sisters?"

It was the usual dance when two people met, the ferreting out of personal information in a social setting. "I have a mother, a sister and two brothers who I only recently met. Don't ask," she said. "It's a complicated family tree. What about you?" She felt far more comfortable when the conversation was about him and not her.

"I'm the only child of two highly educated people who didn't quite know what to do with me." His eyes twinkled with a light of humor. "I'm not even sure they understand what exactly they did to get me."

Dora laughed. "Oh, I imagine they figured it out, since you don't have any siblings."

"True," he agreed. "But they were the cerebral types who were ill equipped to be parents. I was shuffled off to boarding school as soon as I was out of diapers. I suppose I should be grateful that they were wealthy enough to see that I went to the very best schools."

"And then you decided to become an FBI agent?"

"Actually, the FBI chose me, I didn't necessarily choose them. At the time I was involved with several different experimental classes that revolved around the topic of criminal profiling. I excelled and the FBI took notice. They made me an offer I couldn't resist."

"You love what you do?" Once again she could smell the faint scent of fresh soap and shaving cream that drifted off him. In the past she'd been accustomed to men who smelled of grease and sweat and cheap cologne.

"I love it," Mark replied, and his blue eyes deepened in hue. "Although it often takes me to some pretty dark places."

In the next moment Dora realized he'd drifted off into someplace in his head. The focus of his eyes grew fuzzy and his features went a bit slack.

He'd done the same thing the day before, drifted off for several seconds to a place inside his brain where nobody could follow him. She waited for several long moments and then softly called his name. Nothing. Hesitantly, she reached out and touched his forearm and said his name again, this time a little bit louder.

He gave her that heavy-lidded blink as his eyes regained their focus and he grimaced. "Sorry about that. I have a tendency to drift off. It's one of the irritating qualities about me that destroyed my marriage. Sarah used to tell me that I was working half the time and when I was home I was lost in my own head. It didn't leave much time for her."

"Maybe she just needed to learn how to break through to pull you out of your mind. Or figure out how to join you there," Dora replied.

Mark's eyes darkened even more, transforming to the deepest midnight-blue. "I wouldn't want anybody to join me in my head when I'm working a case, but I appreciate anyone who can pull me out of there."

Dora smiled. "Then when you disappear like that I'm going to tap you three times on your arm and if that doesn't do the trick I'm going to grab you by the hair and shake you."

He laughed and it was the first time she'd heard the deep, exceedingly pleasant sound. "It's a deal," he agreed.

They both turned at the sound of the opening of the coffee-shop door. Ben Craig walked in and when he spied Dora he smiled. "Hi, Dora," he said, approaching where she and Mark sat.

"Hello, Ben. Here for a late-night coffee fix?" she asked.

His handsome face wreathed into a wry grin. "For me this is an early-night coffee fix. I've got enough work on my desk to burn the midnight oil for the next couple of weeks."

"Mark Flynn," Mark said, and held out a hand to Melinda's assistant.

"Oh, where are my manners?" Dora explained. She quickly made the introductions and then Ben headed toward the counter to get his drink.

"He's one of the grad students who works with Professor Grayson, isn't he?" Mark asked.

Dora nodded. "He and Amanda Burns are Melinda's go-to people. They come into the bookstore a lot, ordering hard-to-find books for research or whatever Melinda needs. They seem like good kids, although Amanda can be a little intense at times."

"Intense how?"

Dora took a sip of her coffee as she thought of the two students who worked with Melinda. "They're both absolutely devoted to Melinda and I think there's more than a little bit of competitiveness between them. Ben is fairly laid-back, confident, and Amanda seems unsure of herself, more frantic to do whatever is needed to please Melinda."

"What is it about Professor Grayson that inspires such complete devotion?" Mark asked.

She looked at him in surprise. "You saw her. First of all she's absolutely gorgeous and then add in all her achievements and her position of power here at the college. She's an icon that many people admire and want to emulate."

He gazed at her thoughtfully. "Are you one of her groupies?"

Once again Dora laughed. "Not exactly a groupie, although there are many things I do admire about her." She wasn't about to explain to him her familial ties to Melinda or how grateful she was to the sister she'd scarcely known growing up, the woman she still didn't know well at all.

Melinda had been the least-expected person to do anything for Dora, yet she'd been there with Micah to get Dora on her feet and pointed in the direction of success.

"I find her kidnapping intriguing," Mark replied.

Dora frowned. "I thought the general opinion was that it was some of her students who pulled a prank that somehow got out of control. How else to explain the fact that there was never a ransom note and she was released with the worst of her injuries being a broken arm?" Dora fought a shiver as she thought about how scared she'd been for Melinda when she'd been kidnapped.

"The whole thing is just weird." Mark leaned back in his chair and took another drink of his coffee.

"On that, we both agree. I think there are several professors who are concerned that the same kind of thing could happen to them, that there's a mysterious group of rogue students running around plotting the kidnapping of another teacher."

Once again he leaned forward, pinning her in place with the intensity of his gaze. "Is that what you believe?"

Dora considered the question carefully. "To be honest I don't know what to believe about everything that has happened lately here in Vengeance."

At that moment she noticed that the young woman behind the counter was casting glares at them and pointed looks at the nearby wall clock that read eight-thirty.

"I think it's time for us to get out of here," Dora said, and then quickly drained the last of her coffee. She tried to tell herself she wasn't disappointed that their time together had been so brief.

Mark finished his coffee before grabbing both their empty cups and walking over to dispose of them in the trash bin. Dora quickly gathered her things and, with a quick good-night to the impatient counter girl, she and Mark stepped out into the darkness that had fallen.

"As always, it was nice to spend some time with you," he said as they lingered in front of the coffee shop.

"I enjoyed it, too," she admitted.

"You know any good restaurants in town?" he asked, his eyes sparkling in the glow of the moon. "I've had a diet of nothing more than cold pizza and greasy burgers for the last three weeks. It would be nice to get a good steak or maybe some Italian for a change."

"There's Bailey's Steakhouse not far from here, and Manetti's is a great place to go for Italian food." She clutched her laptop close to her chest and held her breath. Was his question a prelude to an offer to join him for dinner? That would be more like a real date.

"A big plate of lasagna and some fat meatballs sound like just the ticket," he replied. "Would you like to join me on Friday night for a good Italian meal?"

She'd hoped he'd ask. She'd hoped he wouldn't ask, because now she had to make a decision. If she said yes, then she'd be going against every rule she'd made for herself three years ago when she began her new life here in Vengeance. Yet, she had a feeling that if she said no, she'd regret it for the rest of her life.

"That sounds wonderful," she heard herself saying, and knew with both dread and a tiny thrill that she was breaking her biggest rule.

"Great, then why don't I pick you up around seven on Friday night?"

"I'll meet you there," Dora countered. Though it sounded crazy, having her own transportation made it feel less like a date, less like a rule broken.

"Okay," he said, obviously surprised. "Then I'll see

you at Manetti's at seven on Friday if I don't see you before then."

"Sounds like a plan," she agreed.

He frowned. "Do you have a way home? I didn't realize how dark it was until just now."

"I'm fine," she assured him. She didn't want him to know that she always walked home from the campus. She didn't want him to be a gentleman and offer to see her home.

Meeting him at a restaurant was one thing, but having him know where she lived was something else. They each murmured an awkward goodbye and then he turned in one direction and she turned in the other.

She cast only one quick glance over her shoulder to find him gone, the night having swallowed him whole. She had a three-block walk to the small off-campus house that she called home.

It had been Micah who had found the house and bought it, telling her that he wanted her to focus on nothing but her studies until she got her degree and was on her feet. She'd never owned anything of her own and cherished everything about the house. She even loved the drafty upstairs bedrooms and the cranky air conditioner, the wooden floors that needed to be refinished and the creak of the staircase.

She started down the sidewalk. She'd often walked home from the bookstore after dark and had always felt safe on the campus. As she walked, her thoughts were filled with Mark.

What are you doing, Dora? The question whirled around and around in her head without any definitive answer. The truth of the matter was she could rationalize to herself all she wanted that it had just been a couple cups of coffee, that it was just a simple meal with a friend, but the real truth was that she felt an intense attraction to the FBI agent.

When he gazed at her with those beautiful blue eyes she wanted to fall into their depths, confess all her sins past and present, and if she did then he wouldn't be able to head for the hills fast enough.

She should go right home and call him and cancel the Friday-night dinner. She should stop this whole thing before it went any further and she screwed up by saying something she shouldn't.

Of course, she couldn't call him to cancel. She didn't have his phone number. Surely she'd see him around in the next couple of days to cancel. It was for the best, she told herself, and yet she couldn't halt the small ache of regret that welled up inside her.

She was about halfway home when she thought she heard someone walking behind her. She stopped then turned around and, in the faint light from the streetlamps nearby, she saw that the sidewalk was empty.

Silly girl. Overreacting, for sure. She turned back around and continued walking. After several more steps she thought she heard the faint slap of a shoe behind her on the pavement. It was just an echo, as if somebody was matching their steps with hers and had missed a beat.

She hurried her pace, her heartbeat accelerating to an unnatural rhythm. Once again she looked over her shoulder and although she saw nobody on the sidewalk behind her, she thought she heard the rustle of the bushes nearby.

She had the distinct feeling that she was being followed. "Mark?" she called out tentatively. But there was no reason to believe that the FBI agent would be hiding in the bushes, shadowing her footsteps. Why would anyone be following her?

As she thought of what had happened to Melinda, a new fear shuddered through her, and her heart nearly exploded out of her chest. She broke into a run and her fear didn't ebb until she was in her house with the door securely locked.

Still, she stood at the window for a long time staring out into the night, wondering if she were simply imagining things or if somebody was stalking her.

It was just after nine the next morning when Mark stepped outside the courthouse and punched in the familiar numbers to the land phone at the house he'd once called home.

He'd been thinking about what Dora had said about fathers and daughters and now an ache of need rose up inside him, the need to talk to his baby girl.

Sarah answered on the second ring, her voice holding vague surprise. "Mark, this certainly isn't an everyday experience." There was a chiding tone to her voice, one he knew she thought he deserved. It had been over a month since he'd last called.

"Hi, Sarah. I know it's been a long time but I was wondering if Grace was around. I thought I might talk to her for a minute." He shifted from one foot to the other, nervous as he thought of the little girl he loved more than life itself.

"I'd say that's a wonderful idea," Sarah agreed. He heard her calling for Grace. "Come on, Daddy is on the phone."

"Daddy?" Grace's little high-pitched voice was filled with excitement and then she was on the line with him. "Daddy, when are you coming to see me again? It's been awful long. You should come right now."

Mark couldn't help the laughter that bubbled to his lips as he heard the mini-diva command in his three-year-old's voice. "I wish I could be there right now, Gracie Ann, but I can't. Daddy is in the middle of a big job."

"You're always in the middle of a big job," Grace said with a bit of a pout.

"I promise when I'm finished here I'll come and see you." Mark clutched the phone closer to his ear. "We'll go get ice cream together."

"Two scoops?" she asked hopefully.

"Two scoops," he agreed.

"Just you and me, Daddy?"

"Just you and me."

"You pinky swear?" Grace asked dubiously.

"I double pinky swear," Mark replied.

"Okay, Daddy, I've got to go now. Mommy wants to talk to you."

"You won't let her down." Sarah's voice filled the line.

"I've never broken a promise, especially not a double pinkie swear," he replied.

"True, but the problem is you never make promises,

Mark. I just don't want this to be the beginning of any heartbreak for Grace. It's bad enough that you see her so rarely as it is."

"I know, I know, and I'm going to do my best to change that."

There was a long moment of silence. "Did you find out you have a terminal disease or something?" Sarah asked finally.

"No, nothing like that," he replied with a wince. "I just had a conversation with somebody who reminded me that little girls need their fathers." Dora's gray eyes filled his head. "She told me that it was important that I be the kind of father Grace needs in her life. I want to be that, Sarah."

"Well, whoever it was, thank them for me," Sarah said drily. "Apparently they got it through your thick skull when I haven't been able to."

"Sarah, you know why I've kept my distance," Mark said softly.

"And I've told you a hundred times that Grace's light is far brighter than your darkness," Sarah said. "You can only bring good things into her life, Mark."

Mark's heart expanded at her words, at the utter faith with which she spoke them. After a few more minutes of conversation, they hung up. Mark remained leaning against the stone building, thinking about what Sarah had said.

She'd never truly understood the grip that darkness and evil had on him when he was in the middle of a case. He'd tried not to bring it home, but it clung to him like a cloak that he was unable to shed.

She hadn't understood that he climbed into the very

skin of evil, that he invited madness into his head. He *became* the killers he sought and there were many nights during their marriage he had stayed in a motel room rather than bring that home with him.

A glance at his cell phone let him know that it was time for a briefing inside. The room smelled of stale coffee and fresh doughnuts, the latter scent drifting from two boxes of the fresh pastries in the center of the tables. One of the boxes was already half-empty. He sank down next to Lori Delaney, who gave him a smug little smile.

"The scuttlebutt is that last night a certain agent was seen having coffee with a certain student in the campus coffee shop," she said.

"Research," Mark replied, despite the flush of warmth he felt climbing into his cheeks.

"Research, my butt," Lori replied as she reached out and grabbed a chocolate-covered doughnut from one of the boxes.

Mark sat patiently while the others gave their reports…reports that led nowhere, as usual. "We're coordinating our investigation with the local law enforcement," Agent Donald Thompson said to the group. "Currently the liaison is Detective Nick Jeffries, and his team is scrambling just like ours with a lot of questions and too few answers."

"What we need to do is find a solid connection between all three of our victims," Richard Sinclair said. "The connection between Peter Burris and Senator Merris is obvious. Sheriff Burris was blackmailing the senator…they were both elbow deep in dirty dealings. But we haven't been able to tie David Reed to either the sheriff or the senator. If we can find a person who had run-ins with all three before the murders, then maybe we'd have a better handle on our killer."

Richard frowned. "I can't tell you how much the pressure is mounting for us to get these cases solved."

Finally it was time for Mark to make his report. "I still believe the kidnapping of Professor Grayson and the murders are somehow tied together," he began, and ignored the groans of some of his fellow agents. "Don't any of you find it odd that when Melinda was kidnapped, all of her notes and lectures for the upcoming semester were already done?"

"Yeah, but there was also a grocery list next to those notes with a word only half-written, as if she'd been interrupted in the middle of writing out that shopping list," Donald reminded him as he swiped powdered sugar from his mouth. "As far as the lectures notes being already prepared, maybe she is just one of those types who is creepy weird and always well prepared."

Everyone laughed, knowing that Donald was a seat-of-the-pants kind of guy who never planned ahead for anything. More than once somebody had to call him to remind him of a briefing because he'd spaced it. His strength as an agent was in forensics, taking apart a crime scene to see what was there and what wasn't.

"I know we ran a cursory background on Ben Craig and Amanda Burns, but I'd like to see a little more in-depth information about them," Mark continued. "We need to talk to their friends, find out exactly what their relationship is between each other and with Melinda Grayson. We also need to look further at some of the other groupies that hung around Melinda at the time of her kidnapping."

"This is one of your famous hunches?" Donald said with a weary sigh.

"Most of Mark's hunches prove out," Richard said defensively. "I say we do what he says and dig a little deeper. If nothing else it might answer some questions about the kidnapping. In the meantime we'll continue to try to find a person who connects to all three murder victims. Somehow, someway, there's got to be a motive that ties to one single killer even if more than one person was involved in the actual murder acts."

"One more thing to consider," Mark added. "There certainly are more people in this little town with scandalous secrets, and yet the killings stopped when Melinda reappeared from her ordeal."

"That just means these murders were definitely personal to somebody," Larry Albright said. "It doesn't point a finger specifically at Melinda, who doesn't appear to have had any personal contact with any of the victims."

"So, we follow Mark's hunch and keep exploring other theories," Richard said.

"Thanks for the support," Mark said to Richard later, after the meeting broke up and all of the agents had gone their separate ways.

Richard clapped Mark on the shoulder. "If there's one thing I've learned over the years of working with you, it's that your hunches shouldn't be ignored. Now, what's this I hear about you cozying up to some student?"

"Dora Martin. She works in the bookstore and she's

enrolled in Grayson's classes. I think she might be a good source of a little inside information as to campus politics and such." Once again a hint of warmth crept into Mark's cheeks.

"Whatever helps break this all wide-open, I'm all for it," Richard replied. "Homecoming may have been pushed back due to all that's been going on, but now it's coming up soon and it would be nice if all of us could be out of here by then. The whole place is going to be crowded with alumni and parades and all kinds of extra people and events. It's just going to make our job even more difficult."

"Then we need to get this all solved before homecoming weekend," Mark replied. He raked a hand through his hair, his brain racing as usual.

Richard grinned ruefully. "From your lips to God's ears. We sure as hell haven't managed to get a break yet."

"It will happen," Mark replied with a confidence he didn't feel. "We're the FBI...we always get our man."

"Uh, I think that's the Royal Canadian Mounties' motto," Richard said.

"It is, but in this case it's going to be ours, too," Mark said firmly. "We're going to figure this out. Somebody belongs in prison in this town and we're going to find him or her or whoever is responsible for those murders."

"On that note, I'm heading out," Richard said. "Pounding the pavement, that's what solves most crimes."

"I think I'll do a little more video watching," Mark replied. It surprised him to realize that what he'd really like to do was find Dora, spend a little time talking to her, just losing himself in the peaceful calm of her gray eyes.

A tool, he reminded himself. She was just a tool to use to further his investigation. Still, he was eager for Friday night to arrive, but in the meantime he had images to watch, images of Professor Melinda Grayson with her captors.

Melinda stood at her living room window and watched the sun slowly sinking in the west. Another day done and it was definitely time for a glass of wine and perhaps a phone call.

She poured herself a glass of Cabernet Sauvignon, admiring the expensive red wine as it splashed into the bottom of the crystal goblet. Thank goodness the cast was on her left arm so she could foist the goblet high in the air to toast her success…her very survival.

Carrying the wine to the sofa, she sank down, placed the glass on the coffee table and then picked up her cell phone. She considered calling her brother Samuel, but with him being in jail at the moment it was sometimes difficult to get through to him and she knew his calls might be monitored. She decided to check in with Micah instead. Although she rarely thought about him and he had no place in her life, she occasionally called him to keep up the pretense of some sort of family normalcy. If she checked in with him, then she figured he'd have no reason to get nosy about her life and that was just fine with her.

A couple of years ago it had been quite a shock to discover that she had not one but two brothers, twins.

Micah and Samuel Grayson were the antithesis of each other. Micah was the good twin, an FBI agent who at this moment was on an undercover assignment pretending to be his twin, Samuel, in the small town of Perfect, Wyoming.

Samuel had built the town into his own personal cult with his charismatic power, wielding complete control. Unfortunately, Samuel had been stupid and arrogant and was now sitting in prison charged with a multitude of crimes ranging from illegal adoptions to murder. Because the corruption in the town had run so deep, the FBI had placed Micah in undercover as Samuel to ferret out the guilty who had avoided capture when Samuel had gone down.

She took a long drink of her wine and then punched in the numbers that would connect her to Micah. He answered immediately, identifying himself as his twin brother.

"Samuel Grayson," he said.

"It's me, Melinda. Can you talk?"

"Yes, Olivia and I are just sitting here alone. The kids are in bed and we're relaxing. I've wanted to call you since I heard about your ordeal. I wish I could have been there for you, but there was no way for me to get away from this assignment. How are you doing?"

"They beat me, Micah. They beat me and they broke my arm." She made her voice sound small and weak. "I'm jumping at shadows and having terrible night-mares and panic attacks where I feel like my heart is going to beat out of my chest."

"Sounds like a case of post-traumatic stress syndrome. Are you seeing anyone? A therapist?" His sympathy was evident in his soft tone.

"I can't do that in this town," Melinda protested, and eyed her glass of wine with longing. "If word got out that I was seeing someone it would undermine me and my power to lead."

"Speaking of leads, do they have any where your case is concerned?"

"Nothing." Melinda reached for her wineglass and took a sip and then continued. "I'd say they have their hands full with the murders. I'm assuming you've heard all about them. My kidnapping seems to be on their back burner."

"They'll figure it out. Eventually they'll get the guilty party behind bars in both cases," Micah replied.

"I don't know. It's been almost a month and neither the FBI nor the local law enforcement seems even to have a person of interest in either of the cases."

"How's Dora doing?" he asked, obviously ready to change the subject.

"She is being a good little soldier," Melinda said. "She was on the dean's list last semester and I'm expecting the same kind of accomplishment from her this year. She never misses a class, works in the bookstore and then goes straight home."

"That's good to hear. It won't be long and she'll have her degree and will begin building a real life for herself, far away from her roots."

"That's what we both want," Melinda replied. She was already sorry she called, bored with the conversation and ready to drink her wine and wallow in her own personal successes. "I just wanted to give you a quick check-in. How are things in Perfect?"

"Definitely un-Perfect, but we're working on it."

"Good luck," she said, and then they murmured goodbyes and she clicked off. Tossing the cell onto the sofa cushion next to her, Melinda once again reached for the wine goblet and made a silent toast to herself, commending her decision to leave her home, to never look back when she'd turned eighteen years old.

She wasn't about to allow an alcoholic tramp of a mother, or an abusive father or a mealymouthed younger sister, who was following in their mother's footsteps, to stop her from achieving the recognition and admiration she not only deserved but demanded.

She'd done it all on her own, with no help from anyone. She hadn't had an older sister or brother to pull her up from her coattails and set her on the road to success. She'd carved her own path.

"Here's to me," she whispered out loud, "the smartest member of my dysfunctional family and the smartest person on this entire campus." She drained her glass and leaned back against the sofa, a smug smile playing on her lush lips.

Chapter 4

She hadn't been able to cancel the meal. Dora hadn't seen Mark all week to get the opportunity to tell him that dinner out together wasn't a good idea.

To make matters worse, she'd arrived at Manetti's fifteen minutes early, like a pathetic loser who was afraid she might be stood up or who feared that if she was a single minute late he wouldn't wait for her.

She sat in her car parked across from the popular restaurant and watched for Mark to arrive. Maybe he'd forgotten about tonight. He was a busy man with lots of things on his mind. The invitation had been three whole days ago. She imagined in Mark's world three days could hold a lifetime of thoughts and actions, things that could drive a simple dinner invitation straight out of his mind.

Dora's life was far less complicated and the idea of dinner with Mark had filled her head for most of the past three days. She flipped down the rearview mirror and checked to make sure she didn't have lipstick on her teeth or hadn't gone too heavy with the mascara wand.

It was ridiculous, the way she felt…the fluttering in her stomach, the sparking nerves in her veins. She wasn't a young girl just beginning to experience the blossom of hormones; rather she was a forty-year-old woman on the verge of kissing her hormones goodbye.

She had many regrets from her past, but the deepest regret she'd have for the rest of her life was that she'd had no children. It had been a selfless decision she'd made because she'd known that the last thing she wanted was to bring an innocent child into the mess of her life.

In another year or two when she finally had her life perfect for bringing in a child, she'd be too old to parent, probably too old physically to have a baby the natural way. She'd long ago made peace with the fact that there would be no children for her, but that didn't stop the wistful bittersweet pang that sometimes clutched at her when she thought about it.

That's why she'd spoken to Mark about his daughter and the importance of him being a part of her life. Children should be considered gifts to take care of, not inconveniences to beat and abuse.

She sat up straighter in her seat as she saw a dark car pull into a parking space near the front of the restaurant. The car looked official and her heart danced as Mark stepped out of the driver side.

He was dressed in a dark suit, white shirt and a black-and-gray tie at his neck. She was grateful that she'd opted to put on panty hose and a dress instead of the less casual slacks and blouse. It was obvious Mark had made an extra effort by wearing a tie for the night.

Her dress was rust-colored, cinched at the waist and with a slightly flirty skirt. Although she was taller than most women to begin with, she wore black heels, knowing that Mark would be taller than her even with her high shoes. And there was nothing better for a woman's confidence than a pair of heels that showcased the length and shapeliness of her legs.

Still, the last thing Dora felt was confidence. The flutter of nerves inside her stomach turned into a full orchestra of drumbeats and a discordant brass section. She could always just drive away, stand him up. That would be the smart thing to do, but surely a simple dinner couldn't be a stupid thing.

Decision made, she got out of her car and headed for the entrance. Even outside the restaurant the evening air smelled of rich tomato sauce, of fresh garlic and spices, and her stomach rumbled shamefully because she'd been too nervous to eat anything all day.

The minute she stepped inside and saw Mark standing in the waiting area, a pleased smile curving his lips at the sight of her, her nerves magically vanished.

His smile was so sexy, so warm, and the light in his eyes as he swept her with his gaze from head to toe whispered of intense approval, of male interest.

"I was beginning to wonder if maybe you were going to stand me up," he said.

"And why would I do that?" she countered lightly, shoving all her previous doubts about the night aside.

"It seemed to be some sort of a rite of passage for girls when I was in high school." Before he could say anything more the hostess motioned to them to follow her. She led them to an intimate table in the back of the busy restaurant. She handed them menus along with a bright smile and told them their waitress would be with them shortly.

"Now, what's this about high school and girls standing you up?" she asked as she shoved the menu aside and instead focused on his beautiful eyes shimmering in the light from the candle in the center of the table. "I thought you went to private schools."

"I did. Until I was a junior in high school and then I begged my parents to send me to public school. They finally relented and I began my junior year at Washington High School in Dallas."

He paused as the waitress arrived with a basket of freshly baked mini garlic loaf. He ordered lasagna and meatballs, she ordered chicken Alfredo. He asked for a glass of wine while she went for a diet cola. When the waitress departed he continued.

"I was nerdier than the worst nerd. To be honest I was too smart for the classes, too stupid to try to fit in. So, I became the class joke without really understanding it." He smiled at her ruefully. "Chemistry I did well, people I flunked. I made a total of five dates and was stood up all five times."

"That's awful, they must have been the mean girls in the class." Dora couldn't imagine a hunk like him being stood up by anyone.

He shrugged and reached for a piece of the garlic bread. "The good thing is after a semester of that I was ready to go back to my private school where the other students were more like me." He cocked his head slightly, his gaze a bit more intense. "What about you? What were your high school days like?"

"Definitely unmemorable." The lie slid easily from her lips. It wasn't really a big lie. She'd spent a lot of time trying to forget that time in her life.

"You mentioned you got married at eighteen. That's really young."

"That was my first marriage," she replied, and then blushed. He raised a dark eyebrow. "I've tried marriage twice and both were dismal failures." The last attempt at a happily-ever-after had sent her descending into the very pits of hell.

"You mentioned the other day that you married a man like your father." He took a bite of the garlic bread and then washed it down with a sip of wine.

"Billy Cook." She carefully unfolded her napkin on her lap, refusing to look up as she continued. "I had just graduated from high school and I thought he was my escape from my father, from my life, but instead he was just more of the same abuse and misery. We divorced when I was twenty and then when I was thirty I decided to try the institute of marriage once again."

She paused and looked at him. "Surely I'm boring you."

"On the contrary, I find you and your life fascinating. Who was husband number two?"

"Jimmy Martin. He worked at the bank in town, had an aura of respect and genuine politeness that was appealing to me. He'd come into the café almost every night and flirt shamelessly with me. One thing led to another and we got married. It lasted for two years before things fell apart and that's when I decided romance and marriage just didn't fit into my life."

Billy had been her need to escape, Jimmy had been her first real love and in the end he'd led to her near destruction.

"I feel the same way," Mark said, pulling her from her teetering on the edge of painful memories. "Been there, done that and made a mess of the whole thing. I wouldn't be too eager to try the marriage scene again anytime soon."

His words put Dora at ease. Knowing that they were both on the same page and that this was just a meal between new friends, she felt her nervous tension ebb.

By the time the waitress arrived with their meals, they were deep in a conversation about college football, the traditions of homecoming and the upcoming festivities.

"Friday night before the game on Saturday they always build a huge bonfire on the right quadrant of the campus. It draws a massive crowd and they burn an effigy of a football player from the other team," she said as she dug into her chicken Alfredo.

"Sounds barbaric," he said drily.

She laughed. "Oh, it is. One of the fraternities sponsors it and there are plenty of keg parties before and after. The college board turns a blind eye to all the shenanigans on that one night of the year."

The conversation remained light and easy as they ate. They both admitted that there were no traditions or rituals where they had grown up.

"I guess the biggest tradition that occurred in my household was that each year at Thanksgiving time my mother would order a turkey already stuffed and cooked from the local butcher," he said. "We didn't actually sit down to eat it at any specific time. It was just left out on the counter for us to help ourselves throughout the day when we got hungry."

"Hello, salmonella," Dora exclaimed, loving the sound of his laughter. "I always worked at my mother's café on the holidays. There were no family gatherings for us, either." Daisy, Dora's mother, did have a tradition, but it was a daily event. She'd start each morning with a cup of coffee and the pronouncement that it was a new beginning. And each day by noon she'd be drinking gin and getting sloppy. Before night fell she would have lured at least one man into the back room for a tumble on the cot that was shoved against one corner.

Once again Dora was relieved when the topic changed to favorite foods they shared, colors that attracted them, and they even learned each other's astrological sign. He was Aquarius and she was Libra.

"Compatible signs," he exclaimed, and gave her a smile that threatened to melt everything inside her.

They lingered over coffee and dessert, chatting about nothing and everything. Only once did he seem to disappear from the conversation, going deep into his head with that unfocused look that was slightly unsettling. She tapped his hand and he returned with a sheepish smile.

"Sorry." He shook his head. "I'm sorry."

"Stop apologizing," she replied as she cut into the thick slice of cheesecake in front of her. "So, how is the investigation going? Anything new?"

He cupped his big hands around his coffee mug as

if seeking warmth from whatever visions had momentarily captured his focus. "Absolutely nothing. I feel like we're all running around like Keystone Cops and the perp is someplace nearby laughing at all of us and the useless effort." He lifted his cup to his lips and then set it back down in its saucer. His frustration was evident in the rigid set of his shoulders, in the dark smoldering of his eyes.

"I just can't buy into the theory that it was a gang of students who kidnapped Professor Grayson as a stupid stunt. If that were the case one of them would have talked by now. Somebody would drink too much beer and brag to a friend or tell somebody else, and that hasn't been the case."

"But why else would anyone want to hurt her? I mean, what's the motive for what happened to her?" Dora popped a bite of cheesecake into her mouth as she continued to gaze at him.

"I have a feeling if we could figure out the answer to that then we'd be able to solve everything." He smiled softly and reached across the table with his finger extended. She froze as he touched the side of her lips. "Cheesecake," he murmured, and put his finger into his mouth.

Dora was so entranced she didn't move, could scarcely breathe, and then his words flittered through to her consciousness. "Solve everything? Surely you don't think the kidnapping and the murders are related?"

"Actually, I do. I don't know how, but there's no doubt in my mind that they are somehow related," he replied.

"You can't think that Melind…Professor Grayson

had anything to do with those men's deaths, do you?" She looked at him, horrified by the very thought.

He studied her for several long moments; once again his piercing gaze seeming to see inside her to her very soul. "We're looking at all possibilities," he answered after a long pause. "Now, take that little frown off your forehead. We'll eventually figure it out and I'd much rather look at your beautiful smile."

"Why, Agent Flynn, are you flirting with me?" she asked with a forced lightness.

He looked at her seriously and a slow grin spread across his lips. "Yes…yes, I believe I am." He appeared exceedingly proud of himself as he tossed a hand through his hair, ruffling the muss into a new style of disarray.

Her fingers tingled with the desire to linger in the silky strands, to make order in the chaos, but she clenched her fork tightly instead. "Harmless flirting," she said, and wondered if she was reminding him or warning herself not to take him too seriously.

"That's the only kind there can be, right? I'm here to solve crimes and you're here to get a degree."

"And neither of us is interested in pursuing anything but a friendship," she added.

"Neither of us is looking for a long-term relationship," he countered, and something in the depths of his eyes made her think of the minty soap fragrance of him, of tangled sheets and soft, low moans. Temporary liaisons, that's what he made her think about, and she didn't want to go there.

"It would be foolish to start anything," she said, gazing down at the last of her cheesecake as her cheeks filled with warmth.

"I'm sure you're right," he agreed easily.

Within minutes their check had arrived and she insisted on going Dutch, telling herself that if she paid her own way then this hadn't been anything like a date at all.

"I'll walk you to your car," he said as they left the restaurant. His voice held a slight edge that made her think he believed she'd refuse his offer.

It had been such a nice evening and she didn't want to ruin it by something so simple. Besides, he was just being a gentleman and what difference did it make if he saw her beat-up old vehicle?

He fell into step beside her. "I've enjoyed the night."

She smiled up at him. "Me, too. I can't remember when I last took the time to eat out other than the vending machines in the student lounge."

"This was definitely better than a cold burger or pizza in the war room," he agreed as they reached the driver side of her car.

"Thank you for the wonderful time," she said.

He nodded and moved close…closer still, making it impossible for her to open her car door and escape from his heady scent, the inviting shine in his eyes. She saw the kiss coming in the dip of his head, in the slight lean of his body toward hers.

She told herself she was trapped, caught between him and the door of her car, but the truth was she had no desire to escape. As his head bent, she raised hers, her lips already open to welcome him.

Mark Flynn might have been a nerdy kid in high

school and he might be a man who easily got lost in his own head, but he definitely knew how to kiss.

His lips were warm and feathery soft as they played against hers. There was no other contact between them. He didn't wrap her in his arms and pull her close or lean against her to make their bodies touch.

It was over almost as quickly as it had begun, leaving her wanting more. She cleared her throat and leaned backward to steady herself against the car door. "I thought we agreed that we weren't going to start anything," she said, her voice huskier than usual.

"That was just the perfect finish to a perfect evening," he replied. "Good night, Dora. Safe travel home."

She watched, weak-kneed, while he turned on his heels and headed to his own car. Her trembling fingers punched the remote to unlock the door.

Oh, the man was dangerous. FBI agent Mark Flynn, with his sexy smile and soft lips, with his bedroom eyes and the ability to pull forth a desire inside her that she'd never felt before.

That desire rode with her all the way home from the restaurant. She'd wanted more. She'd wanted his strong arms wrapped tightly around her as he pulled her against his broad chest. She'd wanted him to plunder her mouth until she couldn't breathe, until she couldn't think. She wanted what she shouldn't have.

She tightened her hands on the steering wheel and told herself that as long as she kept control of her emotions, of her desires, then she'd be fine.

Besides, they'd both made it clear to each other that it would be foolish to pursue anything meaningful. It had been a simple kiss and she needed to stop over-thinking things.

She pulled into the driveway of her house and got out of her car. The night air smelled like autumn leaves and a hint of wood smoke. As she walked to her porch, she caught a movement out of the corner of her eye.

She froze with her house key in her hand, poised to unlock the front door. She gazed over to the neighbor's yard. With her porch light shining a halo of light, it was difficult to discern much of anything about the neighbor's place except for the gigantic tree in their front yard.

Was somebody there? Behind the tree?

Hiding?

Watching her?

With her heart's frantic beat echoing in her ears, she fumbled the key into the lock and quickly stepped into her hallway. She slammed the door behind her, immediately relocked it and then hurried to the front window to peer out the venetian blinds in the living room.

There was nothing to see in her front yard, but she could have sworn that the movement that had caught her eye was a person running from view…a person who at this moment was possibly hiding behind the thick trunk of the tree next door.

Fear torched through her. This was the second time she thought she'd been followed…watched. Was she being stalked?

As she thought of what had happened to Melinda she couldn't help but wonder if somebody was watching her and waiting for the perfect moment to kidnap and beat her.

Chapter 5

Melinda Grayson sat on Mark's chest, her long dark hair wild and free and her large green eyes gleaming in the light of a full moon. She was laughing as something pulled tighter and tighter around his throat, choking him…gagging him.

He could smell the dank earth of his shallow grave, was aware of two dead bodies nearby. His heart thundered in his chest, desperately needing the oxygen he was being deprived by whatever was wrapped around his neck. A male's laughter filled the air, joining Melinda's. She tightened her thighs against his sides.

She then leaned down, her lush lips moist and swollen and repulsive. He knew that if she tried to kiss him he'd vomit and aspirate on his own bile. "Die," she whispered, and then threw back her head and laughed as darkness claimed Mark.

He shot up, his gun in hand and sweat pouring off

his body. It took him a moment to orient himself in the dark room. From a slit in the curtains at the window he could see the yellow neon sign flashing *Vacancy*. The motel. He wasn't in some makeshift graveyard. He was in his motel room in Vengeance, Texas.

He clutched the gun so tightly his fingers ached, making him wonder when he'd grabbed it and how long he'd been holding it. With a hand that trembled he placed it on the nightstand and turned on the bedside lamp. A shudder slowly worked its way up his spine.

Thank God he hadn't fired the weapon. He could have killed somebody in the room next to his. He stumbled from the bed and into the bathroom, where he sluiced cold water on his face. When he was finished he dried his face with a towel and then stared at his reflection in the mirror.

This had never happened before. He'd always been able to easily tap into the head of the killer, but not the victim. But he'd been there as a victim, helpless and choking, feeling the life slowly squeezed out of him and knowing that he would soon join the other two dead men in a shallow grave of his own.

His heart finally slowed to a more normal rhythm and he left the bathroom, his mind twisted in confusion. Why now? Why identify with any of the victims? It was as if he'd been there when those three men had been strangled to death, as if he'd seen the way it had gone down with Melinda's glee and her partner's cool efficiency.

Had the dream simply been a manifestation of his need to be right? Of his desire to make Melinda the guilty party because he didn't believe the whole kidnapping issue that his teammates had bought into so easily?

He got back into bed, his brain refusing to turn off despite the fact that it was just after two in the morning. The dream bothered him despite the fact that it was just crazy and all in his head.

He finally fell back asleep and woke up in a foul mood. As if the wild dreams about Melinda and some unknown male killing him hadn't been enough. When he'd finally fallen back to sleep, he had dreams of Dora.

Erotic dreams of the two of them together in his motel room bed. Her smell had permeated the entire place, and her imagined warmth had been a tangible ache when he'd awakened alone in the bed. His intense physical attraction to her had been so unexpected.

He'd told himself she would be a perfect tool to use in his investigation, but he knew now he was only fooling himself. Dora Martin wasn't about to solve these crimes for him; nor did he believe she had any relevant information that might lead to the killer or killers.

What she did have was hair that looked as soft as silk, eyes that held just enough mystery to make him want to explore and an indefinable spark that kept him wanting more from her...of her.

After rolling out of bed he'd taken a long shower, then had dressed and tried to forget Dora Martin. He attended the usual briefing, where they were all told that there was intense pressure coming from Darby College officials as well as the mayor to clean up this whole mess before homecoming week.

This mess. Mark was sure the powers that be in the small town of Vengeance would like nothing better than to somehow sweep this all under a rug, but three men were dead, one of them a state senator. Homecoming was only two weeks away and nothing new had come to the surface to shed the tiniest light on any of the murders or the kidnapping of Melinda Grayson.

They'd interviewed spouses of the dead men, neighbors and friends. Mark himself had conducted a long interview with Senator Merris's aide, Frank Kellerman. He'd found the thirty-eight-year-old man to be angry and closemouthed despite the fact he was cooling his heels in jail for the kidnapping of Peter Burris's baby and sister-in-law. He refused to shed any information that would help the ongoing investigation of the murder of his boss.

Dead ends, and Mark had seemed to have lost his ability to crawl inside the killer's mind. They didn't even have enough information to formulate a viable profile that fit both the kidnapping and the murders.

The usual murder suspect would be a Caucasian male between the ages of twenty-eight and forty. The consensus was that all three men might have known their attacker and were taken by surprise. Certainly the killer had been privy to the secrets that the men had in their lives before their untimely deaths.

It was late afternoon when Mark found himself once again in front of the video equipment, playing and replaying the images of Melinda Grayson with her captor and trying to forget the alarming nightmares he'd had about her the night before.

He watched all four of the videos that had been sent to law enforcement three times and then leaned back in his chair and rubbed his gritty, strained eyes.

Dora. This was about the time of day she'd be making her way to the bookstore. In the brief kiss they'd shared she'd tasted just like he thought she would, like warm sunshine on his lips.

What he'd like to do was walk over and hang out, talk to her and maybe buy her a cup of coffee again after she was finished for the night. But he wasn't going to do that.

Two weeks before homecoming and in his heart he knew Dora had no information that would move the investigation forward. He could pretend all he wanted that he needed her as an informant, but the truth was it had nothing to do with his job—as a man, he wanted her.

That wasn't fair to her. She'd told him she had no place for romance in her life and the last thing he wanted was to be a meaningless distraction from her studies. She could definitely become a distraction to him in his duties, and he couldn't allow that to happen.

With a disheartened sigh, he leaned forward and punched the remote to watch the videos yet again. He was still there an hour later when Richard found him.

"Richard, I want you to see something." A thrum of excitement raced through Mark's veins, an excitement he was afraid to embrace in case he was seeing something that really wasn't there.

Richard eased down in the chair next to him. "You've got to get away from these videos, Mark. You're driving yourself crazy," he said not unkindly. "You need some distance, to get out of this room and try to get an insight into things through another avenue."

"Just wait." Mark hit the rewind button and waited

until he was at the beginning of the loop of the four videos. "For the first time I think I noticed something that I hadn't noticed before. I just want you to focus solely on Professor Grayson. Don't take your eyes off her while you watch," Mark instructed.

Richard released a long-suffering but tolerant sigh. "Okay."

Mark hit the button to play the videos. Neither of them spoke as each scene played out. When the screen went blue Richard leaned forward, a thoughtful frown on his face. "Play it again."

When it had played once again Richard leaned back in his chair and raked a hand through his salt-and-pepper hair. "She flinched," he said as he looked at Mark with a vague surprise. "Each time before her captor hit her, she flinches, as if she's expecting the blow."

Mark nodded and allowed his excitement free rein. "Exactly, and yet she's blindfolded, so she wouldn't see the hit coming, there's no reason for her to flinch and prepare for the blow."

"Unless the whole thing is scripted," Richard said thoughtfully. "I can't believe that I'm starting to buy into what I thought was your very own personal delusion."

Mark laughed. "All the times I've watched these scenes before, I've been focused on the surroundings, the person in charge. I've been trying to find something that would point to where the video was shot and something to identify the captor. I hadn't really focused my whole concentration on the *victim*."

"But, playing devil's advocate here, she might have

flinched just because she was afraid of being hit, unsure of if or when an attack might come."

Mark shook his head. "The flinches are perfectly timed just seconds before she gets hit. She doesn't flinch any other time. I'm telling you, somehow this whole kidnapping was staged."

"But why? Why would a woman like Melinda Grayson do such a crazy thing? She's an esteemed professor, an icon of success around the campus. It doesn't make sense that she would work with somebody to stage her own kidnapping, allow herself to be beaten and then miraculously be released. There's no motive for her to have done that."

"I know," Mark replied, the excitement he'd felt at his discovery quickly ebbing away. "I just can't figure it out. I think we need to dig deeper into Melinda's background, find out exactly what kind of woman she is."

"And I think you need to get out of here and come with me. Some of the guys are calling it a day and doing a little unwinding at Johnnie's Tavern. Pitchers of beer and New York–style brats with spicy onion sticks that will blow the back of your head off." Richard stood. "Come on, Mark. Take the night off and fill your head with grease and booze. We all need a little downtime."

"Okay," Mark relented. He didn't often join the team for anything but the daily briefings. Mark was a loner who allowed in few people, and he knew it was because so many people found him intimidating with his intelligence and strange because of his abilities and his social awkwardness. Richard understood this. However, at the moment, the offer appealed to Mark because not only did he need a break from thinking about the cases, he also needed something to make him stop thinking about Dora.

A half hour later he sat with Richard on his left and Donald Thompson on his right. Lori Delaney was across the table along with Agents Larry Albright and Joseph Garcia.

Within minutes three pitchers of beer adorned the center of the table and orders had been placed for everything from mozzarella sticks to hot wings and, of course, the onion sticks that were a signature dish of the dingy, typical college-town tavern.

"Hey, Mark, nice of you to climb out of your head long enough to join us," Delaney teased when the waitress had left.

"As long as I don't have to crawl into your head, I'm good," he teased right back.

"Right now my head is filled with thoughts of a bubble bath in my own tub and a full night's sleep in my own bed. I hate the motel we're stuck in. I swear they put the noisiest guests in the room next to mine night after night."

"I never thought I'd say it, but I'm actually starting to miss my wife's cooking," Larry said.

Everyone groaned. It was a well-known fact among their team that Larry's wife was an enthusiastic but very bad cook.

As everyone at the table began to talk about what they missed most being away from home, Mark thought of Grace and the phone call and promise he'd made to her.

He'd forgotten to mention it to Dora and it had been Dora who had prompted him to make the call, to make an attempt at being the kind of father Grace needed in her life.

He gazed across the table at Lori Delaney. She was a nice-looking woman with shoulder-length brown hair like Dora's. But Mark didn't want to tangle his hands in Lori's hair. He didn't want to pull her close against him and feel how well their bodies molded together. He wanted to do that with Dora.

He wanted to feel the strands of her hair whirled around his fingers, pull her close to see if her hair smelled of wildflowers. He could easily imagine how neatly she would fit against him.

Sarah was a short, petite woman, and their embraces had always felt awkward, as if they were two pieces of separate puzzles. He knew instinctively that physically Dora's height would make them fit together neatly, as if they were from the same puzzle.

"Earth to Mark." Joseph's voice pulled him back to the tavern. "You've got to try these onion things. They are mucho hot."

"It's the capsaicin," Mark replied.

"The what?" Richard asked.

"Capsaicin, a molecule that is the main component in chile peppers. It's actually an irritant that causes the burning on the tongue." His cheeks flushed as he realized he'd delivered a short speech on something nobody really cared about.

"I've said it before and I'll say it again, I don't ever want to play trivia with you," Lori replied ruefully, and Mark relaxed as everyone laughed.

He used to think that people were laughing at him, but he knew these people who surrounded him. They were colleagues who knew and appreciated his quirks, people who often came to him for minute bits of trivia when investigating one thing or another.

For the next two hours they sat at the table, eating fried and greasy food and drinking far too much beer. They got loud and laughed often as they all blew off the steam of frustration.

It was the work that brought a team together, but it was times like these that bonded a team forever. When Richard's wife had gone through breast cancer treatment it had been the people at this table who had brought food to his house, visited her in the hospital and tried to ease some of Richard's fears. When Sarah and Mark had divorced it had been these people at the table who had offered him comfort and support.

By the time Mark got up to use the men's room he had a pleasant buzz going on and was grateful that the motel where they were staying was walking distance from the tavern. There was enough trouble in town without the embarrassment of one of them being picked up by a local for driving under the influence.

He'd almost made it to the restroom when a loud, strident voice caught his attention. Blearily he gazed at the table in the back corner where a thirtysomething man appeared to be holding court.

"They all were scumbags," he said to the group of three men who were with him. His words slurred, a definite indication that the man had probably had a little too much to drink. "They deserved what they got. I hope the Feds don't solve the damn murders. Whoever killed those men did us all a big favor."

Mark sobered as he continued on his way, suddenly interested in the identity of the man who was so outspoken and publicly applauding a murderer.

When he left the restroom he went to the bar and waited to catch the bartender's attention. "More pitchers for the table?" the bartender, who wore a name tag that identified him as Mike, asked.

"No, thanks, I think we're good," Mark replied. "I was just wondering if you could tell me who that guy is at the corner table in the back, the one wearing the blue shirt."

"That would be Troy Young. Why, is he bothering you? He tends to be a loudmouth, especially when he's had a few."

"No, nothing like that," Mark hurriedly replied. "Thanks."

Troy Young. Mark turned the name over in his head as he walked back to the table of his colleagues.

If Melinda was somehow responsible for the murders, then she had to have a partner. There was no way she could have killed three men and buried them all by herself.

A person of interest, he thought as he rejoined the group. First thing in the morning he'd do a little digging into Troy Young and see if there was anything there or if the loudmouth opinionated guy was just another person who hated liars, cheaters and thieves.

Amanda knocked on Melinda's door and waited for a response. It was almost nine at night, but it wasn't unusual for Melinda to get a sudden brainstorm and need Amanda to come take notes or sit at the computer and pull up research. Melinda didn't adhere to usual business hours. When she needed her assistants she called, no matter the time of day.

Her stomach clenched in irritation as Ben opened Melinda's front door. "How did you get here so fast?" she asked as she shoved past him and into the living room. It usually took Ben ten minutes longer than it did Amanda to get to Melinda's when she beckoned.

"Actually, I've been here for a little over an hour." He flung himself on the sofa, a smug smile on his face. "Melinda is in the bedroom. She should be out shortly."

Amanda stared at him, feeling sick as she recognized the implication he was trying to give her. The idea of Ben in bed with Melinda made her throw up a little in the back of her throat.

"You're lying," she whispered vehemently, not wanting to believe that her idol, her role model would allow somebody like Ben to even touch her. He wasn't good enough to wash Melinda's feet, let alone be in bed with her.

Ben shrugged. "Believe what you want." He grinned slyly. "I'll just say this, I like being teacher's pet."

"Ben." Melinda's voice thundered as she entered the living room from the bedroom clad in an emerald-green dressing gown. "Stop trying to make trouble or you'll make me angry. And you know you don't want me angry with you."

Her eyes were hard chips of jewels that matched her floor-length silk gown. They glowed with a displeasure that chilled Amanda to the bone. Ben's smug smile disappeared from his face. They both had seen Melinda's rages and Amanda knew she never wanted Melinda angry with her.

"We have work to do," Melinda said briskly. "And we don't have time for childish games." She glared once again at Ben, who appeared to sink deeper and deeper into the brown sofa cushion.

Amanda opened her laptop, ready to do whatever she was told by her mentor.

Chapter 6

It had been a quiet Sunday for Dora, who had spent most of the day off cleaning her house and telling herself she didn't care that she hadn't seen or heard from Mark since Friday night.

She was grateful for the arrival of Monday and her regular routine of classes and work. All she wanted to do was focus on what was important in her life and not keep thinking about that darned kiss she'd shared with Mark.

The kiss…so sweet, so evocative, had shaken the very core of her new world. As she sat in the theater and tried to focus on the lecture Melinda was giving, for the first time in three years Dora had difficulty maintaining her concentration and focus.

A vision of Mark's sexy smile kept coming into her head. The sound of his deep laughter filled her ears, and the memory of that kiss made her lips burn and ache for more.

As she watched her sister pace back and forth on the stage, owning the room with her subtle command for attention, admiration swelled up inside Dora.

She'd never been close to Melinda, who had left their hometown immediately after high school graduation when Dora was fifteen. Neither Dora nor their parents had heard anything from Melinda for many years, not until the time that Melinda and Micah had shown up in the small town of Horn's Gulf, Wyoming, to pick Dora out of the gutter and get her some much-needed help.

Although Dora admired her sister and would forever be grateful to her for helping her get on a healthy path for future success, the truth was she didn't know Melinda very well.

It had been Micah whom Dora often turned to when she was feeling overwhelmed. Although Micah was undercover in the small town of Perfect, Wyoming, to clean up some of the mess their brother, Samuel, had made there, Micah always had the time and patience to talk Dora through any problem.

Dora respected and admired her sister, but she loved the brother who she hadn't known existed when she was growing up. Micah had chosen the right side of the law while his twin brother, Samuel, had chosen the wrong side.

Dora had only met Samuel once and that had been enough. Something in his eyes had made her skin crawl. She was glad he was now behind bars, where he deserved to be for the crimes he'd committed.

She refocused on her note taking. Melinda was a

tough teacher. Her tests were the hardest of all the tests Dora had taken and Dora knew her sister had too much integrity to fudge if Dora blew a test. In any case, Dora didn't want that kind of special treatment. She was doing this alone for herself, to become the woman she was meant to be.

By the time the lecture was finished she left the building, a vague sense of disappointment winging through her as Mark wasn't sitting on the bench or standing tall beneath a nearby tree waiting for her.

"And this is the way it should be," she muttered aloud as she headed toward the bookstore. Mondays were always busy. She had two classes in the mornings before Melinda's weekly lectures and then bookstore duty from two until close.

Traffic in the bookstore was hit-and-miss, leaving her time both to study and to think about the past week. She consciously kept her thoughts away from Mark Flynn. Instead, she focused on the idea that she was being stalked.

Even Saturday, as she'd made her way home from the campus, she'd felt the presence of somebody nearby, somebody watching her, somebody who didn't want her to know that she was being watched.

She didn't know if she was just imagining things because of what had happened to her sister or if there was a real threat to her. She didn't know whether to tell somebody that she felt the whisper of danger breathing softly on the back of her neck. The last thing she wanted was to draw attention to herself or be seen as some sort of hysterical woman jumping at shadows.

The only thing she knew for sure was that at the end

of the night she dreaded the three-block walk back to her house. At exactly eight-thirty she locked up the store and stepped out into the encroaching darkness of the night.

She clutched her laptop to her chest, her purse slung across her shoulder, her heart already beating a fraction too fast. The campus appeared deserted, but in the distance she could hear the sound of male laughter drifting from the area where the fraternity housing was located.

With homecoming less than two weeks away, there was already an energy thrumming in the air, an energy that heightened with each day that passed. Banners and flags in the school red-and-gold colors were appearing from windows, across walkways. Brilliant artwork depicting red-and-gold-clad gladiators crunching blue-clad birds underfoot were nailed to trees and adorned classroom windows.

By the time the actual football game and the usual pregame events arrived, the students would be frenzied with school pride and spirit.

Her heart misfired as she heard the distinct sound of heavy footsteps behind her. She quickened her pace, fear hammering through her veins. *Just get home safely,* a voice whispered in the back of her head. *Just keep moving and don't look back.*

"Dora."

The familiar deep voice made her nearly stumble to her knees in relief. She turned to see Mark hurrying to catch up to her. "Oh, my God, Mark, you scared me to death," she said, half-breathless.

"I did?" He stopped next to her on the sidewalk. "Sorry about that."

"What are you doing here?" she asked, her gaze darting from the sidewalk behind him to the nearby manicured tall bushes.

"I intended to catch up with you at the bookstore, but by the time I got there you'd already closed up and then I saw you walking and here I am." He said it as if it all made perfect sense.

It wasn't fear now that kept her heart beating just a little faster than it should. It was his nearness to her, the scent of him, which had become familiar, and a thrill that he'd sought her out once again.

"Why did you want to catch up with me at the book-store?" she asked as they began a slow walk in the direction of her house.

"Because I wanted to see you again." He looked at her as if she should have known his answer before he actually said the words aloud. "And I forgot to tell you the other night that, because of the things you said about fathers and daughters, I called Grace and made plans to visit her as soon as we wrap up things here. We're going for ice cream…two scoops."

"That's good, Mark. I'm so glad." She was glad for a number of things. She was ridiculously pleased that he wanted to see her again and relieved that she wasn't making this walk home alone in the dark. She was also happy that he was obviously set to make things right with the daughter he so obviously loved.

She felt safe with him at her side and yet knew she was a fool to feel the excitement, the giddy rush of his very presence next to her. Still, she remained acutely conscious of their surroundings as they continued to walk toward her place.

"Are you expecting somebody to jump out of the bushes?" he asked, obviously noticing her nervous gazes. "I can feel that you're on edge, Dora. What's going on?"

"Nothing," she replied quickly, apparently too quickly, as he looked at her in disbelief.

"What's going on, Dora?" he repeated.

She could see her house in the distance, her porch light a welcome beam in the darkness. "Why don't you come in and I'll make us a cup of coffee. We can talk a little more inside."

Even in the darkness she could see the flash of his white teeth as he grinned. "That sounds perfect."

She hoped by the time they got inside and she had the coffee brewing he'd forget that anything had bothered her. The last person on earth she wanted to believe that she was just some paranoid nut was Mark.

It felt odd, unlocking the door and allowing him to step into the place behind her. In the three years she'd lived in the house there had never been a man inside other than Micah.

The house was nothing fancy, just a two-story brick with a kitchen, dining room and living area downstairs and two nice-size bedrooms upstairs. It had been furnished with mostly thrift-store furniture and cast-off items she'd picked up when students were leaving college and no longer wanted their college-dorm-style decor.

The only item Dora had bought new was an overstuffed sofa in shades of yellow and red. It was vibrant and looked like sunshine and poppies. She'd fallen in love with it at first glance.

A small computer table sat against one wall, a bookshelf on the other. She'd added throw pillows and scented candles, a large yellow vase of artificial poppies to warm up the house and claim it as her own space.

There was no furniture in the dining room. The small round table in the kitchen was built for two and she'd found it left out by the Dumpster after the end of a semester.

"It's not much, but it's mine," she said as she led him into the kitchen and motioned him into one of the folding chairs at the table. He took off his jacket and she was vaguely surprised to see his shoulder holster and gun. Of course he'd have a gun, she thought, he was an FBI agent. But she'd never seen it before.

"I think it's quite charming," he replied as he folded his length into the chair at the table. He appeared perfectly comfortable to sit and watch as she shrugged off her cardigan sweater, draped it on the back of the chair opposite his and then busied herself making half a pot of coffee.

"I've never seen your gun before," she finally said.

"Does it bother you?" His brows lifted with concern. "I can take my holster off while we have our coffee."

"No, it's fine. I just never really thought about you being a gun-toting kind of guy. So, how's the investigation going?" she asked once the coffee had begun dripping into the glass carafe and she'd gotten out two mugs and a sugar bowl.

"We have a new person of interest."

His words spun her around to look at him. "Really? Who?"

"His name is Troy Young, a local rancher. He was in Johnnie's Tavern last night spouting off how the killer had done everyone a favor. I decided this morning that we needed to look closer at him."

Dora poured the coffee and carried his cup along with the sugar bowl and a spoon to the table. "And what did you find?" she asked. She quickly grabbed her own cup and sat down across from him.

"We're just starting the dig, but I don't want to talk about that right now. What I want to know is what had you so freaked out when you were walking home."

Dora's stomach tightened and she gazed down into her mug. "It's nothing really." She was hoping he'd forgotten all about it.

"Dora, I felt you. I felt the emotion that wafted off you." She looked up in surprise, right into that piercing gaze of his. "It's what I do, Dora. This is what I'm trained for, to feel emotion, to get into people's heads and to become the killer."

"I'm no killer," she mumbled.

He smiled at her, a gentle smile that threatened to be her undoing. "I know that, but something had you spooked out there as we walked home. Tell me why you were afraid."

His gaze had her captured, like a trembling bird in the palm of his hand, and to her horror tears welled up in her eyes to blur her vision. She hadn't realized how fear had simmered inside of her the past week or so until this very moment with the tall, handsome FBI agent looking at her with concern.

"Dora." He instantly got up, walked around the table

and pulled her to her feet. He cupped her face with his strong hands. "Talk to me. What's going on?"

"I know it sounds crazy, but I think I'm being stalked." The fear she'd tried to swallow against for the past week exploded out of her on a choking sob.

Mark could climb into the head of a psychopath, and he could reasonably anticipate the next move of a serial killer, but despite his brief marriage to Sarah, he'd never known much about women, especially crying women.

As Dora began to tremble and cry in earnest, he acted only on instinct. He quickly took off his gun and holster, laid them on the table and then tugged her against him and wrapped her tight in his arms.

With her shapely body filling his arms, fitting just beneath his chin as he'd thought she would, for a moment all he could think about was the sensory pleasure.

She fit perfectly and, just as he suspected, her hair smelled of the sweetness of a field of flowers. She was warm and soft as she buried her head in the crook of his neck.

He caressed a hand up and down her back, tearing his thoughts away from how right she felt in his arms and instead focusing on why she was crying, what she had just said to him.

Stalked?

Why would somebody be stalking Dora? As she finished her crying she stumbled back from him, her cheeks damp and flushed with embarrassment. "I'm sorry," she said as she swiped her cheeks. She gestured him back to his chair at the table, but he ignored her.

Instead he grabbed her by the hand and led her back

into the living room and pulled her down next to him on the comfortable sofa. "Tell me," he said as he twisted his body to face her and took both her hands in his. "Why do you think you're being stalked?"

She squeezed his hands and gave a small self-conscious laugh. "I don't know, maybe I'm just being paranoid because of what happened to Melin…Professor Grayson." She pulled her hands from his and leaned back against the cushions. "The last week or so when I've walked home after work, I've been sure somebody was following me. I've heard their footsteps behind me, but when I turn around nobody is there. When I'm walking between classes I get that prickly feeling of uneasiness and my chest tightens up with fear. The other night I was certain that there was a person hiding behind the tree in the neighbor's yard, watching me." She shivered and once again released a small laugh as if to dismiss her fears.

But Mark wasn't about to dismiss anything. The prickly feeling she talked about, the tensing of muscles and racing of the heart, were all survival instincts, the call to fight or flight.

"I don't want you walking home alone anymore after dark," Mark said, hoping that the strength in his voice would let her know this was a command not a request. "I'll arrange to be at the bookstore each evening when you get off work and I'll walk you back here."

"Oh, that's not necessary," she protested, her cheeks once again turning pink. "Mark, you're here to catch a killer. You aren't here to play babysitter to an overaged student with an overactive imagination."

"Do you normally have an overactive imagination?"

he asked, although he already knew the answer to the question. In the brief conversations he'd shared with Dora he'd found her to be practical and levelheaded, certainly not prone to dramatic imaginings or suffering from a hysterical personality.

"Well, no, but maybe in this case I'm just hypersensitive or something."

"The bottom line is that you're afraid to walk home alone after dark. I can easily fix that by walking you home each night." He couldn't imagine why anyone would want to hurt her. The murdered subjects had all been men and Dora certainly didn't have the public adoration, the powerful aura that Melinda Grayson had, so he couldn't fit Dora into any kind of a kidnapping scheme.

But he had a killer he couldn't access, a kidnapping that didn't make sense and not enough information to try to guess what might happen next or if the crime spree in Vengeance was really over. He only knew that he'd never forgive himself if Dora was murdered or kidnapped and he'd been warned in advance.

"Mark, you have important things to do here in town." She made one last protest, but it didn't have any teeth. Instead, he could hear the relief that had crept into her voice.

He smiled at her. "It's a done deal. I'm going to escort you home on bookstore nights."

"I'd like that," she agreed, as the last of the fear finally left her eyes. "And now let's get back to the kitchen and have our coffee before it gets cold."

He followed her back into the next room, unable to

stop his gaze from lingering on the soft sway of her hips beneath the black slacks she wore.

"Now tell me about this new suspect," she said when they were once again seated at the table. "You said his name was Troy Young. How does he tie into things?"

"At the moment the only thing we know about him for sure is that he's a rancher, recently divorced and struggling financially." Mark placed his gun and holster at his feet. "He frequents Johnnie's Tavern often, and he and Sheriff Peter Burris had some ugly run-ins when Burris was alive. According to the records we obtained, Troy was arrested or ticketed by Burris over ten times in the last year—arrested three times for public intoxication and once for disorderly conduct, and tickets for speeding and other minor infractions. Troy has made no secret of the fact that he hated Burris. He'd even threatened to kill the sheriff more than once when being arrested."

"Does he have ties to the other two victims?"

Mark looked at her with new admiration. "Ah, your criminal-justice classes are showing. He's only a viable suspect if we can tie him to all three victims and so far we haven't found the connection to the other two, but we've only just starting looking at him. Tomorrow afternoon a couple of us are going to talk to him and see if he has a solid alibi for the time of the murders." He added a teaspoon of sugar to his coffee and then took a sip.

"And the kidnapping? Has there been any progress on that case?"

Mark wanted to tell her that he didn't believe a kidnapping had taken place. That somehow, someway, despite the appearance of Troy Young, in spite of his teammates' views, he believed the beautiful professor was at the center of this whole storm.

"Nothing new. She seems to be a fairly isolated person, other than her two assistants. Nobody seems to know her very well."

Dora cast her gaze toward the wall just over his head, a tiny frown dancing in the center of her forehead. "Her assistants probably know her better than anyone, but I know just before her kidnapping she was kind of seeing Andrew Peterson from the history department."

Mark sat up straighter. This was new information. "None of us has managed to find that out."

"I imagine that's because Melinda and Andrew didn't want anyone to know. Andrew is married and he and his wife have three small children."

"How do you know about this?" he asked. As always, the thought of a new lead to follow shot adrenaline through his body. He'd always assumed that if Melinda was responsible for the murders, then she'd had a male partner…the man who had appeared in the videos to beat her.

It was a devious scheme and he knew few women who had the guts to allow themselves to be slapped across the face, who would abide somebody breaking their arm just to prove an alibi.

"I accidently stumbled on them one night," Dora said, bringing him back to the here and now. "I'd kept the bookstore open a little later than usual. They were standing beneath a tree and I was too far away to hear what they were saying, but they embraced and kissed long and hard before they parted ways."

"Did either of them see you?" he asked.

She hesitated and then shook her head. "I don't think so, but I can't be sure."

"Andrew Peterson? And he's in the history department?" Mark repeated.

Dora nodded, her frown deepening. "It might have been nothing, but if it is something you pursue, I hope you'll be discreet. I'd hate to see Andrew's marriage destroyed, because I'm certain Melinda isn't looking for any kind of a long-term relationship, at least that would be my impression of her," she quickly added.

"We'll try to be as discreet as possible, but we are investigating a crime," he reminded her.

For the next few minutes, they talked about what each had done that day. When they finished their coffees, Mark knew it was time to leave. They both had early mornings the next day and it was after eleven. He grabbed his holster and fastened it back on, then pulled his lightweight jacket on, effectively hiding the weapon.

As she walked with him back through the living room he wondered what her bedroom would look like. He had a feeling it would be a romantic room, with a flowered spread and fragrant candles, the scent of her in every corner.

When they reached her front door he turned to tell her good-night, but instead reached for her, wanting to feel her in his arms one last time before heading back to the motel and his lonely bed.

He thought she might protest, but she came willingly into his embrace, leaning her head into the crook of his neck and once again reminding him of how well they physically fit together.

Desire flared inside him, hot and eager as he'd never felt before. It drove every thought out of his head, something that never happened. He was focused completely on Dora, on the warmth of her curves against him, on her soft breaths that heated the side of his neck.

She stood close enough to him to know that he was aroused, and as she raised her head to look up at him, he took her mouth with his, plundering, exploring. She reciprocated, winding her arms around his neck and pressing more closely against him.

The kiss seemed to last a lifetime and yet wasn't long enough, would never be long enough. It was she who broke it and stepped back from him, her eyes sparkling overly bright and her breathing coming too quickly.

"I want you, Dora. I haven't said those words to a woman for a very long time."

She closed her eyes, as if finding his words almost painful to hear. "I want you, too." The words were a mere whisper. She looked at him once again. "But I can't do this, Mark. I don't want us to become lovers. It will just complicate things between us and make them messy." She took a step backward, as if needing to physically distance herself from him.

"I don't want to lose you as a friend," she continued, her gaze not meeting his. "I know, I'm being selfish. I want to talk to you. I want to spend time with you, but I'm afraid of making love with you. Somehow, someway, that kind of a relationship has always screwed me up and I can't screw up now...I just can't."

"And I don't want you to," Mark replied, despite the

disappointment that slowly drained out of him, taking with it his desire to possess her intimately.

She glanced up at him, her eyes holding such misery he felt it in his soul. "I want you, but it won't be long and you'll be back to your real life in Dallas, and I have my school to finish and a life to begin. Is it too much to ask for your friendship and nothing more?" She bit her bottom lip as she waited for his response.

"Dora, I don't want to take from you any more than you're comfortable giving." He wanted to reach out for her again; instead, he shoved his hands in his jacket pockets. "I like spending time with you, I love seeing your beautiful smile. We can be friends until it's time for me to leave. We can remain friends after I leave here, if that's what you want."

Her features brightened and she released a sigh of relief. "I just want you to understand that my decision not to have a physical relationship with you has nothing to do with you and everything to do with me."

This time he did step toward her and stroked a hand down the side of her face in reassurance. "I get it, Dora, and I'm okay with it."

Minutes later as he stepped out of her house he drew in a deep breath of the night air, hoping to chase away the scent of her that lingered in his head.

He liked her intelligence, her laughter and her ability to keep him outside his own head. But he'd like to have it all—not just those things, but her passion and her desire, as well.

Still, if he couldn't have it all, he'd take what she was willing to give because he couldn't imagine his time here in Vengeance without her as a part of it.

What he wondered more than anything was, what had happened in her past that made her so wary of allowing herself any physical pleasure? What had her ex-husbands done to her that had made her so afraid of love?

Chapter 7

It was just after ten the next morning when Mark and Richard headed out to the north side of town where Troy Young lived. At the briefing that morning Mark had told the other agents about Andrew Peterson and the possible affair with Melinda, but everyone seemed to believe that Troy was their man. By the time the briefing was finished he feared that the information about Andrew Peterson and Melinda had been lost in the shuffle.

"I feel like nobody was listening to me today," Mark said as he rolled down the passenger window of the car to allow in some of the cool, fresh air. "You're the only one who has taken my theory about Melinda halfway seriously."

"You know why nobody was paying attention to your information today," Richard said. "We now have two strikes against Troy Young. If we can figure out if he ties into David Reed, then we've got somebody who is three for three in the motive department, and that makes Troy our most viable suspect."

Mark heaved a deep sigh and focused out the side window. The day before, Joseph Garcia had discovered that Troy Young had written and emailed Senator Merris, the communications filled with vicious words and threats.

Apparently Troy Young's father had worked for billionaire, and Melinda's ex-husband, Gabe Dawson's oil company and had been one of the many men laid off when Senator Merris had embezzled from the company and run it into the ground. Troy's father had committed suicide after his layoff and Troy had blamed the senator for his father's death.

Just three days before the murders, Troy had fired off yet another email, damning the senator and promising that one day he'd pay the piper for his crimes.

Those communications to the senator, coupled with Troy's hatred of Sheriff Burris, had the whole team buzzing with the scent of a solve in their noses.

All they needed to do was tie Troy to David Reed and then they could probably build a case that would lead to an arrest. Had Mark been that wrong in his theory about Melinda? Certainly, he'd been wrong before in his career, but this one felt different. His instincts were still screaming even though a potential viable suspect had emerged.

"Are you going to pursue the Andrew Peterson angle anyway?" Richard asked.

Mark shrugged. "I think it's something that needs to be done. I think it's something I have to do. Even if we make Troy Young as the murderer, that doesn't answer the questions about Melinda's kidnapping. I'm just not ready to let Melinda Grayson off the hook yet. I need to know where this piece fits into the puzzle. If nothing else, he needs to be checked out concerning the kidnapping. Maybe he had something to do with it because she threatened to tell his wife about their affair."

"That's the first actual potential motive that's come to the surface concerning the kidnapping. It would definitely be nice to come up with a solve of both of the crimes at the same time. You need help you let me know," Richard said.

Mark shot him a quick grin. "You going rogue with me?"

Richard laughed and then sobered. "Even if we get the killer behind bars, we still don't have any answers as to Melinda's kidnapping. Your theory of a spurned or scared lover at least makes sense."

"But, once the killer is arrested, we'll be pulled out of here and back to Dallas. The kidnapping investigation might or might not continue with the local law enforcement, depending on the new sheriff," Mark replied. "And I hate to leave unfinished business behind, even if it is deemed not our business anymore."

"I'm like you, I'd like to have all the answers when we leave here." For the next couple of miles they rode in silence. And in the silence, Mark's thoughts turned to Dora and the night before.

Mark had loved Sarah when they'd married, but it had been a quiet love that was comfortable and easy… until it wasn't. She began to resent his long hours, his time away from home, and slowly their love had changed into nothing more than a friendship.

Mark's desire for Dora screamed inside him. There was nothing comfortable or easy about it and that excited him. But she wanted to keep things on a friendship level and he would do that because he had to, because he'd rather have part of Dora than none of her at all.

He sat up straighter in his seat as Richard pulled down the dirt road that led to Troy Young's place. Troy's house was a small ranch bleached into multiple shades of gray and beige by the sun and wind. It screamed for a coat of fresh paint and some basic maintenance. However, the cattle herd in the pasture next to the house looked well fed and healthy, and the nearby barn appeared to be well maintained.

Richard hadn't even turned off the car before the medium height, dark-haired rancher stepped out on his front porch. The man was clad in jeans and a white undershirt. His face was pale and his eyes narrowed as if the overhead sunshine tortured the last vestiges of a hangover.

He didn't move from his planted position in front of his door as Richard and Mark climbed out of the car. There was no question as to Richard's and Mark's identities. The day was cool and each of them wore their dark windbreakers with the bright yellow FBI letters on the front and back.

"Gentlemen," Troy greeted them. He didn't smile, but he also showed no sign of nervousness or anger at their appearance. "What can I do for the FBI this morning?"

Richard made the appropriate introductions. "We'd like to come in and ask you some questions."

Troy hesitated and seemed to weigh the pros and cons of allowing two FBI agents into his home. He finally gave a curt nod and opened the door, going inside ahead of them.

When he disappeared into the dark interior, Richard and Mark exchanged glances. The door remained open in invitation, but invitation to what? Both men drew their weapons and advanced toward the door.

Mark went in first to see Troy slumped against a corner of a sofa. As he saw Mark's gun he raised his hands above his head in alarm. "Look, I know the place is a mess, but I didn't know you shot men for that."

Mark relaxed a bit and holstered his gun as Richard did the same. Troy motioned them to two chairs across from him, one of them holding a take-out pizza container and the other a pile of newspapers. The house smelled of rotten garbage, dirty clothes and stale booze.

"Just toss that crap on the floor," Troy said, and raised a hand to the side of his forehead where he rubbed as if to ease a headache. "My loving wife left me two months ago and I haven't felt like cleaning up since then."

Unlike the night Mark had seen him in the bar, pumped up by alcohol, shoulders rigid with indignation as he spewed vitriol, the man in front of them now appeared smaller, beaten down by life and circumstances beyond his control.

Mark moved the pizza box to the floor and sat in the chair opposite Troy. "We're here to talk to you about your correspondence with Senator Merris."

"You mean all the hate mail that I sent to the bastard." Troy nodded. "I wondered when somebody would be around to ask me about it. I'm surprised you haven't been here to talk to me before now."

Richard sat in the chair next to Mark and pulled out a small pocket recorder. "Do you mind?" he asked as he turned it on to tape the conversation. Troy shrugged, didn't seem to care one way or the other. "You must have a lot of anger directed at the senator."

Troy snorted. "We both know that's an understatement. I won't lie, I hated the man, his policies and his corruption. He robbed good people of their jobs. He destroyed my father with his greed."

"Several of your notes and emails indicated something to the effect that he would 'get his.' What exactly did you mean by that?" Richard asked.

Troy leaned forward. "I sure as hell didn't mean that I intended to strangle him to death. I was talking about karma, you know, that somehow karma would make him pay for his crimes, that eventually something bad would happen to him. Guess I was right, karma got him." He slumped back against the sofa back.

"We're not looking for a killer named karma," Mark replied drily. "It was a real person who strangled the senator and the others."

"And speaking of the others, we also understand that you had quite a few run-ins with Sheriff Burris."

Once again Troy's features darkened. "That man was a bully who liked pushing people around and he seemed to take special pleasure pushing me. I'm the only person in town who got a ticket for spitting on the sidewalk. Now, do you really think I'm the only cowboy in this one-horse town who ever spit on the sidewalk?" His outrage was showing. His face flushed with color and he was no longer slumping into the sofa but rather sat up straight, shoulders tensed.

He gazed first at Richard and then at Mark. "You two think I had something to do with those murders? Anyone in town will tell you I hated both of them. They'll also tell you I'm a drunk, a loudmouthed blowhard, but I'm not a killer."

"Did you know David Reed?" Mark asked. Instantly Troy's shoulder grew more rigid and the flush on his face deepened.

Troy swiped a hand down his jaw, suddenly looking far older than his years. "I'm not going to lie to you. You're probably going to hear about it around town anyway. It was all the gossip when it happened. Yeah, I knew him. He's the reason my wife left me."

A person of interest with personal ties to all three victims. It wasn't looking good for blowhard Troy Young, Mark thought. "What do you mean he's why your wife left you?" Mark asked.

Troy released a deep sigh and once again slumped back against the sofa cushions, a beaten man. "Mr. Slick sports writer seduced her. They had a brief affair and Kathy was stupid enough to think she actually meant something to him. Two months ago she told me I couldn't give her the things she wanted in life and she moved into an apartment in town." He frowned, as if suddenly aware of his precarious position in the investigation. "I'm in trouble, aren't I?"

"Where were you in the twenty-four-hour period that the murders took place?" Mark asked.

"It's been almost a month ago. Hell, I'd have to think about it, and I think I'm done talking to you now." He got up from the sofa and walked to the front door, opening it and looking at them both expectantly.

Richard turned off the tape recorder and tucked it back in his pocket and then together he and Mark left the house and headed back to their car.

"What do you think?" Richard asked once they were on the road back to the courthouse in the middle of town. "Gut instinct?"

Mark cast him a wry smile. "I must be hungry because my gut instinct isn't talking to me right now. He has motive to kill all of them. It's probably going to be difficult for him to provide an alibi for the entire time in question, but somehow I don't think he's bright enough to pull something like this off."

"The team is going to love him."

Mark stared out the passenger window, his thoughts going in all directions. The memory of his nightmare about Melinda suddenly chilled him.

Was it time for him to let go of his idea that she somehow had a finger in the deaths? Had they found their guilty party and all they needed to do was get him under arrest…case closed?

At exactly eight o'clock Dora closed the bookstore and stepped outside to see Mark standing nearby. Relief mingled with pleasure at the sight of him. After the unexpected awkwardness of the night before she hadn't been sure he'd really show up.

"Coffee?" he asked with a smile that warmed her from head to toe.

"Sounds perfect," she replied, and fell into step next to him as they headed toward the nearby coffee shop.

"Good day?" he asked.

"The usual day. Classes and work, but yes, it was good. What about you?"

"We brought in a suspect late this afternoon. He's being held for questioning in the murders."

"Really? Who is it?"

"I mentioned him to you last night. Troy Young, whom we've now discovered had motive to want all three of the murdered men dead. We'll hold him for as long as we can and in the meantime tonight several of the men are conducting a search warrant on his place."

"Shouldn't you be there?" she asked, immediately feeling guilty about taking him away from his work.

"Nah, they can do it without me," he replied easily.

"So, you think he's the one?"

Mark didn't reply and he stopped walking, his eyes with that hazy cast that let her know he'd disappeared into his head where murders were solved and where his desire for her had been stowed away when she'd denied it any life the night before.

She allowed him to stay inside his head for several minutes and then tugged on his arm. "Mark? Come back to me."

He looked at her with the heavy-lidded blink that indicated he was rejoining the here and now. "Do you think you have the right man behind bars?" she repeated.

"To be honest, I don't know. There are still some things that bother me," he said as they continued on down the sidewalk.

"Things like what?"

He smiled. "Things that you shouldn't be worrying about." They passed a new banner that hung between two trees. Go Gladiators, it read. The background was bright red and the letters an electric yellow. "So, tell me about more about these homecoming festivities. Do you usually participate?"

"It would almost be sacrilegious not to," she replied with a small laugh. "I always attend the bonfire on Friday and then go to the football game on Saturday night. That's about the extent of my participating."

"If I'm still in town could I join you for the fun?"

She looked up at him and as always her heart leaped in her chest. "I'd like that," she replied as they reached the coffee shop.

As she took their usual table and he went to get the coffee, she thought of his request. *If I'm still in town...* it was a definite reminder that he was only here temporarily to do his job and then he'd be gone. They already had a viable suspect under arrest. Mark would probably never make it to homecoming. He'd be gone back to Dallas and his life.

A bittersweet feeling of both regret and relief flooded through her as she thought about the near-capitulation of the night before. She'd wanted more than anything to let him take her into her bedroom and make love to her until the morning light.

She knew she'd made the right decision in denying them both what they wanted, and his words about homecoming merely confirmed her decision.

She was used to being with the wrong men. Unfortunately, she believed that Mark might have been the right man, but at the wrong time.

When he returned to the table they sipped their coffee and talked about other cases he'd worked on in the past. Dora found it...him...fascinating. She told herself it was because she wanted to go into his line of work, but she knew it was much more than that.

She loved his clean scent and the way his slow, sexy smile began at the left corner of his lips and then spread out. She liked his abruptness, found his awkwardness in a social setting endearing. She was fascinated by the host of trivial information that occupied so much space in his amazing brain.

She was going to miss him when he left. He'd filled a space in her life she hadn't realized was empty until he'd given her back the pen he'd borrowed.

They were just about finished with their coffee when Amanda Burns came whizzing through the door. She looked exhausted and frazzled as she headed to the counter. After she got her coffee, she turned and appeared for the first time to notice Mark and Dora.

"Hi, Dora," Amanda said, her brown eyes deep with weariness.

"Hello, Amanda. Amanda Burns, this is FBI agent Mark Flynn," Dora said.

"Nice to meet you, Agent Flynn."

"Please, make it Mark." He offered her a friendly smile.

"Amanda, you look absolutely exhausted," Dora said.

Amanda offered her a grim smile. "To tell the truth,

I am. Professor Grayson is on a research jag, and I seem to be the one assigned to do all the work."

"What kind of research?" Mark asked.

"Everything I can find on sociopaths. Sociopathic killers in society, traits and backgrounds of known killers who have been diagnosed as sociopaths." Amanda shrugged. "I think maybe she's secretly writing a book or something."

"Isn't that the name of the course she's teaching? Sociopaths in Society?" Mark asked.

Amanda nodded. "Yes, and she's already gotten everything she needs for the course. She just wants more on the topic."

"She's well published in the industry," Mark said, and both Amanda and Dora looked at him in surprise. He smiled at them. "What can I tell you, I have an eclectic taste in reading material."

"She is well published in psychiatric journals, but I get the feeling that this is for something much bigger than just an article. It's just my guess, but I think it's a book. Maybe she was offered a big deal after her kidnapping." She checked her watch and frowned. "And I better get going." A tired smile curved her lips. "It was nice seeing you again, Dora, and nice meeting you, Agent...Mark."

As she hurried out of the door, Dora watched her go with concern. Amanda was a sweet girl and Dora hated to see her so harassed and stressed-out.

"Poor thing," she said, more to herself than to Mark. "She looked so exhausted."

"Professor Grayson seems to be a tough taskmaster," Mark observed.

"I know she's a tough teacher," Dora replied, always more than a little bit uncomfortable when it came to talking about Melinda with anyone else.

"I should probably get home," she said as she stood. It was time for the coffee shop to close and time for her to allow him to walk her home and then go on about his own official business.

"I can't thank you enough for doing this," she said as they hit the sidewalk outside. Night had tumbled down, darkening the area except for where an occasional streetlamp pooled a halo of light to the ground.

"Believe me, I know what it's like to be scared, and it's not a feeling I'd want anyone to experience if I can help it."

She looked at him, his features cast in darkness. "Does your work sometimes scare you?" she asked curiously.

"Scares me lots of times," he admitted easily. "But, fear is a good, healthy response to a perceived danger. It's a primal response that helps keep us alive."

"In any case, I appreciate you helping to alleviate some of mine even though I can't imagine why I'd be in any danger. I still think it's possible I'm just a little bit on edge and imagining things because of what's happened here in town."

They had almost reached Dora's house when Mark stiffened beside her and grabbed her arm with a sense of urgency. "Your imaginary stalker is at the window on the side of your house," he said softly as he reached inside his jacket.

Dora released a startled gasp as she spied the dark figure at the side of her house.

"When I say go, you run straight to your front door, get inside and lock the door," Mark whispered.

"What are you going to do?" Dora asked in alarm. She wanted him to come with her, to run inside the house and lock the door against any danger to either of them.

"Go," he replied, and gave her a little shove as he took off running toward the house. Dora ran just behind him, her heart beating frantically, her gaze focused entirely on her front door.

Get inside and lock the door. Her brain screamed the command as she hit her porch. Mark had disappeared in the darkness, and the fear that screamed inside her begged to be released as she realized her fears were true…somebody was really stalking her.

Amanda raced back to her apartment, coffee already half-gone and her thoughts spiraling out of control and shooting in all directions. The day before, Melinda had given her the assignment to research everything she could find on the internet concerning sociopaths. Initially Amanda hadn't thought it a big deal…until she'd actually started the daunting task.

There were thousands of articles about the mental illness, thousands of pages about killers, child abusers and other criminals who had been diagnosed with the personality disorder.

Much of it Amanda knew Melinda already had in her books and papers on the subject, so she didn't understand why she had been given a task that felt remarkably like stupid busywork.

And something was definitely going on between

Ben and Melinda. Something wrong. Amanda reached her apartment and sank into the sofa, sipping the last of the coffee as she thought of her boss and her coworker.

Secrets. They seemed to share secrets that didn't include her. If she entered a room when the two of them were there, there was a sudden pregnant silence. They didn't seem to want her to hear them.

Things had just gotten weird and Amanda couldn't quite place her finger on what was going on. She only knew that for the first time since she'd started working for Melinda she'd begun to see some flaws in her idol.

The fact that Amanda was relatively certain Melinda had invited Ben into her bed wasn't just nauseating, but so beneath the brilliant woman Amanda had thought she'd known.

Lately Melinda would occasionally fall silent, as if in her own world inside her head, and a small curve would lift her lips. But when jarred out of her thoughts, there was a second when her huge green eyes looked hard and wicked and frightening.

The truth of the matter was that Amanda had begun to distrust the woman she'd once admired above all others. She certainly couldn't talk about her feelings with Ben, who had always been a besotted fool where Melinda was concerned. If Melinda told Ben to jump off a cliff he wouldn't hesitate if he knew it would make Melinda happy.

She thought about the FBI agent she'd met. Mark. He'd seemed nice and she'd always liked Dora, but what would she tell them? That something strange was going on but she couldn't put her finger on it? That her coworker was sleeping with the boss and Amanda was jealous of the relationship they seemed to have formed? A relationship based on sex and secrets?

She tucked a strand of her long blond hair behind her ear with a weary sigh. Maybe everything seemed strange because she was functioning on empty. What she needed more than anything was about twenty-four hours of uninterrupted sleep. Unfortunately, that wasn't in her near future.

She drained the last of her coffee and headed to the computer where a screen saver of butterflies filled the monitor with splashes of color. It would take all night for her to accomplish what Melinda wanted done by morning and even then it wouldn't be a complete job. There was just too much to do.

Fighting back weary tears, she sat down and got to work.

Chapter 8

Mark raced after the dark figure that he'd seen at Dora's window. It was definitely a man. Clad all in black and with a ski mask on, the man made it difficult to discern anything else about him other than he was fast on his feet.

"FBI…halt!" Mark yelled, but the figure continued to race ahead.

Unwilling to fire a gun in the dark without knowing who else might be around, Mark followed after him, slowly gaining ground in the foot chase that took them from Dora's house, down the sidewalk and across to the campus grounds.

A ping off a nearby tree had Mark jumping for cover as he realized the man he pursued not only had a gun but wasn't afraid to fire it.

He dove behind a trash bin, his heart pounding with the rush of adrenaline. When he saw the back of the figure, he left his cover and once again continued the pursuit.

They were in the middle of the campus now, between the history department building and a row of fraternity houses. When the man in black turned back toward Mark, Mark leaped behind a tree. He heard the sound of a bullet whiz by.

Once again as the figure disappeared around the side of a building, Mark burst out from behind the tree. He ran at full speed, ignoring the stitch that nagged at his side.

His heart pounded so hard it felt as if it threatened to burst out of his chest. His only thought was that he needed to get to the man—he needed to find out who he was and what he wanted with Dora.

When he reached the corner of the building, he paused and then whirled around in a shooter stance. And there was nobody to shoot.

The moon shone down on the empty ground, and Mark had no idea in which direction the man had gone to completely disappear. He searched for another fifteen minutes and then headed back to Dora's house, his heart still banging with fight-or-flight adrenaline.

Why would a man with a gun be at Dora's window? One thing was clear—Dora's imaginary stalker definitely wasn't an imagination. Somebody was after her and what he needed to figure out was who and why.

By the time he reached Dora's house his heartbeat had returned to something resembling normal and his gun was back in his holster. He'd already contacted a couple of the members of his team to do a sweep of the campus and intended to meet them at Dora's place.

Mark wanted to see if they could find the bullets that had just missed him.

With a bullet they would at least find out what kind of gun had been used, and if and when that gun was found the markings on the bullets would match to it.

In the meantime he needed to make sure that Dora was okay and he needed to have an in-depth talk with her about who might want her harmed.

She unlocked her door after he knocked and called out her name. When he stepped inside the entry she fell straight into his arms. Tears streamed down her face as she hugged him close. "I was afraid. I was so afraid for you." She stepped back and gazed at him from head to toe, as if to assure herself that he was truly okay.

"He got away from me. But the man at your window had a gun." He ignored her gasp of shock. "Your imaginary stalker is very real, Dora, and nobody comes knocking on a window on the side of your house with a gun in his hand and goodwill in his heart."

She stepped back from him and stumbled against the sofa, dropping as though she'd been hit with a stun gun. "But, who...why?" She looked up at him with her beautiful gray eyes.

"That's something we need to figure out," he replied. He sat down on the sofa next to her, trying to maintain a professionalism when all he wanted to do was wrap her in his arms and carry her away from any danger. He wanted to take the simmering fear out of those beautiful eyes. "Do you have any idea who might want to hurt you?"

She shook her head, softly at first and then more vehemently. "No, I can't imagine. I mean, I'm just a student here. I mind my own business, go to classes and work in the bookstore. I don't make any close friends, but I also don't make enemies, I just focus on my studies and my job."

He knew that would be her answer because he already knew that about her. He was the anomaly in her quiet, orderly life. He was the friend, the wannabe lover, the only man she'd allowed to get close to her in some time.

"What about your ex-husbands?"

"Oh, Mark, I haven't seen or heard from either of them in years. Billy and I parted ways when I was twenty and Jimmy and I divorced over eight years ago. That can't be the answer. There would be absolutely no reason for either of them to want to hurt me after all these years."

The doorbell rang and she jumped nearly a foot off the sofa. "That will be members of my team." He got up to open the door, and Richard, Donald and Joseph came in. Mark quickly made the introductions and filled in his fellow agents on what had happened.

"Joseph, I'd like you to sit on this house for the rest of the night," Mark said. "I don't think this creep will return, but we can't be sure and I don't want to take any chances." He turned his attention to Richard and Donald. "We need to see if we can find the bullets he fired or anything else he might have dropped while he was running from me."

Dora got up from the sofa as Mark and the other agents prepared to leave. Mark grabbed her by the hand. "You'll be safe for the night. Joseph will be right outside and nobody is going to come near this place."

She leaned toward him, as if needing his arms around her, and he couldn't deny himself or her. He pulled her against him and gave her a kiss on the forehead. "It's going to be okay, Dora," he said as he finally released her. "We're going to get to the bottom of this."

With these words Mark left the house with Richard and Donald trailing just behind him. "Getting pretty cozy with the bookstore lady," Donald observed.

"She's a nice woman," Mark replied, and hoped that particular topic was dropped.

"She's a nice woman who looked pretty much at-home in your arms," Richard said, ignoring Mark's sigh.

"I like her, okay? I like her a lot. She's been a piece of sanity in this whole mess of a case, a person to talk to when I need to unwind and just enjoy somebody's company."

They moved to the window where Mark had first stopped the potential intruder. Richard flipped on a high-power flashlight and together they scanned the area for anything the perp might have dropped or left behind. "I'll print the window," Richard said.

"You won't find anything. He was dressed all in black, like a ninja warrior. I'm sure he was smart enough to wear gloves. Besides, when I saw him he wasn't trying to get inside, he was just crouched down by the side of the house."

"I'll dust for prints anyway and then catch up with the two of you on campus," Richard replied.

"Who would want to hurt a nice bookstore lady?" Donald asked as he and Mark headed toward the area of the campus where the shots had occurred.

"She has no idea. I have no idea, but I can tell you that the gun had a silencer. Whoever it was meant serious business." Mark's gut clenched as he realized how close it had been. The man could have gotten in through the window and waited for Dora in the darkness of a bedroom. Nobody would have ever known until it was too late.

"This is all we need," Donald muttered beneath his breath. "With Troy Young in jail I've been counting the hours until I can get back to Dallas and my own place."

"If the case is built that Troy Young is guilty, then we're still on our way out of here. Stalking issues are not our problems," Mark said, less enthused about getting out of town without everything being tied into a nice neat knot. "The locals will take over the kidnapping of Professor Grayson and this stalking case."

"Could they somehow be related?" Donald asked.

"I don't see how," Mark replied. He stopped by the tree he'd hidden behind when the first bullet had flown. "I'll tell you one thing. Whoever this is, he's in good physical condition. He was fast, faster than me," Mark admitted. "I didn't want to return fire because I didn't know if there might be a student sitting out here somewhere in the dark. Damn, but I wish I would have caught up with him."

"Well, finding a bullet would be a start," Donald said.

After half an hour Richard joined them and they searched for another hour and found plenty of things on the ground and in the bushes. Gum and candy wrappers, a paperback book that was weathered by more than one rainstorm, and a single pink sock. Although the grounds of the college looked pristine on the surface, it was evident that the groundskeepers rarely bent their backs to beat the bushes.

"Ugh, I'm not picking that up," Donald said in disgust as he pointed to a condom. "Why don't we pack it in? Those bullets could have gone anywhere and it's obvious the perp didn't drop anything. We've been back and forth over the territory the two of you covered half a dozen times."

Mark looked at the illuminated dial of his watch. Almost midnight. He stared at the building that housed the history department and remembered what Dora had told him about Melinda and history teacher Andrew Peterson.

Funny that the man he'd chased had run to this area of the campus, as if it were his territory, a familiar place. Was it possible that Melinda and the teacher were behind the murders? A lovers' thrill, the secret of murder could certainly spice up a relationship.

Or maybe it had been Peterson who had kidnapped Melinda, angry that she'd either spurned or threatened him. Maybe he'd kidnapped and beaten her to teach her a lesson and maybe he knew that Dora had seen him and Melinda together. That would make Dora a loose end, and nobody in the game of crime liked loose ends.

Nobody had spoken to Andrew Peterson with all the excitement about Troy Young. That particular piece of information had been deemed unimportant.

Let it go, an inner voice whispered in his head. Maybe it was time to let Melinda off the hook for the murders and pursue another avenue in her kidnapping. Maybe she didn't show as much fear as he'd expected her to because she knew it was Andrew who held her captive, because she knew he was angry and might hurt her but wouldn't kill her.

Maybe she really was a victim and the only reason she hadn't fingered Peterson was because she still had some feelings for him.

He made a mental note to have an interview with Peterson the next day. If nothing else, Peterson knowing that Mark knew his secret might mitigate any threat to Dora, if that's where the threat was coming from.

"Mark!" It was obvious by the aggravation in Donald's voice that this wasn't the first time he'd called out Mark's name.

"Yeah?"

"I said let's call it a night."

Mark nodded and the three of them headed back toward Dora's place, where Richard had parked his car. Donald got into the passenger seat of the car and Richard remained standing by the driver door with Mark. "You've got her covered for tonight, but what are you going to do about tomorrow night and the next night?"

"I'll figure something out," Mark said. If his theory about Peterson had legs, then a chat with the man might possibly put an end to the stalking or any threat to Dora.

"You know she's crazy about you," Richard said.

Mark looked at him in surprise. "How do you know that?"

Richard released a deep rumble of laughter. "I've been around a long time and it was obvious in the way she looked at you, in the way she needed your embrace. I don't know what you've got, man, but you've definitely caught her on your hook."

As Mark climbed into the backseat of the car, Richard's words weighed heavily in his heart. He was pretty hooked on Dora. Now, all he had to do was keep her alive to see if there might be the possibility of a real relationship between them sometime in the future.

Dora woke early the next morning after a night of restless sleep and bad dreams. She stumbled into her kitchen as dawn was breaking and fixed a short pot of coffee, her head filled with thoughts of Mark and the horrifying events of the night before.

At least she now knew she wasn't losing her mind, jumping at shadows and imagining a stalker. The stalker was real. The very idea terrified her and sent an icy shiver up her spine.

Minutes later she sat at her table, her hands cupping a mug of coffee, seeking the warmth that might steal away some of the cold that had taken grip of her since the moment she'd realized somebody was at her window.

Even after downing a full cup of the warm brew the chill inside her remained and she knew there was only one thing that could take it away.

Mark.

How she longed for his arms wrapped around her right now, his body pressed tight against hers. There was passion there, the joy of life, but also a feeling of safety, of security.

In the short time they'd known each other she knew he was nothing like the men in her past. Despite what he did for a living, in spite of his ability to get into the minds of killers, there was a gentleness, a kindness about him that she trusted.

She wondered if she'd see him today. It was her night off at the bookstore and she'd forgotten to tell him. Each week she had a different night off. Last week it had been Wednesday and this week it was today.

He'd show up to walk her home only to be told she hadn't worked that day. Would he come by here to check on her?

She knew in her heart he would. He was that kind of man, the kind she'd never had in her life before. Dependable, trustworthy, with a genuine sense of humor and kindness, and she wanted to hold him tight and never let him go. He was a treasure she'd been seeking all her life.

But she knew she could never have him that long. He was a good, moral man, a man who would never understand who she had been, where she'd come from and the character flaws that had nearly destroyed her.

If he ever found out about who she'd been before she became Dora Martin, student and bookstore clerk, his respect for her would vanish, his desire for her would turn to deep revulsion.

No, he could never be hers forever. But he could be hers for a night, a little voice whispered inside her head, a tiny whisper that echoed in all the chambers of her heart.

Surely making love with Mark one time wouldn't ruin her life plan. Or was it like an alcoholic deciding that a single drink wouldn't mess up their sobriety?

Want battled with fear, a fear of tumbling into nowhere, of falling back to where she'd been in a past she desperately wanted to forget. She finished her coffee and shoved thoughts of Mark out of her head as she showered and dressed for her classes.

What she needed to do was focus on an answer to the question of who was stalking her and why. Who had been outside her window the night before?

It couldn't possibly be anyone from her past. Nobody in the small town of Horn's Gulf, Wyoming, cared enough about her to want to kill her. She couldn't imagine anyone here who cared enough about her one way or the other to go to such lengths.

There had to be a reason this was all happening, but for the life of her she couldn't think of one. But somebody had kidnapped and beaten up her sister and no motive had been presented for that crime, a voice nagged in the back of her head.

She couldn't make that connection to Mark because it would open up all the ugliness of her life, inside her soul. She'd rather be kidnapped and beaten than be exposed to Mark for who she had once been.

Never had she felt the need for a friend as much as she did now. She needed somebody who wasn't Mark to talk to, somebody who could be a voice of reason in the chaos in her mind.

Micah. She needed to talk to her brother.

She normally dressed up a bit when she was scheduled to work in the store. Today she chose a pair of jeans and a coral-colored sweater since she wasn't working later.

With her books and laptop on the table ready to grab and go, she sank down on the sofa and punched in the numbers that would connect her to her brother.

It was after eight, he should be up by now, especially since he had two little stepsons who were probably early risers. She knew Micah had met the woman who was now his wife, Olivia, when he'd first been gone to Perfect to stop Samuel from his evil. Micah definitely had a personal vendetta to settle. Samuel had tried to have him killed and one of Samuel's henchmen had put a bullet in Micah's head, a bullet that hadn't killed him but had put him into a coma for months. When he regained consciousness he was more than willing to work with the FBI to do whatever necessary to bring Samuel down.

Olivia had worked with Samuel and, one night, had seen him kill a man. Horrified, Olivia had fled with one of her sons, little Sam, but her other son, Ethan, had been left behind at the day-care center.

She'd run from town and headed into the wooded mountains, seeking a safe house that she'd heard had been established for people who wanted out of Perfect. Micah found her and vowed to get her son back for her.

He'd not only returned Ethan to Olivia's arms, he'd also given her his heart and the two had married a few months ago in a secret ceremony. As far as the people in town were concerned, Micah was Samuel and Olivia was just Samuel's live-in girlfriend.

"Dora?" Micah's deep voice filled the line, pulling her from where she'd been lost in thought. She almost smiled as she wondered if maybe Mark's plunges into introspection were contagious.

"Micah, did I wake you?" she asked.

He released a deep chuckle. "I was awakened about two hours ago with Sam on my chest poking his fingers in my eyes and demanding that I wake up." There was such happiness in his voice and Dora wished for nothing more for him. "I've heard that you're doing well," he continued.

"I keep my nose to the grindstone," Dora replied, unsure how to broach the topic of Mark and her growing feelings for him.

"All work and no play isn't exactly healthy. I hope you're taking some time to enjoy life. I know homecoming is coming up there. Are you planning on joining in the madness?"

She laughed. "I think the college board would kick me out if I didn't show appropriate school spirit. We're playing our rivals, the Everly College Blue Jays. The Gladiators hate them and they hate the Gladiators."

"Should be a good game. Everyone plays harder when it's against archenemies."

There was a moment of silence and she wondered if he was thinking about how hard he'd had to play to get his archenemy, his twin brother, behind bars.

"There is something else," Dora said tentatively. "I've kind of met somebody."

There was a small pause. "I assume we're talking about a man?"

Dora felt the rush of heat to her cheeks. "A very nice man. He's one of the FBI agents here in town working the murder and kidnapping case. I like him, Micah. I like him a lot and I know he feels the same way about me. We've been going out for coffee together and he walks me home from the bookstore, but nothing more than that," she hurriedly added.

She decided not to tell her brother about the stalking

and the incident the night before. He was working his own case and the last thing she wanted was to worry him about something he could do nothing about.

"What's this all about? Dora, are you asking my permission to have a man in your life?"

"No, I mean, maybe." She released a sigh. "There's a part of me that is afraid, Micah. I don't exactly have a great track record when it comes to men and making good decisions. I don't want to get off track from my goal to get my degree and move on with my life."

"Dora, a lot of women have their career and a man in their life," Micah said gently. "When Melinda and I gave you this opportunity to build something for yourself we put you in a college, not in a nunnery."

Dora couldn't help the laughter that burst out of her. "Maybe a nunnery would have been a good idea." She sobered and continued. "I've had a 'no man allowed' policy in my life since I started here three years ago and this is the first time I'm tempted to break my policy."

"Then break it," Micah replied easily. "You aren't the same person you were three and a half years ago. My wish for you has always been for you to be happy and lead a healthy, productive lifestyle. You don't need my permission, Dora. You just need to trust your own judgment."

A rush of relief shot through her as she realized he was right. She had grown by leaps and bounds in the past three and a half years, leaving behind the woman she'd once been for a smarter, better one.

At some point she had to learn to trust her instincts, to believe that she was capable of making important decisions in her life. She couldn't forever depend on others to guide her. She had to be in charge of her own life and live it with confidence. "You're right," she replied. "And I thank you for reminding me."

They made small talk another few minutes and then hung up. Dora grabbed her things from the table, realizing she'd have to hurry if she were going to make it to her first class of the day on time.

As she left her house she looked around to see if there was anybody nearby who might mean her harm. Twice in the night she'd gotten up to peer outside her bedroom window and had seen Joseph sitting on the curb.

She'd seen nothing of him this morning and could only assume that he'd been pulled off babysitting duty to get some much-needed sleep.

Nobody appeared to be around and even though she knew that, someplace, danger lurked nearby, the thought couldn't stanch the thrum of excitement that warmed her veins as she realized she'd decided to break her rule.

She wanted FBI agent Mark Flynn not just in her house for a cup of coffee. She wanted him in her bed.

Chapter 9

Mark attended the usual morning briefing where they talked about the attack on Dora the night before and how it might play into anything that they were already investigating.

"I have a theory," Mark said to his team. He ignored Larry Albright's eye roll.

"Let's hear it, brain man," Lori said, and smiled at Mark.

Mark reminded them about the information that Melinda had been having an affair with Andrew Peterson, about Dora spying the two of them together and his speculation that perhaps both Melinda and Dora had become a liability in the married man's life.

"You might have something there," Donald agreed, powdered sugar dusting his chin. "At least you aren't still accusing Professor Grayson of being responsible for our murders."

"Unfortunately, the search warrant of Troy Young's place yielded nothing that we can use to build a case against him as far as the murders are concerned," Joseph said, his eyes bloodshot from exhaustion that Mark knew had come from his babysitting duty on Dora's house the night before.

"Right now all we've got is circumstantial evidence and the fact that he hasn't been able to provide any kind of an alibi that can be substantiated. What we have against him probably won't hold up in court. We've got to find something more on him today or he's going to be kicked loose. Donald and I are headed back to the judge to see if he'll extend the search warrant to not just search his house, but also all the outbuildings on the property. There's got to be something there if this is our guy."

"How about Donald goes to the judge and then the house and you get some sleep," Richard said to Joseph.

"I'm all right," Joseph replied with a wave of his hand. "I'll head back to the motel around noon and catch a quick snooze and be back here for the four-o'clock briefing."

"I'm going to the history department and have a talk with Andrew Peterson," Mark said.

"I'll tag along with Mark." Richard reached for one of the doughnuts that had become a staple in the room.

"And I'll hang around the campus and see what kind of information I can get about all the players in this whole mess," Lori added. She was perfect for the job. She was young enough, hip enough, to blend in with all of the other students.

"Then we all have places to go and people to see,"

Mark replied. He checked his watch and wondered what Andrew Peterson's schedule was like for the day.

Within minutes the room had emptied and Richard and Mark headed toward Richard's car to drive the short distance to the college campus. "You haven't given Peterson a heads-up?" Richard asked.

"No. I thought about making an appointment to meet with him, but I'd rather catch him off guard and unprepared," Mark replied.

"It's a good theory of the kidnapping and Dora's stalking," Richard said.

"Yeah, but at this point it's just a theory." Mark stared out the passenger window. He didn't want to tell Richard that he couldn't let go of this theory that Melinda Grayson was the true evil behind everything.

He admitted it, it…she…had become an obsession especially since the horrible dream he'd had about the murders and her and some unknown male.

Still, that didn't explain why anyone would be after Dora. No matter how he moved the pieces around, he still couldn't fit everything into a completed puzzle or find an adequate profile of the perp in his head.

Richard parked along the street a block from the campus. There was definitely a crispness to the air this morning, the familiar scents of fall in the air.

Mark remembered Dora telling him she loved autumn, and like Dallas, Vengeance would enjoy a pleasant fall that would last long into the months where other states were seeing snowfall.

Of course, Mark wouldn't be here when winter officially began in Vengeance. He'd be on another case, back working out of the Dallas field office and coming and going to the small apartment that had never really felt like home. The house he'd shared with Sarah had also never felt like home. It had always felt like Sarah's home and then later Sarah and Grace's home, but never his own.

Funny, he'd only been inside Dora's house a couple of times, but there had been warmth and welcome there, a sense of home that he'd never felt before.

As he and Richard headed toward the building that housed the history department, he shoved thoughts of home and Dora away. He hadn't even called her to check in on her this morning, knowing that she would have survived the night safely with Joseph on duty. Mark was a fool to think about her as the place where he belonged, as the home he'd never had.

It was time to solve this case and get out of Vengeance, leave Dora behind. It was time to gain some distance from her for his own sanity's sake.

She'd made it clear on several occasions that there was nothing there for him but friendship, that the last thing she wanted in her life right now was the complication of a relationship.

"You're unusually quiet this morning," Richard said, pulling him out of his thoughts.

"I'm just ready to get this case solved and get back to Dallas," Mark replied.

Richard raised an eyebrow. "And here I thought maybe you'd want this case to go on for a long time due to a certain bookstore lady."

Mark gave him a pained smile. "She's not ready for a man in her life and we both know that I don't do relationships very well."

"Mark, you didn't fail at your marriage," Richard said as they paused outside the history building. "You married a woman who never understood who you are at your core and what you do. You aren't like ordinary men who work nine-to-five jobs. You have a special gift that doesn't always fit in the outside world but makes you invaluable as an FBI agent."

"And a bad choice as a boyfriend or husband," Mark replied ruefully.

"Not true," Richard said firmly. "All it means is that whatever woman eventually winds up in your life has to be somebody who can embrace all that you are, a woman who doesn't expect you to be a normal man."

"You're making me sound like a freak," Mark exclaimed.

Richard laughed. "There's a difference between being a freak and being special. You're special, Mark, and you deserve a special woman, and I hope you find her someday."

Someday, but not here and not now...not Dora, he thought as they entered the building. He focused on the task at hand, eager to find out what he could about the supposed relationship between Andrew Peterson and Melinda Grayson.

It took them several minutes inside the building to find Andrew Peterson's small office on the second floor. There was a note on the door that indicated he was currently teaching a class and would be back in his office and available at ten-fifteen.

Mark checked his watch. "Fifteen minutes. Should we just hang out right here?"

"Sounds good to me," Richard said, and leaned back

against the wall to make himself comfortable. Mark did the same on the opposite wall, gathering together in his mind the questions he wanted to ask Andrew Peterson.

Students swept past the two agents, hurrying toward a class or escaping to the building exit. They carried with them an energy that filled Mark's veins as he thought of a scenario where Andrew Peterson had been the man outside Dora's window the night before.

Mark knew the man he'd chased had been medium build and in good shape. If Andrew Peterson ambled in fat or skinny, with sagging or bulging muscles, then it would instantly prove his innocence in the scene the night before and would also discount him as the man in the tape with Melinda. Melinda's captor had also been medium build and in good physical condition.

Nick Jeffries had been invited to the four-o'clock briefing. Mark and his team had managed to play nice with the local law enforcement, and Nick had made it easy as the liaison between the two.

Certainly Nick had a personal interest in seeing the crimes solved. Not only had he made notification of death to Peter Burris's wife, but when Suzie Burris's life had been threatened, Nick had not only protected her but also had fallen hard for the new mother and recently widowed woman.

The nice thing was that unlike what so often happened in cases where the FBI was brought in, there was no pissing contest between the two law enforcement agencies.

They were all working for an arrest and conviction and it didn't matter who got the job done or who took the glory, just as long as it got done. It was a united effort. Unfortunately, the Vengeance police force hadn't been able to come up with any more than the FBI.

A dark-haired man who appeared to be in his early forties hurried toward them, his arms full of papers and a couple of textbooks.

"Excuse me," he said to Richard as he unlocked the office door and disappeared inside and then closed the door behind him. Richard looked at Mark.

"Could be him," Mark said softly. Andrew Peterson couldn't be ruled out by his body type and size alone. Mark knocked on the door.

"Enter," Andrew yelled through the door.

As they opened the door and stepped inside the small office, Andrew looked up from his desk, his gaze narrowing slightly as he faced the two men. He rose to his feet. "I was expecting it to be a student. Can I help you, gentlemen?"

As Richard made the introductions, Mark stared at the man who might or might not be part of the puzzle. Andrew Peterson was a nice-looking man. His blue eyes held a touch of wariness, which wouldn't be considered unusual in the circumstances of being confronted by two FBI agents.

Andrew motioned them to two straight-back chairs in front of his desk. "We thought it was time we had a little chat with you," Richard began as he and Mark sat down.

"About?"

"Melinda Grayson," Mark said flatly, watching Peterson's features carefully for tells. There was a faint flare in his eyes and his mouth tightened. The tells were barely discernible, but Mark had been trained to watch for them, to recognize them.

"Professor Grayson," Andrew replied. "A terrible thing that happened to her, but what does that have to do with me?"

"We were just wondering who broke off the affair, you or her, or if the affair is still ongoing?" Mark went straight for the man's jugular.

Andrew sputtered incoherently and blinked several times like an owl unexpectedly caught in the daylight. He turned his gaze from Mark to Richard and then back again. "I have no idea what you're talking about."

"Oh, we think you do," Richard replied smoothly.

"We know about the affair, Mr. Peterson. What we need to know now is if it has ended or if it is still ongoing," Mark said, his gaze pinning the man in his chair. "Or perhaps you'd feel more comfortable answering our questions down at the courthouse."

Andrew jumped out of his chair and for an instant Mark thought he intended to run from the office. Instead he walked over to the door and closed it, then returned to his seat behind his desk, his eyes glimmering with the shame of a guilty man.

"Please, I'd much rather answer your questions here. This is rather a delicate situation."

"Adultery is usually a delicate situation," Richard said drily.

"So, tell us about you and Melinda," Mark said, noting that a fine sheen of sweat had appeared just above Peterson's upper lip.

"There really isn't much to tell," Andrew replied. "I knew Melinda around campus, but our paths rarely passed because we're in different departments, housed in different buildings."

He leaned back in his chair and stared at a photograph on his desk. Although Mark couldn't see anything but the back of the picture frame he guessed that it was the requisite photo of Andrew's happy, smiling family.

Andrew shook his head and instead focused his attention out the nearby window, as if unable to look at the picture while he talked about Melinda.

"The *affair* began about a month before she was kidnapped." He spoke the word as if it left a nasty taste in his mouth. "About three weeks before that I found myself next to Melinda at a staff meeting for the department heads. I'd been to plenty of such meetings with her, but this time she sat next to me and was being very flirtatious. You've seen her, right?"

He looked back to Richard and Mark, who both nodded, and Andrew hurriedly continued, as if he'd just been waiting for somebody to ask, as if he needed to confess his sins.

"She's smoking hot and things at home weren't going so well. I had a harassed, nagging, exhausted wife dealing with three children under five years of age, and there was Melinda, making me feel like I was the smartest, most desirable man in the entire world."

"And so you two began an affair," Mark said.

Andrew gave a curt nod. "We were so careful. We didn't email each other, didn't leave any kind of a phone trail. We'd see each other on campus and then plan to meet up at a motel just outside of town. She was like an intoxicating addiction to me for a couple of weeks.

I lost sight of everything that would be destroyed in my life if my wife or colleagues found out. I lost sight of everything that was important to me. Nothing mattered but being with Melinda."

A dry, humorless laugh escaped him. "And then one day she just ended it. No explanation, so emotionless, she just told me she was tired of me and it was time for her to move on."

"And that made you angry," Mark replied.

Again Andrew laughed, the sound brittle and false and with a touch of genuine humor. "Actually, it shook me to my core. It made me realize I'd been a stupid fool and I went home and hugged my wife and kissed my kids and thanked God that I'd come to my senses about what was important in my life."

"So, you felt no anger toward Melinda," Richard said, his disbelief evident in his voice.

Andrew leaned forward in his chair, a new alertness in his eyes, his lips slashed to a thin line once again. "What's this all about? Why are you here talking to me about all of this? I've had nothing to do with Melinda since our breakup."

"We need to know where you were and what you were doing on the day that Melinda disappeared."

Andrew's face flushed with color. "Surely you can't believe I had anything to do with that. I'm a respected teacher here. I've always been a law-abiding citizen."

"This wouldn't be the first time a seductive, beautiful woman shoved a man over the edge," Richard replied coolly.

The flush on Andrew's face deepened. "I can't tell you where I was that day just off the top of my head.

I'd have to check my day planner, reconstruct my activities, and I have a class to teach in five minutes."

"Then we'll be back later today to get that information from you," Richard said as he stood. "I would recommend your full cooperation with us, Mr. Peterson. I'd hate for any of this to get out to the press."

It was a barely veiled threat, for Mark knew that the last thing Andrew Peterson wanted was for anyone to find out about his illicit affair with the beautiful professor.

"By the way," Mark said as they reached the office door, "where were you last night between the hours of eight o'clock and ten?"

Andrew frowned. "I taught a class at seven and then came back here to the office and spent the next couple of hours grading papers. I went right home from here. Why? What happened last night? Is Melinda okay?"

"She's fine. Did anyone see you here when you left?"

Andrew shook his head. "Not that I know of. The building was closed by that time and I used my pass card and code to get out. I didn't see any security as I left."

"Somebody will be back later this afternoon for the information we've requested," Mark said.

"So, what do you think?" Richard asked Mark as they stepped out of the building and began the walk back to where they'd parked their car.

"I found it interesting that he didn't ask us how we knew about the affair."

"Indicating he already knew that Dora had seen him and Melinda together?"

"Possibly," Mark agreed. "I also doubt that the transition between being Melinda's besotted lover and returning to loving husband to his wife was as smooth as he'd like us to believe."

"What's our next move?"

"I'd like to contact Nick Jeffries and see if one of his men can put a tail on Peterson for the next couple of days. I'm not convinced he wasn't the perp at Dora's window last night. His alibi seemed a little shady." Mark frowned thoughtfully as he got into the passenger side of the car.

"If we separate the two crimes, as most of the team has already done, then potentially we have our murderer, Troy Young, behind bars now and we have Andrew Peterson with motive and opportunity to teach Melinda a lesson by kidnapping her and busting her up a bit," Mark said.

"Feels good to me. So, why don't you sound happy?"

"I don't know," Mark admitted.

"Personally, I'm smelling the end of things here in Vengeance." Richard shot him a quick, knowing glance. "Maybe that's why Mark isn't a happy camper? Because he likes a certain somebody here in Vengeance and isn't quite ready to tell her goodbye?"

Dora. Thoughts of her exploded in Mark's head. Maybe she was the reason he was trying to make the case more difficult than it was, buying him more time here in Vengeance, time he could spend with her.

"This is the first time I've allowed personal feelings to get twisted up with my investigation," Mark admitted.

"Then she must be a special woman," Richard returned.

A special woman. Dora was that and more, but she'd

told him both in actions and with words that she didn't want a real, in-depth relationship at this point in her life.

Even knowing that, he had a swift desire to see her. Joseph had let him know she'd weathered the night all right and had gone to class this morning, despite the fact he'd already told himself it was time to start distancing himself from her. He was being pulled in too deep and didn't want to get hurt, but he knew before the night was over he'd seek her out.

She might be a special woman and Richard had said that Mark was a special man, but at the moment he simply felt like a fool. He was unwilling to give up seeing a woman who had told him she had no place for him in her life.

He'd go back to Dallas and continue to be special… and alone.

Chapter 10

As evening fell Dora found herself restlessly pacing from the kitchen to the living room and back again. Would Mark stop by to see her tonight or wouldn't he? Would the stalker from the night before once again show up to terrorize her?

Agent Larry Albright had called her earlier to let her know that they'd made arrangements with campus security to keep an eye out for her and had also arranged for hourly drive-bys throughout the night by the Vengeance Police Department.

She should be safe, but that didn't stop the edginess that kept her from completely relaxing, the tension that rode her shoulders like a wild cowboy she couldn't throw off.

By the time eight o'clock came and went she considered changing out of her jeans and sweater and into her nightgown. Before she could put the action to her thoughts, a soft knock sounded on her door and she peeked out the window to see Mark standing on her porch.

The tension fluttered out of her, replaced by a simmering excitement. She opened the door and he gave her the sexy grin that moved her, that thrilled her.

As he stepped inside she closed the door and immediately moved to stand against his body. She closed her eyes the instant his arms wrapped around her. "I wasn't sure I'd see you tonight," she said, her face nuzzled into the crook of his neck.

"It's been a busy day," he replied.

"Coffee?" she asked. "I already made it."

"I'm good right here," he said, not releasing her from his embrace. "But, coffee is probably a better idea for us." He dropped his arms from around her and stepped back, his eyes midnight-blue. "I want to play by your rules, Dora, but when you let me hold you, it's hard to remember the rules."

"Maybe I've been reconsidering my rules," she said, her voice surprisingly breathy to her own ears.

His eyes flared a bit but he remained in place and stuffed his hands in the pockets of the dark windbreaker with the bright yellow FBI letters on the back and front. "Several of the men searched Troy Young's outbuildings today and found a pair of shoes that appear to have the same kind of soil as the place where the murdered men were buried. I doubt I'll make it to homecoming."

"Then I think maybe we should take advantage of what time you have left here in Vengeance," she replied. She stepped closer to him once again, so close she could feel the warmth of his breath on her face, see the desire that darkened his eyes. "I want you, Mark. I know you won't be here for much longer. I'm not looking for a forever, but I'd like one night with you, a sweet memory to hold tight to when you're gone."

"I swore to myself that I was going to stay away from you, that there was no point in continuing having coffee and conversation with you when I wanted so much more. I swore that I wasn't going to be here tonight and yet here I am." He pulled a hand from his pocket and raked it through his hair. "Dora, I don't want to get in your way, to block the path you've set for yourself."

She smiled and a confidence and strength she'd never felt before filled her up. "Nothing and nobody will block my path." It was true. Only she could screw up her plans for her future—nobody else—and she had no intention of screwing up.

She placed a hand on his chest, where she could feel the strap of his shoulder holster but wanted to feel his heart. "One night, Mark. No promises necessary, no looking forward and no looking back. Just one night."

He grabbed her to him, and before she could say another word, his mouth slashed down on hers, hot and hungry and filled with the desperate need of a man starved for her.

And she was starved for him. She leaned into him and raised her arms so she could tangle her fingers in his thick hair. At the same time she opened her mouth to him, allowing the kiss to become deep and hot as their tongues explored.

The kiss went on until she was breathless. Finally

she broke apart and took his hand in hers. She pulled him toward the stairs, which led up to the bedrooms.

He came willingly with her, and when they were halfway up the stairs, she smelled the scent of lilacs, the candles that she'd lit in hopes that this would happen.

Her heart fluttered rapidly with each step they took. She wanted this, she wanted him, more than she'd ever wanted a man in her life. He would be the first man she'd brought into her life since her rebirth and she knew she'd remember him long after he left Vengeance and her behind.

She pulled him into her bedroom, decorated in lavender and white and lit only by the five fat candles she'd placed around the room. The bed was turned down and beckoned for their bodies, naked and writhing against the pristine white sheets.

She dropped his hand and turned to face him. The stark hunger she saw on his features torched a heat through her that threatened to consume her. As she stared at him, he unzipped his windbreaker and took it off, then unfastened his shoulder holster and laid it and his gun on the top of her dresser.

Only then did he open his arms to her once again. This time when they embraced there was nothing between them, except his T-shirt. She felt the wild thunder of his heartbeat against her own.

Their mouths met in another kiss as his hands caressed up and down her back, molding her to him. She felt his hard arousal and it only shot the desire inside her to a higher level.

As he grabbed her buttocks and pulled her tightly against him, she rocked her hips back and forth, the friction of her jeans and his hardness spiraling her up and half out of control.

His lips left hers and blazed a trail down her jawline and into the hollow of her throat. She dropped her head back, dizzy with pleasure as his lips teased and nipped erotically against her sensitive skin.

"Mark." She finally managed to breathe his name. Things were moving so fast and they weren't even partially undressed. She didn't want this fast and over. It had been so long, and she wanted him slow and in bed with her. She wanted to savor every kiss, each caress.

He stumbled back from her and grinned. "You make me crazy," he said in a husky voice.

She grinned back. "The feeling is more than mutual," she replied. She reached out and unfastened the top button of his white shirt. When she unfastened the second one she moved the material aside and pressed her lips against his muscled, hot skin. He stood so still it was as if he had stopped breathing. She continued one button at a time, one kiss for each button, until the shirt was completely unfastened and he shrugged it to the floor. She grabbed the bottom of her sweater and pulled it off over her head then sought the warmth of his arms once again.

With only the thin material of her white lacy bra between them, she loved the feel of him, the muscled planes and warm skin. Her breath caught in her throat as his fingers worked the fastener of her bra. The garment came loose and she shrugged it from her shoulders. His hands moved around to cup her full breasts. She closed her eyes as his fingers rubbed across her taut nipples, creating a coiling heat that pooled in the very core of her.

He dropped his hands from her and unfastened his slacks at the same time he kicked off his shoes. "If I don't get you into that bed right now, I'm going to be insane," he whispered.

She stepped back from him and tore at her jeans, wanting nothing more than to be naked with him and beneath her sheets. Within mere seconds they were there, bare limbs tangled together as their mouths once again melded together.

With each stroke, with every touch of his hands and mouth on her, she knew the rightness of her decision to be here with him now. She knew there was no chance of a future with him. She'd never have a future with any man, for she'd never share enough of her heart, her soul, her past with anyone. But for now, it was perfect, Mark was perfect and she reveled in him.

Their caresses grew more heated and more intimate as he slid his hand down her stomach to tease her inner thighs with feather-soft strokes.

In turn she reached down and encircled his hardness, loving the feel of him pulsating in her hand. He hissed with pleasure and his fingers slipped into place at her center. Rubbing in small circles, he brought her to climax with a quickness that left her gasping.

Then he was inside her, stroking slow and deep, his eyes glittering as he gazed down at her. Tenderness was in those beautiful eyes of his. His gaze held tenderness and caring and the need to please, all emotions that fed a hunger that burned inside Dora's soul, emotions that filled spaces inside her that had been empty since her youth.

She clutched at his shoulders as he continued to possess her, his stokes beginning to accelerate, his breathing harsh and ragged. She raised her knees, allowing him deeper penetration. A rising storm built up inside her and she bucked her hips to meet his.

The storm centered and swept over her, shuddering her from head to toe and leaving her gasping in its wake. At the same time Mark stiffened and groaned, reaching his climax.

He collapsed at her side and the room held only the sounds of their quickened breaths slowing to normal. She'd just assumed that now that they were finished Mark would slide out of the bed, get dressed and leave her, like all the men in her life had done before him.

She released a small sigh of surprise as, instead, he rolled over on his side and leaned in to give her a long, tender kiss. "That was unbelievably amazing."

What was amazing was that they were finished and his eyes still held a sheen of desire coupled with such tenderness it threatened to force tears of joy.

"It was wonderful," she agreed. "And thank goodness you didn't drift off in the middle of it."

He laughed and ran a finger down her cheek, grazing her skin softly. "There was no way I was going to miss one moment of loving you. I was happily present for every single second."

"You know I would have slapped you otherwise," she said teasingly.

"And it would have been a deserved slap." He moved

his fingers to thread through her hair. "So soft, so silky," he murmured.

As he pulled her back into his arms, she snuggled against his warmth, wishing she'd met him years ago, wishing he'd been her first, before the other men who had made it impossible for her to ever think about a forever with any man.

There was no question about it, Mark was on the precipice of being completely in love with Dora Martin. As her warm curves filled his arms and she fit so neatly against him, he knew she was the woman who would complete him.

She got him. She got his dry sense of humor, his quirkiness, and most importantly, she understood and didn't resent his momentary absences when he drifted into the deep thoughts inside his own head.

They were counterparts in many ways. She was outgoing while he was more of an introvert. She was filled with a light that drew him out of the darkness. She was good for him, and she made him want to be good for her.

He knew the moment she fell asleep, and he tightened his arms around her, as if to capture her close to him forever. He had no intention of sneaking out of bed and leaving her and returning to his motel room. He wanted to wake up to the morning with her still at his side.

The candlelight cast dancing shadows all around the room. He thought about getting up to blow out the candles, but they were in big jars and he wasn't concerned about a fire hazard. Besides, he didn't want to wake her now. He was afraid if he did she might decide to send him on his way.

He admired her desire to get her degree, to better her life, and he understood with two failed marriages behind her that she was gun-shy about relationships. But even if this case was solved and he returned to Dallas, that didn't mean things between them had to end.

Dallas was only a short commute from Vengeance and he would never get in the way of her life plan. He'd like to think he could walk beside her on her path through the rest of her life.

Sleep came and with it the nightmare of Melinda. Once again she was heavy on his chest, her lush lips red and wet, as if she'd just eaten somebody's soul. Her eyes glittered with the harsh glint of madness released and her laughter held an edge of both intense pleasure and hysteria. Mark felt the tightening of something around his neck. She was mocking him.

He couldn't move his arms and he wasn't sure if it was the strength of Melinda's thighs that held them tight against his side or if he was bound in some way. He only knew he couldn't defend himself against her... against them. Helpless, he was utterly helpless as Melinda and a man laughed while he slowly died.

He came awake with a frantic gasp, his heart racing painfully and a choking sensation in the back of his throat. He fought the need to cough as he felt the warmth of Dora still in his arms, as he oriented himself to the single flickering candle that had not gone out.

Closing his eyes once again despite the fact he knew it would be some time before he fell back asleep again, he went over what apparently was becoming a recurring nightmare.

Despite the fact that they had a viable suspect in jail, his mind refused to let go of the theory of Melinda's involvement in the murders.

Mark had never considered himself an exceedingly stubborn man. When presented with facts that countered his thoughts, he always capitulated on the issue. Facts trumped theories in any case. So, why this continued obsession with Melinda, an obsession that obviously was still at work someplace in his unconscious brain?

By tomorrow they should all know if there was a workable case against Troy Young or not. If they couldn't build a case against him except through the circumstantial evidence that he hated all three of the murder victims, then Mark had a feeling the district attorney wouldn't go through with a charge and Troy would be released.

He didn't have a lot of faith in the fact that Troy Young had a pair of old boots that had traces of the red earth and mineral content of the area where the murder victims had been found. That particular mix could be found in lots of places in and around Vengeance.

If Troy was kicked to the curb, then the team would be back where they'd started, with no other viable suspects. And Mark had a feeling his obsession with Melinda would only continue to grow.

He must have fallen back asleep for when he opened his eyes again the faint stir of morning light filtered in through the nearby window.

He was on his back, Dora by his side, her hand on

his chest as if at some point through the night she'd sought the feel of his heartbeat.

She was beautiful in the morning light, not like a twenty-five-year-old woman might be beautiful, without lines or character on her features. Dora looked like the mature woman she was, with tiny faint laugh lines radiating out from her eyes even in sleep. Mark found each and every one of those lines beautiful.

Emotions he'd never felt with Sarah buoyed up inside him as he remained motionless, watching Dora sleep. He wanted to be inside *her* head, know every thought in her brain, each and every desire she entertained. He wanted to know every inch of her both inside and out.

He'd told her he wasn't eager to try a relationship again, but he realized now he'd been wrong. He and Sarah had known they'd made a mistake in the first year of their marriage, but by that time Sarah had discovered she was pregnant.

They'd agreed to try to work it out for the baby's sake, but ultimately they had never been right for each other and he was only grateful they'd escaped the marriage relatively unscathed, with Grace as a bonus prize.

Dora felt right in the way Sarah never had. He could look forward ten years in time and see her by his side. He could look forward twenty years and she was still there.

All he had to do was figure out how to make her see what he saw so clearly at the moment—that they belonged together, that they were two halves of a whole.

Suddenly he was looking into the depths of her soft, sleep-laden gray eyes. "Good morning," he murmured softly.

"Hmm." She closed her eyes and snuggled closer against him, as if reluctant to have a new day begin.

He was definitely reluctant to begin a new day. The last thing he wanted to do was leave this bed, release Dora from his arms. But he had an early-morning briefing and could only indulge in this sweet existence for a little while longer.

He breathed in the scent of her, the faint wildflower fragrance that he knew would haunt him for a long time after he left this small town and this woman behind.

Unless he could somehow make her see that they belonged together, that it was okay for her to let down her guard, to let him into her life completely, when it came time to go, he'd leave here all alone.

"I wouldn't mind waking up right here every morning," he said softly.

"Hmm, nice," she replied, obviously still half-asleep.

They remained like that for another twenty minutes or so and then Mark knew he had to get up and get ready for the day ahead. He needed to get back to his motel room, shower and change into clean clothes before heading to the war room in the county courthouse.

Reluctantly he withdrew his arms from around her and rolled away. She mewled like a kitten who had just lost a ball of yarn. "I've got to get back to the motel and head in for work," he said as he got out of the bed.

She rolled over on her back, her sleepy gaze watching him as he grabbed his clothes off the floor and began to dress. "This is the best way ever to start a new day," she said while he pulled on his slacks.

"The feeling is mutual," he replied with a grin. He wanted to say more. He wanted to tell her that his wish was that they start every day this way, but he was afraid of her response, afraid that by pushing her too quickly he'd never have a chance for something more.

He grabbed his shirt and pulled it on, and realized that he had fallen off the cliff, that he was in love with Dora Martin and he wasn't sure what to do about it, wasn't sure there was anything he could do about it.

When he was dressed, he walked over to her side of the bed and pressed his lips firmly against her forehead. "I'll check in with you later today, okay?"

"I'll be at the bookstore tonight until eight-thirty," she replied. "And if I was a good woman I'd get up right now and fix you a quick breakfast before you leave."

He smiled down at her. "You are a good woman, Dora, and I'll grab a doughnut at the briefing." With a murmur of goodbye, he walked out of the bedroom.

He left the house with a vision of her snuggled beneath the sheets, a vision he wanted to hang on to forever. But he knew all too soon it would be shoved to the back of his head when he focused again on murder and kidnapping.

The sun streaked pink and orange bands of welcome across the eastern sky as he walked toward his car parked at the curb in front of her house.

Autumn was in full swing, with a bracing nip in the air that made him want to whistle with a kind of happiness he'd never known before. Funny, he'd never wanted to whistle in his life, but Dora made him want to whistle…and sing…and dance.

When he reached his car he was about to get in behind the steering wheel when he saw a white piece of paper stuck beneath his windshield wiper.

Was it a parking ticket? He looked around but didn't see any no-parking signs in the area. He plucked the paper out, and the words written there caused him to reach for his gun, to lower his body and gaze around himself with narrowed eyes.

His heart pumped adrenaline through him, but he saw nobody in the area. The street was deserted and there was no movement anywhere in his sight to indicate that whoever had left the note might still be in the area.

He holstered his gun and slid into the driver seat, the note still clutched in his hand. He laid the note on the passenger seat and grabbed his cell phone from his pocket and punched in Richard's phone number. When Richard answered, Mark spoke only four words.

"We've got a problem."

Chapter 11

"Troy Young is innocent and you are in danger, Mark"

Mark stood in front of his team and read the note that had been left under his windshield wiper, now in a clear plastic evidence bag.

"Crap," Donald muttered to everyone and nobody. "Where was your car parked when you found the note?" he asked.

Mark felt the warmth that crept into his cheeks. "I was parked in front of Dora's house. Apparently the note was left at some point during the night."

"Attaboy," Lori said with a grin.

Mark ignored her as the flames in his cheeks grew hotter. "I found it when I left this morning, tucked under my windshield wiper, but I have no idea exactly when it was left or who put it there."

"Troy Young remains in jail pending charges right now, but I have a feeling before the day is done he's going to be kicked loose. The D.A. isn't comfortable with what evidence there is against him and he's already been held as long as possible. Even so, he remains our main person of interest," Richard said.

He looked at Mark and continued, "The fact that whoever wrote the note believes that Troy is innocent is less concerning to me than the statement that you're in danger."

Mark nodded. "I've been thinking about that and I'm wondering if the stalker that Dora has is really my very own personal stalker."

"Just what we need, a new mystery," Larry said with a groan.

"I haven't hidden the fact that I've been spending my downtime with her," Mark said, ignoring Larry's pained expression. "So, I now think it's possible that if I take this note at face value, then somebody is after me, not Dora."

Mark wasn't a coward, but he also wasn't a foolish man. He took the threat to himself very seriously, especially considering the fact that the author who had penned the note had given no indication where the danger might come from or who might want him hurt or dead. Still, there was a certain amount of relief in the realization that the danger was pointed at him and not at Dora.

"But if that's the case, then why didn't the stalker just shoot you when he was by Dora's house?" Donald asked, his brow wrinkled into a thoughtful frown. "Why wait until you gave chase?"

"Maybe he didn't want to take a chance at shooting Dora. If I was the primary target, then it makes sense that he wouldn't have fired his gun then, but would rather wait until the two of us were in the middle of the campus and he had a clean shot at me," Mark replied.

"I don't like anyone threatening my men," Richard said, his voice deeper and with a touch of anger. "We'll see if we can pull prints from the note. I want the writer of that note found. Whoever it is seems to have information we don't have."

"Maybe it's just another student prank," Joseph suggested.

"Those weren't prank bullets that were fired at me the other night," Mark replied tersely. "And I still haven't bought into the theory that Melinda Grayson's kidnapping was some stupid student prank."

For the next hour the team threw around theories, talked about what little information they'd managed to glean. The frustration in the air was a living, breathing entity that displayed itself in how quickly the doughnuts disappeared from their boxes. Nothing like a sugar rush to attempt to stanch short tempers and the dissatisfaction with how things were proceeding, Mark thought.

The meeting dragged on and on, with the final decision for everyone to look at the case as if it had just been handed to them. Joseph was assigned to redo background searches on everyone involved with both the kidnapping and the murders, Larry was to reinterview everyone who had already been talked to initially when the cases broke.

Lori was to reexamine what little evidence they had

and find a chink in anyone's alibi that had been provided for the time of the crimes.

Richard would coordinate and Mark was left to do what he did best, put together the facts that the team brought to Richard and him and get them a profile that would eventually lead back to Troy Young or to another suspect or person of interest.

It was almost noon when the team went their separate ways, discouraged that they were at a place where they had to doubt and reexamine every move of their own earlier investigation. But Mark knew as well as the others that the smallest overlooked detail often broke a case wide-open.

As he left the courthouse, he realized he needed to find Dora and let her know that it was quite possible she wasn't being stalked, that it was Mark somebody might be watching and waiting to harm.

Not only would he get to see her again, he'd be able to bring her a small measure of comfort in this new information that took a target off her back.

With only a week and two days to the annual bonfire and homecoming festivities, Mark noted that more red-and-gold banners and signs seemed to have appeared overnight on campus. Go Gladiators signs hung out dorm windows and fluttered from fraternity and sorority house porches.

When in college Mark hadn't participated in the extracurricular activities. He was too busy being tested and taught to achieve his full potential. When he wasn't in the classroom he was in the library, soaking up what he could learn about serial killers and their patterns, their thoughts and actions.

By that time he'd known there was a place for him with the FBI and he knew this job was his calling, his reason for being. But Dora had reminded him that there were also other things important to him…like being the man his daughter needed in her life…things like love.

Despite the tense meeting he'd just endured, he was aware of the jaunt in his steps as he walked across the campus to the place where he knew he was most likely to meet Dora coming or going from a class.

He sank down on the bench where he'd sat the first day he'd met her to wait to give her back her pen. His thoughts immediately went to the note on his car.

Who had left it? If they took the note at face value then it was obvious the person who had written it had information to exonerate Troy Young and knew of a specific threat to Mark. The writer had warned Mark, but hadn't given enough details to allow him to know what was going on.

Why would anyone come after him? There was a whole team of FBI agents working this case, so why single out Mark? His thoughts whirled around in his brain.

Because he'd never believed the theory of the crime that the others believed, a small voice whispered inside his head. Because he'd always maintained and been vocal about the fact that he believed Melinda's kidnapping was staged and she had something to do with the murders.

Could that be the reason Mark had been targeted? Because somebody in the Melinda camp wanted him silenced? Were the nightmares he'd had starring Melinda his imagination mirroring what was really reality?

He didn't know how in-depth the background search had been on her considering that most of the team considered her a victim, not a suspect. He wanted to know everything about the beautiful professor, from the day she was born until she'd arrived here at Darby College. Even though his teammates didn't believe it, she was the key to everything. All he had to do was somehow prove it.

All thoughts of Melinda bounced out of his head as he spied Dora coming out of a nearby building. Clad in a pair of brown slacks and a rust-colored lightweight sweater, she looked stunning amid the fall colors. Her hair glinted in the sunshine and for a moment he remained seated on the bench, just watching her as she walked, obviously not seeing him.

She appeared deep in thought, her laptop case against her chest and her purse slung across her shoulder. He stood and their gazes met. She appeared to hesitate a moment and then her beautiful smile stretched across her lips. But in her momentary hesitation, Mark smelled morning-after regrets that hadn't been there when he'd left her house earlier that morning.

"I didn't expect to see you hanging around here today," she said as she approached where he stood.

"I wanted to find you to tell you that there's been a new development that suggests the stalker isn't after you, but rather is after me."

Her eyes widened as she gazed up at him. "Really?"

He nodded, when he'd rather pull her into his arms. But the laptop remained against her chest in a defense position and she was standing a couple of inches away. "I don't think you're in any danger, Dora. I think whoever was watching you was actually looking for me and knew we'd probably be hanging out together."

"Well, that's a relief for me, but what about you?" Her concern for him was evident in the deepening of her voice.

He gave her what he considered his most self-assured smile. "I'm a big, bad FBI agent. I can take care of myself." His smile fell away as he eyed her intently. "You aren't entertaining any day-after regrets, are you?"

She stepped closer to him, as if afraid that one of the passing students might hear their conversation. "Yes and no," she confessed. She released a sigh. "I didn't expect you, Mark. I'd made decisions about my life and one of those decisions was no men, no relationships. I just didn't expect you to sneak into my bed."

He gave her a crooked smile of amusement. "As I remember it, I didn't exactly sneak. I was willingly dragged up those stairs by you."

She nodded in acknowledgment. "I know. What I don't know is what to do with you now. We have no future, Mark. I don't want a future with you or any man."

Her gaze didn't quite meet his, making him wonder about the truth of her words. "What are you afraid of, Dora?" he asked softly.

"Nothing." She raised her gaze to meet his, a hard defensiveness in her eyes he'd never seen before. "I'm not afraid of anything. I just know what I want, what I'm willing to give to somebody else, and I'd never be able to give what it takes to make a successful relationship. I know my limitations, Mark."

"But, I don't think you're aware of your strengths," he replied.

Again she looked at him in surprise and then released a deep sigh. "I don't want to be hurt, Mark, and I don't want to hurt you."

A beat of panic boomed in his chest. Was she somehow calling a halt to everything? Would he not have the opportunity to spend more time with her, to make her realize that somehow, someway, they could make a relationship work between them?

"Let's just enjoy our time together while you're here in town," she continued, making the boom of his heart quiet. "I'm offering you coffee and conversation—nothing more." Her cheeks bloomed with splendid color. "Last night was wonderful, Mark, but we can't have a repeat. It just wouldn't be right."

"I'll play by your rules for the time I'm here," he said, although it was difficult to capitulate to her wishes in this area. "I just want to spend my downtime with you, to enjoy your presence, and we still have a bonfire date for next Friday night," he reminded her.

She smiled then, a full, warm smile that gave him renewed hope that eventually she'd understand that he was in this for the long run and that she could trust him with her heart, with her future.

"I've got to get to my next class," she said with a glance at her delicate gold wristwatch.

"Go," he replied. "I just wanted to let you know that I don't believe you're in any danger."

She started to leave and then turned back to him, her eyes shimmering with the emotion she refused to allow into her heart. "Watch your back, Agent Flynn."

"Always," he replied.

There was no question that Mark had been on her mind since the moment Dora had crawled out of bed and stood beneath a warm shower spray that morning. Her body had tingled and sung with the memory of his touch. The most difficult thing she'd had to do was tell him that she didn't want him in her bed again even though it was a lie.

Having Mark in her life for a finite period of time was safe, but inviting him in forever would be a disaster. Secrets and lies, that was the sum of this new life Dora had built, and she wasn't about to take a chance on destroying it.

If she were smart, she would tell him that she didn't want to see him again. She'd tell him that there was really no reason for them to have coffee or any further conversation, except she didn't want to deprive herself of him completely.

She knew it was selfish of her, sensed that Mark was developing real feelings for her that went beyond friendship. She felt the same thing toward him, but loving any man for any length of time was impossible for her.

As she hurried toward her next class she once again told herself she was being a bit self-indulgent, flirting with a bit of emotional danger, but couldn't bring herself to cut it off cleanly with him. At least she was grateful to learn that the stalker wasn't after her, although she was concerned that somebody was apparently after Mark.

He was trained for danger and she hoped he'd utilize all of his skills, all of that training to keep himself safe.

She couldn't imagine anyone who would want to hurt Mark unless it was the same person who had killed all three men, unless somebody thought he was getting too close to them.

She figured they'd pretty well solved the murders by holding Troy Young for the crimes. So, if it wasn't Troy threatening Mark, then who?

Questions continued to haunt her through the day and into the evening as she began her shift at the bookstore. It was another quiet night, with few customers coming in. Dora used the quiet time to study and refused to indulge in thoughts of anything else except the class work in front of her.

It was only at eight that she finally closed her laptop and sat back in the chair behind the register and allowed her thoughts free rein.

There had been so much ugliness when the personal details about the victims had come to light. Dora had shied away from hearing all the sordid details. She'd had enough ugly in her life to last forever and the last thing she wanted to do was ruminate over the ugly in her past.

The fear of tainting Melinda had kept her mute about the two women's personal relationship, and the shame of who Dora had been kept her from ever wanting to share that time in her life with anyone.

That was why there could never be anything lasting between her and Mark. That's why she could enjoy his company while he was in Vengeance but had no intention of pursuing a relationship of any kind once he left town.

She would always have to be on her guard, afraid

to share too much. She'd seen revulsion in the eyes of a man she loved once before and it had driven her to the edge of ruin.

She'd truly believed Jimmy Martin would be her salvation, her defense and protector in the town without pity that had spawned her. But ultimately the damage he'd done to her had been devastating.

For the past three years her single goal had been to learn to find the happiness within, to not need anyone else to fulfill her. It had been an empowering lesson to realize she didn't need anyone but herself to navigate in the world. If she chose to allow somebody to walk with her, then it was a choice, not a need.

She would never need a man again.

Still, at eight-thirty when Mark walked through the bookstore door, she couldn't help the jump of her heart, the giddy happiness that accompanied the accelerated heartbeat.

"Hi," she greeted him.

"Hi, yourself," he replied with the easy grin that fired warmth through her entire being. "Good day?"

"Yes, it's been a good day," she replied as she locked up the cash register and prepared to leave for the night. "What about you?"

He raked a hand through his messy dark hair. "Another day of frustrations, but I don't want to talk about work."

"You look tired," she said as they stepped out of the store and into the night air.

"I am tired," he confessed. "The whole team is tired. They cut Troy Young loose today because of a lack of evidence. Everyone on the team believes he's guilty and are scrambling to find the kind of evidence that would make the D.A. bite on a murder charge. In the meantime we're reinvestigating everything about the cases, starting at the beginning to see what we might have missed. We're also checking out any friends Troy might have that could have left the note on my car."

"Sounds daunting," she replied.

"And discouraging," he returned.

They walked silently for a while, but Dora knew Mark hadn't disappeared into his own thoughts. She felt his energy, and noted that his jacket was open, providing easy access to his gun. His eyes never stopped moving, checking first one side of the sidewalk and then the other, both ahead of them and behind.

The stalker was a third person on the sidewalk with them and Dora's muscles tensed. At any moment she expected somebody to jump out of the bushes or appear from behind a tree.

She didn't relax until they were inside her house and Mark had slumped into the sofa. She sank down next to him, deciding she wasn't even going to offer him coffee. It was obvious he was exhausted and needed to go to his motel room and get a good night's sleep.

Although she'd love to sit and talk to him, to drink in his very presence, she also wanted him at the top of his game so that nobody was able to sneak up on him and hurt him because he was too physically exhausted to be careful.

"You need to go," she said firmly. "You need to go and get some sleep. You look like you haven't slept for weeks."

"I slept fine last night," he said with a sly smile.

The smile slowly fell from his lips. "Until the night-mares started."

"Nightmares?" Dora looked at him with concern.

He waved a hand as if to dismiss the subject. "It's no big deal. I always have nightmares when I'm work-ing a case."

She frowned, not sure she believed him. "Mark." She placed a hand on his forearm. "Go home to the motel and go to bed. As much as I'd like you to spend some time with me, I'd rather you get some much-needed sleep."

He took her hand in his and squeezed it, the gesture coupled with the warmth in his eyes speaking words she didn't want him to say aloud. "You're right. I need some sleep. I don't think I'd be very good company to-night anyway." He released her hand and stood.

She got up to walk him to the door, wondering when she'd come to care enough about him to worry about his sleep habits, any nightmares he'd suffered or any-thing else.

She was going to get hurt. As he kissed her on the forehead and then stepped outside and back into the night, she realized that no matter how much she pre-pared herself, no matter how often she told herself she had it all under control, when Mark Flynn left Ven-geance, her heart was going to break in half.

Amanda watched Mark leave Dora's house from her hiding place in the bushes across the street. She remained there as she watched a second figure dash from one tree to another, shadowing Mark as he made his way down the sidewalk to where his car was parked.

Ben.

She knew it was Ben shadowing Mark at Melinda's behest. But why? She didn't want to believe what her head had been telling her ever since she'd found the small note card on Melinda's desk that had *Mark* written on it. The only Mark Amanda knew was the FBI agent and the minute she'd seen the note she'd felt that he was in danger.

Now she had proof that Ben and Melinda were up to something. Otherwise, why would Ben be out here in the dark, watching and following the tall agent?

Amanda had put the note beneath Mark's windshield the night before after she'd found the card on Melinda's desk. That had been as far as she'd been willing to go in an effort to stop whatever might be happening.

The truth was, in the past twenty-four hours, since she'd found that little note card on Melinda's desk, Amanda had been afraid, afraid of her boss and afraid of Ben.

She feared what might happen to her if Melinda or Ben knew that she had suspicions about them. She'd begun to think that Melinda's kidnapping hadn't been real, that somehow she and Ben had plotted the whole thing.

Thinking back, during Melinda's captivity Amanda remembered now that Ben would disappear from campus for long periods of time. Amanda couldn't find him at his apartment; nor was he in any of his usual haunts. Had he been with Melinda? Pretending to be a kidnapper?

What she couldn't figure out was why, but when she thought of the murders that had taken place during that time a true terror she'd never felt before seared through her.

She now breathed a sigh of relief as she saw Mark climb into his car and drive off. The dark figure that she knew was Ben disappeared into the night, either heading back to his place or to Melinda's.

Amanda remained in the bushes for a long time, nibbling a nail as horrible thoughts went around and around in her head. She didn't know who to trust, who to tell her crazy suspicions.

She stared back at Dora's house. She liked Dora a lot and she knew Dora and the handsome FBI agent had something going on between them. But how could she tell Dora her suspicions when she knew what few other people knew about Dora's relationship to Melinda?

She'd found out that Dora was Melinda's sister just before Melinda had gone missing. Melinda had accidently slipped up and mentioned the fact at one of their late-night work sessions. As far as Amanda was concerned she and Ben were the only people on campus who knew that the two women were related.

So, talking to Dora was out of the question. Talking to anyone felt like a dangerous risk. Tears blurred her vision. She was twenty-eight years old and yet at this moment she felt like a frightened child left all alone in the dark.

She shivered in the cool night air and fought against the horrifying belief that something very bad was about to happen.

Chapter 12

Melinda Grayson sat on a stone bench beneath a tree sporting red leaves and watched in the distance as the young college students worked to build the fire pit. It was the pit that would contain not only a bonfire in three nights, but also the traditional burning at the stake of an effigy of the Everly College's blue-clad quarterback.

The Blue Jays. What a ridiculous name for a college team; what a ridiculous mascot for a football team. Birds had such fragile little bones, so easily crushed.

She leaned back against the bench, knowing that nobody would dare approach her here. Even without her two little minions surrounding her, she didn't worry about being interrupted by any students. Passing students might shoot her sidelong glances and shy smiles, but they respected her and perhaps feared her power too much to disrupt her moment of peace.

Speaking of minions... Her gaze was caught by the sight of Andrew Peterson walking across the campus, his shoulders hunched slightly forward as if anticipating a blow. He'd been unimaginative in bed, but a good little soldier for as long as she'd wanted him.

She thought about calling to him, just to see how long it would take to get him under her thumb again, but she'd been bored with him long before she'd kicked him to the curb.

Unfortunately, he was a weak man who might occasionally wander out into the world of illicit sex and subterfuge but ultimately would always run home to the safety of his wife and children. He certainly wasn't a match, or in Melinda's league at all.

Still, if she needed him again, if she wanted to have a little fun, she was confident that it would take only a few minutes to get him back under her spell once more.

A smile curved her lips as she anticipated the Friday-night fun. She always loved the homecoming bonfire and the wildness that reigned on that one night of the year. It called on a primitive wildness inside her.

On a whim she pulled her cell phone from her purse. She hadn't spoken to her brother Samuel since the kidnapping, and she found herself in the mood to talk to the family bad boy.

It took several minutes before she was connected. "Melinda, my dear sweet sister, how are you?" Samuel's deep, pleasant voice slid smoothly through the phone. "I heard through the grapevine that you'd been through a terrible ordeal." His voice held no pity, no real concern for her. In truth she hadn't expected any from him. Still, she made her voice small and hesitant when she responded.

"It was horrible," she replied, admiring a student's muscled back as he took off his shirt while he worked. "I've been having nightmares for the last week."

"Darling, you don't know a nightmare until you've tasted the food in this place," he replied.

"Did the gossip you heard about my kidnapping mention that I was beaten? That my captor broke my arm?" Melinda snapped, unable to contain a flash of irritation.

"I believe I did hear something about it, but broken arms heal and bruises go away. At least you aren't locked up like I am."

Melinda sighed, wondering why she'd called him in the first place. He was such a narcissist. It was always all about him. He had no empathy for anyone else on the face of the earth. "You were stupid, Samuel. You did bad things and you were stupid enough to get caught."

Samuel sighed. "Yes, I admit that mistakes were made and lessons were learned. I won't make the same mistakes the second time around."

"From what I hear you aren't going to get a second time around," Melinda replied. "They're never going to let you out of there."

Samuel laughed. For a narcissistic sociopath, he had a nice, rich laughter. "I'm not counting on them letting me out of here, but that doesn't mean I won't get a second time around."

So, he was working on an escape, she thought. If he did manage to escape from wherever they were holding him, she wondered where he'd go to build a new kingdom where all who lived there would worship him.

"You could at least ask me about the other members of our family," she said, knowing Samuel hated talking about Dora and Micah.

"Why would I want to know about them? One is a loser and the other is a traitor to the Grayson name." His tone of voice was one of distinct disgust. "Dora is a twit you should have left in Horn's Gulf and Micah will someday pay for putting me here. You and I are the only ones with any guts in our family tree, Melinda. We're strong. I built an empire and look what you've survived. We're two peas in a pod."

"There's one big difference between you and me," she replied with a hint of smug satisfaction in her voice. "I'm out here and you're locked up." She knew her words would make him angry and she disconnected the call before she heard his response.

She didn't need him to tell her she was strong, that she had guts. She'd survived her father's brutality and her drunk of a mother; she'd survived out in the world all alone and had worked her ass off to become the great professor Melinda Grayson.

She didn't need a loser like Samuel to tell her who she was and what she deserved from life. She was owed everything good that came her way. She'd built her own little kingdom here at Darby and she was the queen who wielded the power.

Samuel was wrong. The two of them weren't peas in a pod. She was better than him…smarter than him, and only losers went to prison.

Thinking about losers, she checked her watch. It was

time for her to head to her next class. As if on cue she saw Ben and Amanda approaching from the distance. Dependable, malleable and fiercely loyal, the two assistants had been a good choice of hers.

As always, Ben looked cool and relaxed and Amanda was one step ahead of him, her pretty face pale with exhaustion and strain. Melinda knew the two were at odds with each other, and she'd done nothing to ease the tension between them.

Amanda reminded Melinda of Dora…weak and eager to please, while Ben reminded Melinda more of herself. His laid-back aura hid more than a touch of arrogance and a hunger for power of his own.

Melinda stood as the two reached where she'd been seated. She said nothing to them, but turned and headed toward class, confident that they would follow close at her heels.

The past week had been a blend of everything good and everything bad that could happen in an ongoing investigation and in Mark's personal life. He now sat in the briefing and listened to Richard rail about the fact that somehow it had been overlooked that Troy Young had been in jail on drunk-and-disorderly charges at the time of the murders. This unbreakable alibi had come to light the night before and had taken him off their suspect list completely.

Richard was angry with not only the men and woman who sat before him, but also the Vengeance Police Department where Troy had enjoyed accommodations for the twenty-four-hour period when the murders had been committed.

"What I don't understand is why Troy didn't remember that he'd been in jail when he was first questioned," Larry said.

"He drinks almost every night. Sheriff Burris had him on a revolving door down at the jail. He has trouble remembering what he did yesterday. It was his lawyer who discovered the jail records that exonerated him."

Richard glared around the room, as angry as Mark had ever seen him. "We should have been the ones who found this information, not some damned lawyer. We should have had that information the day Troy Young hit our radar." He slapped his hands down on the table before him. He then visibly drew in a deep breath and released it slowly.

Nobody in the room spoke a word as they waited for him to continue. Richard turned to stare at the whiteboard, where the photos of the victims stared back. He turned back to his team. "They haunt me as I'm sure they haunt you. We need to find who was responsible for this." His voice was calm now, his anger in check. "We need to bring whoever is guilty to justice."

Mark realized this wasn't so much an ass-chewing or briefing as it was a motivational meeting. The feel in the room was tired, dispirited, and nothing had come to light in the past week to buoy the agents' flagging spirits. Joseph had whispered earlier that he thought this perp had beaten them, that they were never going to solve these crimes. He'd given voice to what Mark suspected the others felt.

There had never been a real trail to follow and now with Troy Young out of the mix they didn't have anyone on a short list of potential suspects.

Mark was still convinced of his theory of the crime, that Melinda Grayson had staged her kidnapping with a male partner and had somehow played a role in the murders, but nobody wanted to listen to him.

He'd been shut down by his teammates, who he could tell were frustrated with him because he hadn't come up with any other viable theory of the murders. They didn't want to hear any more of his feelings where Melinda Grayson was concerned. As far as they were concerned she was a separate victim of a different crime.

There had been moments in the past week when Mark thought maybe his teammates were right and he was not only losing his mind to an obsession about the professor, but also losing his touch as a profiler.

For the first time in his work, he felt like a failure. The only thing that had kept him from plunging into depression the past week had been Dora.

He'd spent a little bit of time with her each night, not talking about work but rather talking about music and movies and good books. She was a puzzle he put together with each bit of information he gleaned.

She loved reading romance novels, letting him know that there was someplace inside her that still clung to the idea of a happily-ever-after. She loved old rock-and-roll music, especially the ballads about angels and teens...the kind of music meant for slow dancing and holding tight.

"Mark!"

His attention was snapped back to the present as he blinked and looked at Richard. "Sorry, what was the question?"

"I asked you if you've come up with anything more on the note left on your car and the threat to your well-being?"

"Well, the good news is I'm still alive," Mark replied. Everyone laughed and some of the tension slid out of the room. "Nobody has taken any shots at me, no mysterious cars have tried to run me over and I haven't sensed anything out of the usual around me."

"I don't want you dropping your guard for a minute," Richard replied.

"Don't worry, I have no intention of being taken off guard," Mark said. He'd been careful lately, constantly checking his surroundings, monitoring any people who might get too close. His gun only left his body at night when he slept, and even then it was within reach on the nightstand.

"And still no ideas who might have left it for you?" Richard asked.

Mark hesitated only a beat and then shook his head. The truth was he had some suspicions about who might have left the note, but he didn't intend to share his instincts with the rest of the team because it went back to his theory of a guilty Melinda.

He'd given a lot of thought to the note left on his car. Whoever had written it had known that Troy Young wasn't guilty, which implied the writer might know something about who was guilty. There were few people in the town who would write a note of warning to *Mark* rather than to Agent Flynn.

With startled surprise he realized the meeting had ended and everyone was leaving the room, apparently assigned by Richard to specific tasks.

Richard remained in the room and sank down next to Mark, his weariness showing on the lines that appeared deeper in his skin and the pallor that had taken over his complexion.

"The tail on Andrew Peterson has been pulled off," Richard said. "According to the sheriff, he can't justify one of his men tailing a person who has no known connection to the crimes, a man who for the past week has gone to work in the morning and then home every night."

Mark frowned. He wasn't convinced that Andrew Peterson wasn't the man in the videos of Melinda, that the history teacher wasn't Melinda's partner in Mark's nightmares.

"Give me something, Mark," Richard said in a low voice. "Give me anything that we can work with."

Mark looked at his friend and mentor in frustration. "I can't give you what I don't have. I can tell you what you don't want to hear, what everyone refuses to believe, but I'm not pretending to toe the company line here."

Richard leaned back in his chair and released a deep sigh. "So, you still continue to believe the kidnapping and murders are connected and Melinda Grayson is at the center of it all."

Mark gave a curt nod of his head and Richard sighed once again. He leaned toward Mark, his gaze hard and demanding. "Then get me proof. Get me something that proves this theory of yours."

Richard stood and walked to the door of the war room and then turned back to Mark. "Leave all other theories to the other agents. I want you to focus solely on your idea of the crimes. Either prove it or disprove it, but get me something other than your gut instinct, Mark." With these final words Richard left the room.

Mark leaned back in his chair and tried to focus on what his next move should be. The new pressure that had just been laid on his shoulders once again made him feel as if he was failing the entire team.

Prove it or disprove it. The words rang in his ears. Richard had basically just given him free rein to work the investigation of Melinda his own way, without the support of the team.

That was fine with Mark. He didn't have to pretend anymore that any other theory made sense, and he didn't have to put in hours of investigative work trying to prove anything that he didn't believe.

Prove it or disprove it.

That was exactly what Mark intended to do once and for all, and he would start by talking with the two people closest to Melinda…Ben and Amanda.

He left the courthouse with a new sense of purpose and a burning desire to find answers. He headed for the campus, a fresh determination in his soul.

It was time to fish, not cut bait, to either put Melinda in the middle of the murders or find the proof that she had nothing to do with them.

There was no question that the initial background check they'd done on Melinda had been sketchy and half-assed. At that time she'd been viewed as a victim, not a suspect.

Mark intended to ask her assistants some hard questions, to learn what he could from them, and then he would interview Melinda to fill in her background information, to find some definitive answers.

He knew the trick would be to see if he could connect with each, Ben and Amanda, by themselves. Dora had mentioned that the two assistants were competitive with each other. He could probably use that to his advantage, playing one against the other.

He settled on the bench outside the building where Melinda taught her classes, the same bench that had brought Dora into his life.

He closed his eyes for a moment, invoking a picture of Dora in his mind. The past week with her had only confirmed to him that he wanted her forever and always in his life, although he hadn't told her that yet.

They hadn't made love again, although they had shared several long, soulful kisses. It was so difficult when he was with her not to touch her, not to want to kiss her, and he knew she battled the same demons of desire. But he was playing by her rules until he got up the nerve to tell her how he felt about her, how much she meant to him.

He'd come to her each evening feeling like a failure, disappointed in the investigation and filled with the residual darkness of the nightmares. He left her place several hours later, restored by her laughter and strengthened by her nearness.

In three nights he and Dora planned on attending the bonfire and festivities of homecoming together. He'd thought the team would be back in Dallas by now, but with Troy Young off the suspect list, Mark had no idea when they would leave Vengeance.

He'd called Sarah the day before to set up an ice-cream date with Grace for Sunday. He'd already spoken to Richard about taking off for a couple of hours for family time on that day.

He couldn't wait for this case to end to start being the man he wanted to be for his daughter. He had no idea how long this case would continue. Dallas was less than an hour's drive away. He'd drive there, pick up Grace and eat those two scoops of ice cream he'd promised while reveling in the wonder of the child he'd helped to create.

As he saw Ben Craig rushing out of the building doors, he stood and raised a hand to motion to the younger man. "Agent Flynn," Ben said with an easy smile.

"Hello, Ben. I was wondering if you had time for a few questions."

"Actually, I don't right now. Professor Grayson is in the middle of her lecture and she sent me on an important errand. Can it wait until later today or maybe sometime this evening?"

Mark saw no tell on Ben's face, no subconscious nervous gestures, nothing to indicate that a chat with Mark might be stressful to him. "Later this evening would work. What would be a good place and time for you?" Sometimes it paid to be accommodating.

"You can come to my place. I rent a little house off campus." He rattled off an address that Mark easily stored in his memory bank. "Why don't we say around seven?"

"Sounds good to me," Mark replied.

With a hurried goodbye, Ben continued on his way. Mark watched him go, aware of the fact that like Andrew Peterson, Ben had the same medium build, medium height, as the person on the kidnapping videos.

Knowing that with Ben gone it was doubtful Melinda would send her other minion away, Mark pulled out his cell phone and punched in Joseph's number. Joseph was the one who had done the background checks on Ben and Amanda.

"Yo, brother, where are you?" Joseph said when he answered his phone.

"On campus…what about you?"

"At the sheriff's office with Nick Jeffries checking and cross-checking facts. What's up?"

"Do you have Amanda Burns's address?" Mark asked. He figured the best place to catch the assistant alone would be there. Sooner or later she would have to go home.

"Hang on." There was a rustle of papers and then Joseph gave him the information he needed.

After thanking Joseph, he disconnected and headed off campus toward the apartment building where Amanda lived alone in apartment 114.

As he walked he picked through the information the morning meeting had yielded. Pulling the tail off Andrew Peterson didn't mean the man was innocent. The fact that Peterson had been a good boy all week, coming and going to work and back home, didn't clear his name. He was still definitely a potential player on Mark's radar.

Mark knew Melinda's class schedule was light on Wednesdays, but he also knew there was no telling what the taskmaster might have in store for Amanda throughout the day. The lecture they were currently in would only last an hour and he was hoping Amanda would return to her apartment after that.

It wasn't a long walk to the apartment building, and once there, Mark found a shady place to sit near the door of Amanda's and watch for her arrival.

It didn't take him long to get lost in thoughts of both the murders that had occurred and his relationship with Dora. It was a strange mental combination that brought him both frustration and pleasure.

He had no idea how long he'd been seated when he saw Amanda approaching. She looked worse than the last time he'd seen her in the coffee shop, more exhausted, more stressed.

When she caught sight of him, she stumbled and righted herself. Her gaze shot all around and then back to him. "Agent…Mark," she said. "Wha…what are you doing here?"

"I was wondering if I could have a chat with you?"

Once again Amanda looked around the area, as if afraid she might be seen with the FBI agent. She hurriedly unlocked the door to her unit and motioned him inside.

"A chat about what?" she asked once he was inside the small living room and the door was closed behind him. She laid her laptop and purse on a chair but offered no invitation for him to have a seat.

He took the initiative, sitting on the sofa and then pointing for her to sit down, as well. She seemed to slink across the room and sat on the farthest end of the sofa from him. She didn't relax against the cushions but rather remained on the edge, as if poised to run at any moment.

She stared over his head at some indefinable point and waited, her silence like a scream of tension in the room.

"Amanda." He said her name firmly, hoping to force her gaze to his. It worked. Her eyes met his and she reached a hand up to tuck a strand of her hair behind her ear. "You seem nervous."

In truth she appeared to be a woman on the verge of a nervous breakdown. He couldn't help but notice the ragged fingernails, bitten below the quick. Her eyes held the look of startled panic as a short burst of laughter escaped her.

"I am nervous," she replied. "I'm not used to being questioned by the FBI. Have I done something wrong?"

Mark shrugged. "You tell me."

She laughed again. "No, I can't be in trouble because I haven't done anything."

"Actually, I'm here to talk to you about Professor Grayson," Mark said, and instantly felt the tension in the air heighten.

"What about her?" Amanda's face had paled slightly and once again her gaze shot over Mark's head. No doubt, she was afraid of what Mark might see in the depths of her eyes.

"I heard she's a tough taskmaster."

"She is, but she's also brilliant."

"What do you know about her personal life?"

Amanda shrugged. "Not a lot. I heard rumors that she was having an affair with somebody, but that was before she got kidnapped. I've never seen her with anyone. I really don't know what she does when she isn't with us."

"Us…meaning you and Ben."

Amanda's features darkened even though she nodded affirmatively. "We spend a lot of time with Melinda." She sighed and once again met Mark's gaze. "Lately Ben spends more time with her than I do."

"And that upsets you?"

She hesitated. "It used to, not so much anymore," she admitted. She closed her mouth, lips tight as if afraid she'd said too much.

"Are you and Melinda having problems?"

"No, nothing like that," she said hurriedly. "Things are fine between us, great really. She's a wonderful mentor."

It was too much of a protest, instantly letting Mark know that there was an issue, at least for Amanda. He wanted to know what it was, but he was also afraid of pushing her too hard, too fast.

She appeared as fragile as a leaf barely hanging on to a tree in the center of a storm. He had a feeling if he pushed her too hard she would slam to the ground in a crumpled heap.

"Are you going to the bonfire on Friday night?"

She nodded. "And the game on Saturday. It will be my first real time off in a while." She offered him a small smile. "I'm really looking forward to it."

"Sounds like it's going to be fun," he replied, and then leaned toward her. "Amanda, did you put a note on my car last week?"

Her cheeks flamed with color and she got up from the sofa. "I don't know what you're talking about. I don't know anything about a note."

It had been a fishing expedition on his part, but he

knew she was lying. She'd put the note on his car to warn him that he might be in danger.

"What do you know about Melinda's past? Does she talk about her time before she came here to Darby?" he asked, thinking that would be a safe enough question to hopefully put her at ease.

Amanda stared at him for a long moment. "I thought you and Dora Martin had something personal going on between you."

He frowned at her. "What does that have to do with anything?"

"Why don't you ask her about Melinda's past?"

Mark felt like he'd suddenly been cast out into an ocean with a lifeboat that had a hole in it. "Why would I ask Dora about Melinda's past?"

She looked at him in startled surprise. "You don't know?"

"Don't know what?" Mark's heart began a thunder he couldn't control.

"That they're sisters. Melinda is Dora's older sister."

Sisters? Dora and Melinda? Mark got to his feet, the world tilting beneath him as he mentally tried to make sense of what Amanda had just told him.

He reeled to her apartment door, his heart pounding so loud in his head he could hear nothing else. It wasn't until he hit the sidewalk outside that he realized it was anger that drove him away from Amanda's apartment.

Why hadn't Dora told him? She knew he was investigating the kidnapping. Why in the hell hadn't she ever mentioned that she was Melinda's sister?

Why hadn't the background check into Melinda

brought this information to light? Had it been sloppy work on the part of his team?

As he raced toward the campus his anger built as he wondered what other secrets Dora had kept from him. What role did she play in this whole thing?

Chapter 13

Dora was feeling good about her life, about herself. The past week she'd felt stronger than she ever had in her entire life. She was focused, driven to succeed, and had the additional pleasure of Mark's company in the evenings.

She'd tried not to look forward to or worry about where things were going between herself and Mark. She knew their case against the drinking rancher had fallen apart and she had no idea how much longer Mark and the other FBI agents would be in town. She was simply enjoying taking things one day at a time.

She refused to allow herself to love him, even though there were quiet moments in the middle of the night when the emotion fluttered inside her heart. She knew better than to embrace it.

As she walked on the sidewalk from one class to her next, she passed the bonfire site and smiled to herself. She thought of sharing the night of craziness and school spirit with Mark.

What had been on her mind throughout the morning had been the idea of making love with Mark again. They'd managed to get through the week with just enough physical contact between them to set her on a simmer that begged for release.

As if he'd been conjured straight out of her mind, she saw Mark approaching in the distance. Despite the fact that she couldn't be in love with him, her heart lifted at the mere sight of him.

She smiled and waved as he drew closer, close enough that she could see the fire in his eyes and the determined set of his jaw. Uh-oh, somebody was having a bad day.

"Hey, you," she said as he walked up to her. She smiled up at him, but no answering smile lit his stone-hard features. Instead, he took her by the upper arm.

"We need to talk." He started to tug her down the sidewalk.

"Mark," she protested, "what are you doing?"

"We're going to your place. I have some questions to ask you."

"I can't go now," she exclaimed. "I have a class to get to."

"Forget your class." He released his hold on her. "I need to talk to you now. It won't wait until after your class."

She stared at him, suddenly afraid as she saw no kindness in his eyes, only hard, cold orbs piercing through her. Whatever conversation he wanted to have with her, she knew she didn't want to have it here in the center of the campus.

"Okay, let's go," she said.

It was the longest walk of her life. Mark didn't speak a word and she didn't, either. He had found something out, something about her...about her past. With every step they took she realized that he knew she wasn't the woman she'd portrayed herself to be to him. He knew what she had been and now he wanted to tell her what he thought of her.

Her steps began to drag the closer they got to her house. She didn't want to hear the disgust, and she didn't want her last vision of him to be one where his eyes were full of revulsion.

Tears stung her eyes and she quickly blinked them away. It didn't really matter what he thought of her, she told herself. He was only temporary in her life anyway.

She didn't care what he said to her. She'd give him all the ugly he wanted. If he couldn't accept who she had been, and who she was now, then to hell with him anyway.

It took her two stabs to get her key into the lock of her front door. She opened the door and stalked into the living room and then turned to face him, her chin lifted in defiance.

"So, exactly what do you want to talk about? The fact that I was a drunk or the fact that I was a whore?"

He blinked twice and appeared speechless. "Dora, I don't know—"

"You're right, you don't know," she said, interrupting whatever he was about to say. "You don't know what it was like for me in that small town where my father was an evil, hateful man and my mother was an alcoholic who bedded every man in town in the back room of the little café she owned."

To her horror the tears she'd been determined not to shed stung her eyes once again. She swiped at them angrily and realized she had come to a place in her life where she would own what she had been, but she refused to allow anyone else to tell her what she'd been.

"You don't know what it was like, to be branded just like your whore mother before you've ever kissed a boy, to let a town label you as a bad girl when you've done nothing wrong. I was Horn's Gulf's dirty little joke, along with my mother. Despite everything I was a virgin on my wedding night to Billy Cook, who was supposed to be my knight in shining armor. Instead, he beat me and told me every day that I'd come from dirt, that I was nothing but dirt."

Mark remained standing frozen in place, his features reflecting nothing as the words tumbled out of her. "My life in Horn's Gulf was not a safe place to be. When I finally married Jimmy I thought I'd found my safe place, a man who might respect and love me, but when he told me I was nothing more than my mother's daughter and nothing could make me respectable or clean, I lost my heart, my soul, my very mind. I crawled into the bottom of a bottle of gin and wanted to die."

For the first time since they'd stepped through her front door she stopped long enough to draw a deep breath. "So, I'll ask you once again," she said softly. "What do you want to talk about, the fact that I was a drunk or the fact that I was rumored to be the town whore?"

Mark appeared shell-shocked. "I actually came to ask you about Melinda."

"Melinda?" Dora looked at him blankly. She backed up a couple of steps and when her legs hit the sofa she sank down. "What about Melinda?"

The anger that had sparked in his eyes when he'd first approached her on campus, before her diatribe on her past, was back. "When were you going to tell me that you and Melinda Grayson were sisters?"

"Probably never," Dora replied truthfully. Everything was out of kilter. She felt like she'd just laid her heart, her very soul, bare for nothing, and his only response was to ask her about her sister. "It's not something I broadcast. We aren't close and I never wanted Melinda's star to be tarnished by me."

"Her star? I'm trying to take her down for the murders of those three men," Mark replied.

Dora gasped in shock. "What are you talking about?"

"I believe she staged her own kidnapping with a partner and then while she was supposedly kidnapped she and her cohort murdered those three men."

"You're crazy." Dora stared up at the man she thought she knew, the man she'd fought not to love. "Melinda would never be part of something like that. She's the one who saved me. If not for her and my brother Micah I'd still be in a gutter somewhere in Horn's Gulf drinking my life away."

"I'm telling you, Dora, she's in these murders up to her neck. It would have been nice if you'd told me about your relationship with her. The fact that you didn't makes me wonder what other secrets you have."

Dora laughed, an edge of frantic hysteria rising up

inside her. "I'd say I've pretty much spilled all of my secrets now." He'd come here to ask about her relationship with Melinda and she'd given him every piece of her squalid past. "The only thing you might not know about me now is that I was born Isadora Grayson. But, I've always been Dora."

"What I'm trying to figure out is how we missed this when we ran a background check on Melinda. I believe she is involved in these crimes and I'm going to work my ass off to prove it." He raked his hand through his hair. "And now I've got to enter you into the murder mix. You should have told me, Dora. You should have been up-front with me from the very beginning when you knew I was in town to solve the crimes."

"I should have done a lot of things differently," Dora replied with a sudden onset of bone weariness. "Get out, Mark. I think we're done talking now."

He didn't hesitate. He turned on his heels and left the house, slamming the door after him.

Dora stared at the place he had stood, a wealth of emotions welling up inside her. Grief ripped through her heart, the easiest emotion to identify.

He'd never said a word while she'd spewed the sordid details of her past. His expression had never changed. There had been no hint of compassion, no spark of any understanding. There had been absolutely nothing at all.

He'd shut down, turned off, and he hadn't even been here about her past. Another burst of hysterical laughter blurted from her and she shoved her hand against her mouth to stanch it as tears began to fall.

She'd worried about how their relationship would

end, afraid that he was getting closer than he should, that it was going to hurt to let him go.

Now she didn't have to worry about any of that anymore. She hadn't let him go. He'd run from her just as she suspected he would if he ever found out about the woman she'd once been, the woman she vowed never to be again.

She curled up in a fetal position in the corner of the sofa. Mark thought Melinda had something to do with the murders. That was impossible...wasn't it?

She had to admit that Melinda's assistants probably knew Dora's sister better than Dora did. Even though Melinda had appeared with Micah a little over three years ago to rescue Dora, Melinda had been distant, cool, and had made it clear that she was disgusted with Dora's state and was there just to do what had to be done.

When Dora had finished her rehab stint, it had been Melinda who had picked her up from the rehab and brought her here to Vengeance to start fresh with a new life plan.

Throughout the time that Melinda had guided her through the paperwork of scholarships and class choices, she'd remained cool and disconnected, obviously not interested in pursuing any kind of relationship with Dora.

The cool professionalism had been part of the reason Dora had decided not to tell anyone on campus about their relationship, because there was no relationship except in the accident of their births to the same people.

Who was Melinda Grayson? Truthfully, Dora didn't know. She had no idea what Melinda had experienced between the time she left the family ranch at the age of eighteen and when she'd appeared to help Dora. Years had gone by between those times, years when Dora had no idea what her sister was doing beyond building her career.

In those missing years Dora had no idea where her sister had lived, who had been her friends or what morals and values she had embraced.

But Mark was talking about Melinda staging a kidnapping where she allowed herself to be beaten. He was accusing her and a male partner of strangling or suffocating three men and burying them in shallow graves. Only a monster would be capable of that.

Immediately, she thought of Micah and Samuel, one hero and one monster. Was it possible that Melinda was just another monster in the family?

She thought about picking up the phone and making an appointment to meet with her sister. And what would she say to her? Dear sister, did you do all the terrible things the FBI believes you did? Did you know the agent who was my friend, my lover, has vowed to bring you down?

Samuel had been evil enough to try to kill his twin brother, Micah, among all the other heinous crimes he'd committed. Did that same evil run through Melinda's veins? An unexpected shiver worked up her spine. She was suddenly afraid, but she wasn't sure what she feared, who she feared for.

Tears once again trekked down her cheeks as she thought of Mark. She would only see him again now as part of his investigation. He might think she knew something about her sister, but she couldn't help him.

Once he realized that she knew virtually nothing about Melinda's life, past or present, then there would be no reason for him to ever see her again.

Not that he would want to.

The absurdity of what had just taken place might have been funny if her heart wasn't breaking. In the past she would have headed for the nearest bar, eager to numb the keening death of her heart.

Instead, she got up from the sofa with a final swipe of her tears, grabbed her books off the chair and then headed out the door.

She had classes to attend, a life to build, and this was just a reminder that she was meant to be alone... and she was okay with that because she had to be and because she was strong enough to remain alone.

Mark meandered along the paths of the campus, his head spinning with all the words that Dora had spoken and all the information he hadn't asked for but had received.

The anger that had driven him out of Amanda's apartment to find Dora was mixed up now, and he desperately wanted to find that anger again. He wanted to be enraged with Dora and the fact that in all the time they had spent together she'd never told him about her sibling connection to his number-one suspect in the case.

Granted, when they had been together they had spoken little about the cases and had instead talked about other, pleasant things. But in their first get-to-know-you conversation he'd asked her about her family. It had been a perfect opening for her to tell him about her relationship with the esteemed professor Melinda Grayson. Why hadn't she?

What could she know about her sister's crimes and how far would she go to protect a woman she saw as her salvation? There was no question that Dora admired and worshipped Melinda.

He finally set himself on a course to head back to the war room where he could use his laptop. There was now a new player in the game…the woman he'd fallen in love with, a woman he now realized he didn't know at all. He had to run a thorough background check on Dora. As an FBI agent he would be remiss in his duties if he didn't.

She was now an unknown entity in the case.

Consciously he shoved all thoughts of anything else he'd learned about her out of his mind. He couldn't think about that now. The case was all that was important. If he allowed himself to linger on the images Dora's words about her past had evoked, if he embraced the torturous emotions that had shimmered in her eyes, then he'd be distracted from what had to be done.

He couldn't afford to be distracted any longer. Prove it or disprove it. Richard's words rang in his ears. He had to lay aside any feelings he'd entertained about Dora. From this time forward she could be nothing more to him than a piece of the puzzle he needed to solve.

In his deepest, darkest thoughts, he wondered if the man he'd envisioned in his head as Melinda's partner, if the deep laughter he'd heard in his dream, had actually been a woman. Two sisters playing a deadly game?

Before the thought could truly take hold he dismissed it. Melinda's partner was a male from the videos, but more importantly he believed he knew Dora well enough to discount her as a suspect in all of this. Unfortunately, he couldn't use just his gut instinct to make that decision. Once again he had to prove it or disprove it. Either Dora was involved or she wasn't, but he'd have to use cold, hard facts to make the call.

He hated this. He hated the position he now found himself in, questioning the guilt or innocence of a woman he'd come to care about deeply, a woman he thought might have a place in his future.

It was obvious she hadn't wanted him to know anything about her past and now he was going to dig into it, find out everything he could about her. Then he would have to question her once again, to find out where she'd been during the twenty-four hours that Melinda had been gone and three men had been killed.

The war room was empty when Mark arrived. The first thing he did was call Ben and cancel the appointment he'd made with the young man for that evening.

As he remembered the suppressed fear that had shone from Amanda's eyes while he'd questioned her, the potential of Ben Craig being the man involved in the murder had become a more viable scenario. The last thing he wanted to do at this moment was spook the cool, slightly arrogant young man who was so close to Melinda.

What he'd like to do was question the cool, beautiful professor herself, but that option had been taken off the table when she'd mysteriously returned after being "released" by her captor. The police and the FBI had gotten one shot apiece at questioning her and at that time she'd been considered nothing more than the victim of an unusual crime. He could have sworn that during that initial interview she'd mentioned that she'd had a sister who had died years ago. Maybe that's why nobody dug too deeply into Melinda's familial relationships. Still, it should have been done more thoroughly.

Unfortunately, since that time, Melinda had gotten a lawyer, compliments of the Darby College legal team, who wanted no hint of blemish about the illustrious professor. It had definitely hindered the investigation going forward having Melinda protected by a lawyer.

Still, Mark felt as if the dots were beginning to connect. He was gut certain that Amanda had placed the note of warning beneath his windshield. He was also equally sure that the young woman was terrified and obviously didn't know whom to trust. She'd implied a distancing of herself from Melinda and a closeness between Melinda and Ben.

Those were the pieces of the puzzle. Ben and Melinda. Amanda and Dora. Somehow, they were all connected, and he just needed to find how they fit together and then he'd have his answers. Hopefully he would be able to prove that Ben and Melinda were guilty of staging a kidnapping and killing three men. And he was equally hopeful that he could disprove any theory that took Amanda or Dora to the wrong side of the law.

He got out his laptop and began the search to find everything he could about Dora Martin, who he now knew had been born Isadora Grayson.

He was still seated there hours later when Richard came in just before the four-o'clock briefing. "Working hard or hardly working?" Richard asked with a touch of humor.

Mark leaned back against his chair and stretched his arms overhead, trying to digest everything he'd managed to glean both in his time hunting via the internet and by making a few phone calls to Horn's Gulf, Wyoming.

"Dora Martin is Melinda Grayson's sister," he said to Richard.

"Your bookstore lady?" Richard sank down in the chair next to Mark. "How did we miss this? How did you miss this?"

"She never told me," Mark said, fighting against a trace of bitterness. "And it's not in any of the background work we did on Melinda." Mark shoved the laptop away and turned to look at Richard. "I've spent the last couple of hours finding out everything I could about Isadora Grayson Cook Martin."

"And what have you discovered?"

"Their father is named Buck and her mother was Daisy. Buck is still alive but Daisy died two years ago of alcoholism. Daisy had a total of four children. The two girls she and her husband raised and two boys she apparently gave up to their father to raise on a neighboring ranch. Dora never knew about her half brothers until they met a few years ago. One of her half brothers is Samuel Grayson."

Richard raised an eyebrow. "The creep running the show in Perfect, Wyoming. I've heard stories about our work there, but I don't know much about it."

Mark nodded and then continued, "Dora and Melinda were raised in Horn's Gulf, Wyoming, and although I wasn't able to get a lot of information online except official public records like birth, death and marriage certificates, I have made a few phone calls and gotten a better picture of Dora's life before she came here to Vengeance."

"Anything jump out at you that can be tied into what's happening now with the murders and Melinda?"

"Nothing concrete, although I'm certainly beginning to develop profiles on both Dora and Melinda based on their histories." He tried not to allow his compassion, his grief for Dora, to play into his.

"I spoke to a schoolteacher who taught both of the girls in grade school. Mrs. Carlson is retired now, but she had a keen memory of the Grayson girls. She said that Dora missed a lot of school, and when she was there she was always sporting some injury or another… a broken arm, smashed fingers, a black eye. Mrs. Carlson said Dora tried to make friends, but because of the reputation of her mother, most of the other children either bullied or made fun of her."

"What was wrong with her mother?" Richard asked.

Mark's stomach tightened. "She was an alcoholic who ran a small café on the outskirts of town. According to Ida Carlson, Daisy Grayson was a disgrace, a mother who rarely parented, but spent most of her days drunk and bedding down men in a back room of the café. Dora worked part-time for her mother from the time she was fourteen until she was eighteen and married Billy Cook. That marriage ended two years later due to irreconcilable differences. After the end of the marriage Dora returned to working at the café."

"And what about Melinda?"

"Ida said Melinda was in school almost every day, focused completely on her class work. She made no friends, but also wasn't bullied or bothered by the other students. Ida said she thought the other children were afraid of Melinda, but she never saw Melinda do anything to warrant the fear. The day that Melinda graduated she left Horn's Gulf and nobody heard from her again."

"So, tell me about these developing profiles," Richard prompted.

Mark frowned, thinking about the call from the old teacher and all the information she'd willingly shared with him about the Grayson girls.

"It's obvious they both came from abusive backgrounds, but it's equally obvious the two of them developed differently. I would guess that Dora was the scapegoat for much of the physical abuse, probably from the father. She's the one who often showed up at school with signs of the abuse, while Melinda managed to skate under the radar. What's interesting is that many times in cases that this, it's the eldest who gets beat the most, and takes the beating to protect a younger sibling, but it sounds like that wasn't the case with Melinda and Dora."

Once again Mark fought against an overwhelming sadness as he thought of the child Dora had been and the brutality that had made her childhood "not a safe place to be," as she'd described it to him.

"My initial thought is that Melinda developed coping skills very early. Those coping skills might have been the ability to scare the hell out of her fellow students, to isolate herself and focus only on her own needs and wants and the desire to escape. She apparently didn't step in to help Dora in any way, which leads me to believe she lacks empathy."

He frowned. "Dora, on the other hand, seems to have developed no coping skills. Despite the attitude of her friends, she continued to attempt relationships, leading to two bad marriages. She, too, was isolated but not by choice. She became an alcoholic and spent six months in a rehab center and that's when her half brother Micah and Melinda got her set up here to start over."

"So, what's the bottom line?" Richard asked, obviously wanting to cut through the fat to get to the meat.

"With what I've learned so far, I believe that Dora Martin was a likely candidate to commit suicide."

"And Melinda?"

Mark hesitated a moment and then looked at his superior. "Melinda was the most likely to be a full-blown sociopath."

Chapter 14

The afternoon and evening had crawled by with agonizing slowness for Dora. Her last class of the day had gone by in a blur as she played and replayed her last moments with Mark.

Her mind could scarcely wrap around everything that had occurred in the conversation that had taken no longer than fifteen minutes or so.

By the time she reached the bookstore, she was exhausted. It wasn't a physical exhaustion but rather a mental one, an emotional one. The good thing was she knew with time it would ease. In time she would forget the handsome FBI agent who had filled her life with laughter and a gentle caring.

But tonight the wounds were still too fresh, the pain too deep. She sat behind the cash register, just waiting for the time she could close up shop, head home and get a good night's sleep.

Tomorrow would be a better day, she told herself. *This darkness will pass.* It was one of the things she'd learned in rehab, that if she just waited the world would change to bring back the sunshine.

Funny, since the day she'd left rehab she'd never desired another drink. She'd had no desire to anesthetize her emotions, to drink away her pain. She had learned that was the answer to nothing. It was important that she embrace her emotions and deal with them rather than shoving them or drinking them away.

That was the way she had lived her life for the past three and a half years, and that was the way she intended to continue living her life.

Certainly the healthy philosophy didn't ease any of her pain, but now she understood that with life came both pain and pleasure and eventually she would find her pleasure again.

Tonight she would walk home alone from the bookstore. There would be no handsome FBI agent to walk beside her, to make her laugh and feel safe and secure. She was no longer afraid of the walk home. She believed that the stalker had been after Mark. It was really the only thing that made sense, that somebody close to the crime would attempt to take out one of the agents working to solve the crime.

The crimes. She still couldn't believe that Mark thought Melinda was behind the murders, that she'd staged her own kidnapping to provide a sick but seemingly solid alibi.

How she wished she knew more about her older sister. How she wished she'd had the guts to ask Melinda questions, to attempt to forge some sort of bond. But there was no question that Melinda was cold and distant and had never encouraged any kind of personal relationship during the three years Dora had lived within spitting distance of her.

Dora wondered now why she'd decided to help Dora in the first place. Was it possible Micah had made it impossible for Melinda to resist? Or had Melinda wanted Dora close enough to keep an eye on her, to make sure she told nobody about the horrible roots they had shared?

She leaned back in her chair as a couple of male students came through the door. They were rowdy and laughing, trying on a variety of hats in the school colors and bearing the Gladiators logo.

"You going to the bonfire, Dora?" one of the boys asked as he took a school ball cap off one of the shelves.

"I'm not sure." It had sounded like fun when she'd thought she was going to enjoy the evening with Mark.

"You've got to come," the other boy said. He grabbed a plastic Gladiator helmet and woofed several times as he pumped his arm in the air. "We're going to kick some birdie butt on Saturday night, but we've got to burn a few feathers on Friday." He set the helmet on the counter for her to ring up. "You've got to come. Our fraternity is providing free marshmallows."

As Dora saw the sparkle in the young man's eyes, the youthful energy that wafted from him, it was impossible for some of that spirit not to be contagious. "I'll probably be there," Dora replied with a laugh. "Free marshmallows are a hard thing for me to pass up."

Once the customers had left the bookstore, Dora made her decision to attend the bonfire and the game on Saturday night as she always had…alone. Just because she'd made plans with Mark, plans that were now destroyed, didn't mean she should deny herself the pleasure of the traditional fun.

At eight-thirty she turned the Open sign to Closed and then gathered her things to leave. She stepped out into the encroaching darkness and saw the tall figure that stood nearby.

Her heart both fluttered and sank at the same time. He was the person she least wanted to see right now with her heart so bruised and battered, with the spectrum of her past like a ghost between them.

"Mark, what are you doing here?" she asked, her voice filled with weariness.

"I figured you might like the company on the walk home." He stood in shadows, making it impossible for her to see his features, to gauge his mood.

"It isn't necessary," she replied, forcing a coolness into her tone. It was at that moment she realized he hadn't only hurt her, but she was angry with him. It was the irrational anger that he knew the worst of her, that he knew all her ugly secrets.

He stepped out of the shadows and into a stream of moonlight that came from the near-full moon overhead. His features were expressionless. "Actually, it is rather necessary," he replied. "I have some questions to ask you and I'd much rather do it at your place instead of dragging you down to the courthouse."

Dora stiffened. "Does this mean I'm somehow a suspect in the murders? Do you think I kidnapped my own sister and plotted with her to commit some heinous crime?"

"I don't think that," he replied, and for the first time his features softened. "But your relationship with Melinda has brought up questions that have to be answered. It's placed you in the person-of-interest category within my team."

Dora considered forcing him to drag her to the courthouse, to do his business officially, but then she thought of how that might reflect on Micah, on everyone who respected her.

"Come on, then." She finally relented and started down the sidewalk.

He hurried to catch up with her and, as they had earlier in the day, they suffered a silent walk to Dora's house. Dora tried to ignore the scent of him, which smelled of soap and shaving cream and the kinds of things she'd once wanted in her life.

She tried to forget how it had felt to be held in his arms, to taste the passion on his lips and go to sleep with him by her side.

Rather, she wanted to stay focused on the stunned surprise that had lit his features as she'd told him about her past. She wanted to remember that after she'd spewed everything that had been inside her, he hadn't mentioned a word about it, he'd simply asked her about her relationship with Melinda.

She knew what that meant—that he'd rejected her past, that he'd rejected her. Even though in her long-range planning of her life it shouldn't matter, that didn't stop the pain. That didn't stop the old, hurtful memories from playing in her mind.

Despite her efforts to the contrary, thoughts of her past had intruded into her afternoon. She'd mentally wrapped her arms around the little girl she had been, comforting the child who had never had a chance, who had only wanted to be loved.

When they reached her house, she unlocked the door and entered. She left the open door behind her as the only invitation to him. She didn't want him here but recognized he wasn't here as Mark Flynn, friend and lover. He was here as FBI agent Mark Flynn seeking answers to a crime.

When she reached the living room she shrugged out of her lightweight brown jacket and turned to face him, steeled for whatever might lie ahead.

He sat on the edge of the sofa as if he had a right to be there, and that only stirred the edge of irrational anger a little bit higher inside her.

"So question me," she said, refusing to sit. She just wanted this over. She wanted him out of here, where he no longer belonged.

He frowned and, with a deep sigh, pulled a small notepad and pen from his pocket. "I need to know where you were on the day of Melinda's disappearance." He stared down at the paper, as if unwilling to meet her gaze.

"That's easy to answer. The semester hadn't started yet, but I was working six days a week at the bookstore, which was open. After my bookstore shift I was back here alone. It's going to be a little difficult to provide an alibi for that time because I don't have friends I invite over to my house. As you should know by now I don't go out and hang with the younger students. Before you I was completely focused on work and school, not on kidnapping and murder plots."

She couldn't help the bitterness that laced her tone. Even though she understood he was here to do a job, she resented the questions, the inquiry into her very character. It would have been better if the questions were asked by another agent…not Mark, who should already know the answers.

"Dora." For the first time his gaze met hers and in the deep depths of his eyes she saw sorrow and regret. She hated him because he was going to make her cry, because even though she refused to be in love with him, he was breaking her heart all over again.

"Dora," Mark repeated, his heart heavy as he saw the tears that filled her eyes. "You know I don't believe you had anything to do with any of this, but the questions have to be asked to make a complete record."

He patted the sofa next to him. "Please sit down."

She resisted for several heartbeats and then eased down on the opposite end of the sofa from him. She didn't want to sit close enough to him that she could smell him, that she could feel the body heat she knew radiated from him.

"Let's just get this over with and then you can be on your way," she said.

For the next few minutes Mark asked her the questions he needed to ask to prove that she had nothing to offer the case, that she had nothing to do with whatever theory of the crime Mark believed or that the team believed.

Her alibi of working in the bookstore was an easy one to check. In the couple of weeks before school began, the bookstore would be a busy place as students prepared for the coming semester. There would be hundreds of witnesses who could place her there during the time of Melinda's kidnapping and the murders.

"Tell me about your relationship with Melinda," he asked.

"We don't really have one." Dora remained tensely curled up in the opposite corner of the sofa, as if allowing herself to relax would bring about complete disaster. "She's almost four years older than me and we were never close even as children. When she left Horn's Gulf at eighteen she never looked back. I didn't hear anything about her until she appeared in town to grab me by the arm and throw me in rehab."

Her cheeks flushed with color and she drew in several deep breaths, allowing the pink to slowly ebb from her cheeks. "When I got here, she made it clear she wasn't looking for a sisterly bond and I was just so grateful to be here I didn't pursue one."

"Why didn't you tell me about your relationship with her? You knew I was investigating her kidnapping."

Dora shrugged. "I also knew I couldn't help you, that I didn't know about what happened to Melinda. I've never told anyone that she's my sister. I never wanted her to be embarrassed that her forty-year-old sister was finally getting her life together. The last thing I wanted to be was an embarrassment to the person who gave me a second chance at life."

"Sounds to me like you deserved a do-over in life," Mark said softly. He couldn't get out of his head what she'd told him about her former life, coupled with what he'd discerned from his talk with her old schoolteacher and the new owner of the Daisy Café.

She frowned, her eyes the color of dark metal. "Melinda managed to get out. I managed to make bad choices. Despite the fact that my mother was a raging alcoholic, I somehow felt bound to stay in town and take care of her. I'd clean her up when she got sick, I'd sober her up to get her back to my father at the end of the night."

She grabbed a bright orange throw pillow to her chest and wrapped her arms around it, her gaze downward as she continued. "I managed to hold things together through my miserable childhood. I even managed to survive the abusive marriage and divorce from Billy Cook. It was Jimmy Martin who was the straw that broke my back."

"Tell me," Mark said softly, and inched closer to her on the sofa.

She toyed with the fringe on the pillow and he noticed the faint tremble in her hand. "I loved Jimmy— at least I thought I was in love with him, and when we got married I thought he loved me. I truly believed he'd managed to overlook my reputation, my background, and saw the heart and soul of me shining through all the muck."

Mark wanted to say something to ease the pain that sparked in her eyes, but he could tell by their unfocused glaze that she'd gone backward in time, apparently remembering things she'd tried hard to forget. Her fingers tightened on the fringe.

"The first year of our marriage I thought everything was perfect. Jimmy worked at the bank and I was a stay-at-home wife. I tried to do everything I could to make him happy. He came home to a clean house and a home-cooked meal each night. I was a willing and eager lover. I thought we were on our way to building a life together, becoming a family."

She fell silent and there was a stillness about her as if she'd disappeared from this place and this time. Mark knew all about falling into the rabbit hole of his own mind and he sat patiently for what felt like forever before he gently called her name.

She jerked and glanced at him with embarrassment. "Sorry." She drew a deep breath. "It was in the second year of our marriage that things started to go bad, or at least I started noticing things that bothered me. Jimmy never struck me—he never even showed that he had a temper—but he used words to chip away at my confidence. I'd get dressed to go out and he'd tell me it was a shame I had my mother's taste in clothes or he'd mention that it wasn't any wonder I was drawn to whore colors and gaudy jewelry. He never stopped reminding me of where I'd come from, that he was the only man in town who would marry Daisy's daughter. I was just one step from a heathen, needing reminders about manners and why didn't I know how to throw a successful cocktail party…and on…and on."

Mark slid closer to her, close enough that he could smell both her wildflower scent and her sorrow. He wanted to touch her, but she remained in a defense position and he had a feeling any touch from him at that moment would be unwelcome.

"I tried. I tried to be everything he wanted, but one night as we were making love he whispered into my ear that I really was my mother's daughter, just a whore with bad taste."

She sucked in her breath, as if feeling a physical blow to her stomach. "I let him finish with me and then I got out of the bed, got dressed and walked down to my mother's café." Her voice was flat, without affect. "I went into the back room where my mother kept her bottles of gin and I drank until I couldn't feel anymore, until I couldn't think anymore."

Her gaze finally met his and he realized she was back in the here and now. "I stayed my mother's daughter until the day Micah and Melinda plucked me out of the gutter and put me in rehab. That's where I came from, Mark. And that's why I didn't want anyone to know that I was the great, illustrious professor Grayson's sister."

His heart was so filled with her damage he couldn't speak. The great brainiac couldn't find the right words to verbalize the depth of his sorrow, of his grief for her.

"Just go, Mark," she said, the weariness back in her voice as she raised a finger to point at the door. "I was fine before you and I'll be fine after you. Get back to your crime investigation and tie things up here in a neat knot so you can get back to your life and I can continue with mine."

"I wish I would have been there for you." He finally found his voice. "I wish I would have been there to beat up all the children who bullied you, to shoot your father dead the first time he broke one of your bones. I wish I would have been there to sweep you out of town and save you from the horrors you went through."

Her eyes widened in surprise and then immediately narrowed as she shook her head. "I didn't need to have a hero in my life, Mark. I needed to figure out how to be my own hero. I took the easy way out. I allowed small-town people to label me and then I did my very best to live up to the label they'd provided. It's taken me thirty-seven years to realize I don't need a hero. I'm all I need and I'm strong enough to build the rest of my life alone."

"But, you still need a date to the bonfire on Friday night. Why not allow me to accompany you?" He couldn't just walk away from her now. It all felt so unfinished.

"Why would you want to do that?" she asked. She lowered the pillow from her chest and set it on the sofa between them.

"Because for the last week I've heard nothing but how amazing the bonfire is, how the burning of the effigy isn't to be missed, and I can't think of anyone I'd like to share the evening with more than you." There were so many more things he wanted to say, but she looked beaten and bruised from her walk down memory lane.

"It's foolish for us to have anything more to do with each other," she countered.

"I don't want it to end like this, Dora. Come to the bonfire with me. Let's have one more night with no past and no future between us, just the here and now. It will be a night to enjoy together as friends."

Her eyes filled with a swift yearning, only there a moment and then hidden as she blinked it away. "Won't that somehow compromise your investigation if I'm a person of interest?"

"You're only a person of interest to me, and that has nothing to do with the crimes," Mark said truthfully.

He held his breath, wanting, needing her to give in to this final wish. He needed one last night with her, a night of laughter and fun before she kicked him to the curb to get on with her new life.

"Okay," she said, although it hurt him that there was no joy, no sweet smile accompanying the word. She stood as if to indicate that she was done, fried to a crisp and more than ready for him to leave.

"Why don't you come by here at seven on Friday? The bonfire is lit at nine and that will give us a couple of hours to mingle and hang out with the crowd." She looked at the door, an obvious indication that she had said her piece and now it was time for him to leave.

Reluctantly he got up from the sofa and walked to the front door. "Then I'll see you Friday night at seven," he said. She nodded and he realized that was all she had left.

He stepped outside her door and gently closed it behind him. Failure. Somehow he knew he'd failed Dora and for the life of him he didn't know how to fix it.

Chapter 15

Dora awoke Thursday morning after a night of bad dreams. In her dreams she had been back in Horn's Gulf and she'd awakened with the bitter dredges of memory in the back of her throat.

Buck Grayson had been a brutal man, but through the first ten years of her life Dora had learned what set him off, how to dodge and weave most of the physical blows he tried to deliver to her. By the time she was fourteen she was spending almost no time around Buck at the family ranch, rather she spent most all of her time with her mother at the Daisy Café.

She now recognized that her mother had been as, if not more, abusive than Buck. Her mother hadn't hit her or broken any bones, but she'd bound Dora to her and her lifestyle through threats and guile, through manipulation and guilt.

She'd stopped asking herself a long time ago why,

when she was young, nobody had stepped in to save her from her father, from her mother or from herself. She knew most of the people in the small town had been afraid of Buck, which made it easy for them to turn blind eyes when Dora showed up with yet another bruise or a broken bone.

She rolled out of bed and headed for the bathroom. Minutes later as she stood beneath a hot spray of water, she thought about the night before and Mark. The questions he'd had to ask her as part of his job hadn't really surprised her, although she didn't like the fact that by mere accident of birth she was now on some sheet of paper in the war room of the courthouse.

What had surprised her had been Mark's gentleness, the compassion she'd seen in the depths of his eyes as they talked about the childhood that should never have been. There had been none of the revulsion she'd expected to see, no judgment of her at all.

Of course, it was easy to feel compassionate for somebody who wasn't going to be a permanent fixture in your life, she told herself as she got out of the shower and dressed for the day.

He hadn't run for the hills; rather he'd renewed his desire to spend the homecoming festivities with her. And she wasn't sure why she'd agreed to the idea.

Because you're in love with him, a little voice whispered in the back of her head.

She grabbed her computer and purse from the table and headed out the door for her early-morning class.

Her brain rejected the very thought of loving Mark. It would be just another study in heartbreak. It would be a repeat of the heartbreak of Jimmy, and she refused to put herself in a position to care that deeply about a man again.

She was confident in her own strength, in her ability to walk the path of the rest of her life alone. She would never again allow a man to define her.

The morning air was unusually brisk for October in Vengeance. A cold front had moved through that made it perfect football weather. Everywhere she looked were signs of the big game and reminders of the bonfire the next night.

There was a restless energy pulsating, as if even the building and the trees were eagerly anticipating the imminent celebrations of school spirit.

She saw Ben Craig in the distance and waved to him. He waved back as he scurried in the opposite direction of her. Strange, it used to be Dora never saw him without Amanda by his side. The two assistants had been like conjoined twins whenever they were out. But lately Dora rarely saw them together.

As she walked up the stairs into the building where the first class of the day took place, she steadfastly refused to think about what Mark had said about his suspicions of Melinda.

She didn't know the truth and, thankfully, it wasn't her job to try to figure it out. She'd leave the investigation to the professionals. There was no way she could guess about Melinda's innocence or guilt. She could only hope that her sister had nothing to do with her own kidnapping or the murder of the three men. Knowing that there was one sociopath, Samuel, in the family was quite enough.

Throughout her class she stayed focused on the material, refusing to allow her mind to drift in any other direction.

If she continued to pursue her career in criminal justice then maybe sometime years from now she'd find herself working with Mark on a case. By that time she hoped he'd be remarried to a wonderful woman who understood his quirks and foibles, a woman who could chase the darkness away from him when necessary.

He deserved that. He deserved a safe place to fall, next to a warm, loving woman at the end of his long and dark days.

She would never be that woman, but she wanted that for him.

By the time she'd finished her second class of the day, the mood of the campus was already half-mad. Students dressed in Gladiator garb and raced after others who wore jaybird feathers in their hair or pinned to their clothes. Laughter rang out from every corner of the campus and she passed several students who already wore the eau-de-beer scent that would prevail from now until Sunday, when those students awoke with sick stomachs and worse headaches.

She tried not to imagine how different things might have been between her and Mark at the bonfire the next night if the specter of her past wasn't between them, if he hadn't learned about her connection to Melinda and if she didn't know his single goal was to attempt to arrest the sister whom Dora had always looked at as her savior.

It would be so easy if she could see Mark as the enemy, a man attempting to destroy the sister she loved. But Dora had no real depth of feeling toward Melinda other than gratitude. In the very depths of her heart, she couldn't get past the fact that while Melinda was kidnapped three men had been murdered, and since her miraculous release from her captives, nobody else had died.

Mark knew that Melinda had an afternoon lecture and that probably her two assistants would be in their usual seats in the front row. That worked fine with him. In fact, he was counting on that very scenario.

He'd lain awake for half the night, most of his thoughts filled with Dora. His heart had ached for the little girl who'd suffered so much and had sought escape first in the arms of a physical abuser and then with a man who'd emotionally stabbed the last of her life out of her.

As a profiler, he understood very well the forces that drove people onto different, varying paths of life. It was little wonder that Dora had found solace in the bottle. He had no doubt that her unconscious desire had been to drink herself to death, to disappear from the pain.

He'd seen her pain the night before, had felt it radiating so strongly from her it had made him almost physically ill. He'd wanted to sweep her into his arms, hold her tight and assure her of her value as a woman, as a person. He wanted to give to her the validation and love she'd never received as a child.

But he hadn't. She hadn't given him any opening to offer solace and in that he'd seen her strength, a strength that would see her well through the rest of her life.

He probably shouldn't have asked that they spend the

homecoming celebration together. It had been a selfish request. He wasn't ready to tell her goodbye just yet.

He'd finally fallen asleep and had immediately drifted into the same nightmare about Melinda. The weight of her on his chest, the laughter of male and female mingling into a sound of horror and the slow cutting off of his air supply, had finally jerked him awake, sweating and cursing.

It was only then, as he sat up in bed waiting for the nightmare's hold to release him, that he realized he wanted to get into Melinda Grayson's office.

First thing that morning Mark had obtained reluctant permission from the dean of the college to do a search of Melinda's office, which was deemed to be a public place with no expectancy of privacy.

However, Mark knew the permission would not include searching any of Melinda's personal belongings, including any laptop she might possess.

As he made his way across the campus, he felt the wildness in the air, but for him it wasn't just the antics of the students winding up for homecoming, it was the thrum of anticipation that something bad was going to happen.

Whoever had killed those men definitely already had or had instantly acquired a taste for murder. Mark had interviewed too many killers to not know that in most cases a taste of murder quickly became an insatiable appetite.

He was surprised there hadn't been any more murders. As he thought of the note that had been left on his windshield, he wondered if he was Melinda and her partner's next intended victim?

Amanda certainly hadn't told him all that she might know about her boss. She hadn't even admitted that she had been the one to leave the note of warning for him.

It was probably a simple matter of no opportunity that had kept any more deaths from occurring. Melinda and everyone in her intimate sphere had to know they were under his microscope.

As he reached the building where Melinda's next lecture would occur, he sat on the familiar bench outside and checked his watch. He had about ten minutes before he'd feel secure in sneaking into Melinda's office and trying to find something, anything that might point a finger of guilt in her direction.

He had no idea what he was looking for, but knew he'd recognize anything that might tie into his theory of the case. He also didn't know what the other agents were assigned to do today, as he'd skipped the morning briefing.

Patting his jacket pocket, he assured himself that a pair of latex gloves and several evidence bags were still there. Just in case he found something to carry out.

When he was sure Melinda had begun her lecture, he went into the building and to the second floor where her office was located. He'd taken a chance, not bothering getting a key from the dean. If his instincts were correct about Melinda's personality, then she wouldn't bother locking her door because she knew nobody would dare breach her privacy without invitation.

When he reached her office door he was grateful to find himself alone in the hallway. He grabbed the knob and twisted, a sigh of satisfaction escaping him as it twisted easily beneath his grasp.

The fact that she didn't lock her door affirmed the profile of her that had begun to emerge. He found it ironic that she was teaching a class about sociopaths in society, especially given the fact that he believed Melinda was the truest form of a sociopath.

He eased the door open and slid inside, then quietly closed the door behind him. The corner office was large, with windows on two sides. The furnishings were sleek, black and chrome, cold and impersonal. A large desk faced the door, with a leather chair behind it. Two uncomfortable-looking straight-back chairs faced the desk, set at a distance so as not to invade in any way the professor's personal space.

The walls held her degrees and awards she had received in her field of study. There was nothing personal anywhere in the room. A bookcase held only books, no knickknacks or souvenirs that might hint of the person who occupied this space.

He moved around the desk and looked down at the papers that were strewn across the top. A psychology journal was open to an article on treatment plans for the sociopath; student papers were in a stack, the top one sporting thick red slashes where corrections had been made.

Sticky notes littered the bare space, detailing the minutia in a life. *Pick up dry cleaning. Check with B about pit. Get lettuce and eggs.* Pink and yellow notes pinned to the top of the desk by a strip of adhesive. There was nothing here that clenched Mark's gut or that raised any alarm at all in his head.

He slid open the top desk drawer to see an array of paperclips and pens. A red pair of scissors was nestled next to a black stapler. He closed the drawer and opened the second one.

Where the first had held the tools of a teacher, the second contained the tools of a beautiful and vain woman. The drawer held a hand mirror, makeup, a tube of red lipstick and a hairbrush, certainly nothing that would prove or disprove his belief.

He opened the third drawer, which was deep enough to hang files. Inside were files neatly labeled with colorful plastic tabs. He riffled through them, finding them to contain research on a variety of psychological subjects.

Aware of the ticking of time, knowing that he only had a total of about forty minutes to search and then get out of the office and away from the building, he was about to close the file drawer when something caught his eye at the very bottom.

The stack of small cards like those that had been found on the victims was nearly hidden by the files. He quickly yanked on his gloves, his heart beating a rapid response.

As he picked up the stack held together by a rubber band, he noticed that the first one had writing on it. He straightened and stared at the top card.

"Failu." He frowned, his brain working overtime to make sense of the letters. Failu? His heart chilled as he realized he might possibly be looking at the card that had been meant to be left on his dead body.

Failu…an interruption of the word that had been meant. *Failure.* Had that been her intention? If that note card had been found on him after his death, it certainly would have been true. It would have meant he'd failed to capture her. He'd failed to avoid his own death.

Failure.

The word shuddered through him as he clasped the stack of cards in his gloved fingers. Failure as a profiler, failure as a father…and failure to make his case…. How she must have delighted at finding the perfect word to describe him.

With trembling hands he quickly removed the rubber band and plucked the card off the top. He riffled through the rest of the cards but saw no more that contained any writing.

Aware of the passage of time, he quickly placed the "Failu" card into one of his evidence envelopes and then checked his watch again and decided it was time to boogie out of there.

The card in his pocket legally proved nothing, at least not yet. The team had already asserted that these particular note cards were a popular item for sale in the bookstore. The fact that Melinda had the cards proved nothing. But he was eager to get back to the war room and compare the handwriting to the notes that had been found on the dead men.

It was possible Melinda's card would have to be seen by a handwriting analysis.

It might be nothing, or it might be something that would explode the case wide-open. There was no question in Mark's mind that the card had been meant for him, that Melinda and her partner had been plotting Mark's death and this "Failu" card would label him what they believed him to be. However, believing and proving legally were two very different animals.

While Mark hurried out of the building, he realized that as far as he was concerned there were only two people he believed could be Melinda's partner. The first was Ben Craig, the assistant who was devoted to her, and the second was Andrew Peterson, who had been besotted with her. Either man could have been manipulated into helping her commit murder.

At the moment his first goal was to get this note into evidence with the others and find out if they'd all been penned by the same person.

He couldn't get to the war room fast enough and when he finally arrived he found Richard the only person there. Richard looked up from his laptop as Mark came flying through the door.

"You look like you've just won the lottery," Richard said.

Mark flashed him a grin. "Money never makes me this excited. Potential evidence is what makes a happy dance in my heart."

"Potential evidence?" Richard closed his laptop and looked at Mark expectantly.

"I just finished doing a short search of Melinda's office here on campus and I found this hidden in the bottom of a drawer." Mark pulled the plastic evidence bag from his pocket and set in on the table next to Richard.

Richard stared down at the card with a frown. "'Failu'? What the hell is that supposed to mean?"

"I think she was writing *failure* and got interrupted." Mark's heart banged hard against his chest. "I think that card was meant to be left on my dead body."

Richard shot him a sharp look. "Why would she think you're a failure?"

Mark sat in the chair next to Richard. "Probably for several reasons. I've been a profiler without a profile, an agent coming after her but unable to connect all the dots." He didn't mention that Melinda could have found out from somebody that he was also a failure as a father figure in Grace's life and completely stank at being what a woman needed.

"It makes sense if you remember that I got a warning note on my car that said I was in danger," Mark continued.

Richard looked at the card in the plastic bag and then at the board that held photocopies of the notes that had been found on each dead man. *Liar. Cheater. Thief.*

Mark studied the notes, as well. Certainly *failure* worked into the basic theme of the other cards. They were all character flaws defined by a killer.

"It's hard to tell just by looking if the writer is the same," Richard finally said.

"I'd like this one to be sent to the lab and compared for handwriting analysis. If all four cards are written by the same person, then there's no question that the person is Melinda." Mark felt a burst of triumph wing through him. For the first time since they'd arrived in Vengeance, he smelled the end of the case with the guilty party behind bars.

"What about the fact that there was a man with her when she was kidnapped?"

"Her partner in crime," Mark replied without hesitation. "I've narrowed it down to two men, either Ben Craig or Andrew Peterson. I think either of those males could have been easily manipulated by Melinda to do whatever she demanded of them."

"But Andrew Peterson told us he and Melinda broke up before she disappeared."

"He could have lied. The day we spoke to him, despite his protests about reclaiming his love for his wife and children, his obsession with Melinda was still there and burning bright. I think he would have done anything to continue to have her."

"But we've had no indication of anything going on between them since the murders," Richard replied, obviously playing devil's advocate.

"Melinda's smart, too smart to tie herself to her partner while we're still here in town and have our eyes on her."

"And yet she hasn't distanced herself from Ben."

"If she did, then it would look equally suspicious," Mark replied. "He's her assistant. He has a reason to be in her life. She couldn't kick him to the curb without answering a lot of uncomfortable questions."

"Is your gut telling you which man is guilty?" Richard asked.

Mark shook his head. "Unfortunately, no. But before we can really try to figure that out, we have to prove that this note and the others were all written by Melinda."

Richard frowned thoughtfully. "I'll have Lori see if she can dig up a couple of student papers that have Melinda's writing on them and then she can take this card, along with the samples, to Dallas. It will probably take a day or two for us to get a definitive answer."

Mark nodded. It would take some time to get information back from Dallas and one of the FBI handwriting specialists.

"Good work, Mark."

Mark stood, unsure what to do next, but aware that he was too energized to simply sit. "Thanks. It's not a solve yet, but the fact that we've found no connection to Melinda and the victims only makes me more suspicious and more inclined to believe she is incredibly smart."

"And there's nothing worse than a killer who is brilliant."

"And beautiful," Mark added. Thinking about beautiful women brought a vision of Dora to his mind. He should probably warn her that he'd found something that might tie her sister to the murders, but he decided to wait.

Maybe by the next night when they went to the bonfire together he would hear back from the experts. In the meantime it was a wait-and-see situation.

A thrum of unexpected anxiety whirled inside of him. He just hoped the killer was taking a wait-and-see view on things, as well. He now believed there was a solid target on his back, and Professor Melinda Grayson didn't strike him as a woman who liked to leave loose ends or incomplete projects.

As he left the building, heading to a nearby drive-through for an early dinner, he thought about Dora once again. If he arrested the woman she believed was her savior, then what did that make him to Dora? Judas? Traitor?

Certainly by doing his job he could kiss goodbye

any hope for any future with Dora. A pall of depression settled over his shoulders despite the fact that they were one step closer to getting the guilty party behind bars.

Chapter 16

Friday afternoon Dora's phone rang and to her surprise it was Mark. When she first saw his name on her caller ID, she assumed he'd called to cancel their date of sorts for the night. She figured everything she had told him about herself, about her past, had finally sunk into his overworked brain and he'd realized she wasn't the kind of woman he wanted to spend time with.

Reluctantly she answered. "Dora." His warm, deep voice swept over her and she closed her eyes, steeling herself for what she assumed was about to come.

"Hi, Mark." She was grateful her voice sounded strong.

"Since I didn't see you yesterday I just figured I'd call to confirm the plans for the night. I'll be at your house around seven and then we'll head to the bonfire together."

Relief shuddered through her. Just one more night.

She wanted just one more night to be in his company, to watch that slow, sexy smile steal across his features. "That sounds perfect," she replied.

"I can't tell you how much I'm looking forward to it," he replied.

"Me, too."

"Then I'll see you tonight," he replied, and after murmured goodbyes they hung up. Dora sat on the edge of the sofa with her phone still in hand.

Tonight. She would spend the night with a man she shouldn't love, a man who would leave her heart wounded when he returned to his life in Dallas.

He was a highly respected FBI agent, not the kind of man who would want to continue to pursue any sort of relationship with her after this evening. Tonight was their swan song and while the very thought caused her heart to ache, she was comforted by the knowledge that she was strong enough to survive Mark Flynn.

Over the past couple of months she'd recognized that she had become the woman she'd always wanted to be, strong and self-sufficient and without the need for a man or anyone else to define or complete her.

She'd invited Mark into her life because she'd wanted to, because she'd known nobody could throw her off her determination to build a healthy, productive life. And she knew she'd be fine without Mark in her life. But she couldn't help that the thought created a pool of sadness inside her.

She rose from the sofa and placed her phone on the end table. She wanted to leave tonight with her house clean and at some point work in a long, luxurious bubble bath.

Yesterday she'd even gone off campus to a local dress shop and had bought a beautiful bright red sweater with gold-trimmed V-neck. That, coupled with a pair of skinny jeans, would be perfect for displaying school colors during a fun night.

She ate a light lunch knowing that there would be hot dogs, marshmallows and other treats at the bonfire. She consciously schooled her thoughts away from the murders and Mark's suspicions about Melinda.

She wanted nothing negative to screw up what would be her final time with Mark. Even if he wanted to continue their coffee drinking and friendship for the remainder of his time in Vengeance, she couldn't.

As far as she was concerned the moment she'd told him about where she'd come from, the moment he'd told her he thought Melinda was responsible for the crimes, it had ended with a whimper. Tonight would be the final cut.

She would bow out of attending the football game with him tomorrow night. She would no longer require him meeting her at the bookstore to walk her home and she definitely wouldn't give him an opportunity to sit at her table, where she'd begun to believe he belonged.

It was time to let go.

The afternoon whizzed by as she cleaned and did laundry and tried to keep her mind focused only on positive things. In May she would graduate with a degree in criminal justice and then it would be job-hunting time.

The world would be an open canvas for her to paint what she would do for the rest of her life, and although the blankness of the canvas was daunting now, the idea was also exciting.

A part of her wanted to remain in Vengeance, but her job opportunities would be limited here.

Hours later, as she luxuriated in the old tub full of bubbles, she thought about her future. The good thing was, unlike so much of the housing market around the country, her house value had gone up due to the influx of people returning to college and the home's prime location.

She would be able to sell the place and pay back Micah every cent he'd invested in her, although she would never be able to repay his unwavering belief in her.

It was just after five when she finished her bath with a quick shower to wash her hair. When done, she dried off and pulled on a lightweight navy shift to wear until it was time to get dressed for the evening.

She turned on her old stereo unit and tuned to an easy listening channel, then made herself a cup of tea and sat at the table where she'd spent so much time in the past couple of weeks with Mark.

If he took nothing else away from the time they'd spent together, she hoped he'd take a new understanding about how important good fathers were in the lives of their daughters.

Dora had no idea how her life might have been different if she'd had a loving, caring father and if her mother hadn't been an alcoholic.

She still occasionally checked out the newspaper for the small town of Horn's Gulf that was available online. Two years ago she had seen her mother's obituary and she'd tried desperately to summon sorrow, but she'd only managed an uncomfortable relief.

She hadn't gone to the funeral and had spent a long time trying to figure out who might have been in attendance for the alcoholic who had bedded half the town's men. Certainly Daisy hadn't had any female friends who would have shown up to shed a tear. Most of the men Daisy had slept with had been married and wouldn't be attending her funeral.

It was the sad ending to a sad life and Dora had only been grateful that she'd finally managed to break the chain of alcoholism and abuse in her own life.

Glancing at the clock on the oven, she sipped her raspberry tea and listened to the music dancing through the room. She was tired of thinking about everything. Tonight she would feel, not think. Tonight she would laugh and have fun despite the coming heartbreak of Mark.

Tonight there was no past, no future, just the moment and the fun of celebration. Then it would be time for Dora to put all things Mark behind her and get on with her goals.

She'd just about finished her cup of tea when a knock fell on her door. Startled, she glanced at the clock to see it was not quite six o'clock, far too early for it to be Mark.

A peek at the window showed Ben Craig standing on her porch. She opened the door and he offered her a wide smile. "Dora, I'm sorry to bother you, but could I come in for a minute?"

She opened the door wider to allow him inside. "I

figured you'd be frantically finishing up the last-minute things at the bonfire pit," she said, wondering why he was here.

"I am," he replied as he followed her into the living room. "I just have a few more things to take care of and then we'll be ready to roll. It's going to be an awesome night." His eyes glittered with excitement. "I'm really only missing one thing."

"And what's that?" Dora turned to face him.

He took a step toward her. "You."

Before Dora had a chance to protest, he grabbed her, twirled her around and then slammed her against him as he held a strange-scented cloth over her mouth and nose.

Don't breathe, a voice screamed inside Dora's head as she struggled vainly against him. His body was hot against her back, his arms strong as they struggled.

Don't breathe, Dora. The words played and replayed in her head. She attempted to twist out of his grasp, kicked one leg out as she lost her balance. The clumsy kick only managed to connect with a small accent table and she heard the pretty vase on top of it thump and roll on the floor.

She had no idea what was happening, why this was happening. The only thing she knew was she had to hold her breath until she could get away from him. Yet, even as she thought this, she felt the burn of her lungs, the desperate need for air.

Don't breathe, she thought, and did just the opposite. She breathed and immediately her head spun, her brain losing focus as she slumped against him and dove into the awaiting darkness.

* * *

Mark drove his car to Dora's with the intention that they would leave his car there and walk to the celebration on campus. There had been no word back from the handwriting expert and so everyone and everything was in a wait-and-see mode. He was determined to keep his work out of his head for the remainder of the night, although he'd opted to wear his windbreaker with the bold FBI letters on the front and back.

There was no way he wanted the local law officials or campus security to mistake him for one of the drunken revelers. He'd heard that stun guns would be the weapons of choice for the students who got out of control.

Despite the limbo that the investigation was in, in spite of his feeling that Dora intended to kick him to the curb, he was looking forward to the night with her.

The sidewalks were already filling with students and alumni, clad in Gladiator garb and shades of red and gold, making their way toward the campus as Mark pulled up to the curb in front of Dora's house.

It promised to be a perfect-weather night, although several clouds skittered across the sky, bringing forth a false sense of early night.

He'd seen the fire pit earlier in the day and it had reminded him of something out of Old Salem when they'd burned witches at the stake. Tonight a straw-stuffed Blue Jay football player would be the official guest of honor.

Already the scent of beer and popcorn filled the air, but what he wanted to smell more than anything was the scent of Dora, that wildflower fragrance that drove him half-mad.

He got out of his car and walked to her front door with a simmering excitement inside. Tonight he had to somehow make her realize that they deserved a future together. He had to make her understand that he didn't give a damn where she'd come from or what had happened before he met her. Her past meant nothing to him. He was only interested in her future.

A glance at his watch let him know he was precisely on time. It was exactly seven o'clock. He knocked on her door, surprised when it eased open on its own.

"Dora?" He stepped inside as he called her name. There was no answering response. He stepped into the living room and called her name louder. Still no reply and that's when the first stir of anxiety shot off in his stomach.

A quick glance showed him that her purse was on the table, along with a teacup of half-drunk tea. He touched the cup. Cold...as cold as his heart as he cried out her name yet a third time.

She should be able to hear him, no matter where she was in the house. He raced up the stairs to the bedrooms, looking first in the spare room that only held a chair and a single bed and then in her room, where a sweater and jeans were neatly laid on the bed as if just awaiting her to pull them on.

He stared at the clothes and then focused his attention on the closed bathroom door. Was she running late? Still doing makeup or finishing up a shower?

It was completely out of character for her to be late.

Heart thudding an anxious rhythm of dread, he advanced on the closed door.

He knocked on the door, a firm rap that would wake the dead. When there was no immediate response he flung open the door and gasped a sigh of both relief and alarm as she wasn't there.

The room held the trace of her in the lingering scent of her perfume, but other than a damp towel that spoke of an earlier shower or bath, there was nothing to tell him what had happened to her.

He raced back down the stairs, his brain firing on all cylinders. The half-empty glass of tea, the clothes ready to wear and the purse on the table...all were indications that Dora had left the house unexpectedly.

Gone. But where? And why? She had no friends and she certainly wouldn't have left the house on her own volition with the door open and her purse on the table. She knew he'd be here at seven, and there was no way she'd left the house and stood him up.

He looked around the middle of the living room. When he spied the poppy-colored vase half-hidden at the foot of the sofa he realized there had been some sort of struggle and that she'd been taken from here. For a moment he was frozen, his brain not working like a seasoned FBI agent, but rather like a man missing his mate.

Panic set in. Where was Dora? Something bad had happened here. He could smell the evil in the air, as the hairs on the nape of his neck raised in fear.

Do something, Mark, a voice screamed inside his head. That scream snapped him into action. He quickly checked all the windows on the ground level and found them locked and intact. She'd known whoever had come in. She'd apparently opened her door to the person, allowed them into her living room.

Failu.

The letters on the small card he'd found in the bottom of Melinda's drawer suddenly flashed in his head, like a neon sign blinking over and over again. *Failu.*

Failure. Maybe he'd been wrong in thinking the card was meant for him. Maybe somebody who knew about Dora's past had just been waiting to label and get rid of her.

The great Melinda would see the sister who had stayed behind, who had become an alcoholic, as a failure. Although she'd helped Dora escape from Horn's Gulf, she might only hold disgust and embarrassment for Dora.

And what better night to murder again? With the throngs of people on campus, with the law and security on babysitting duty for the students and out-of-town guests, it would be easy for two people to disappear for a night of murder and madness.

Amanda. She held some of the answers, and without full knowledge of what the assistant knew, there was no way for Mark even to begin to know where to look for Dora.

As he ran down the stairs to his car at the curb, he pulled out his cell phone and called Richard. With clipped, terse words he told his boss what was happening, what he believed and that he was on his way to Amanda's place for a shakedown.

"I'll send Albright and Thompson to Dora's place to check for forensic evidence. Lori and Joseph are already somewhere on the campus. I'll tell them to keep an eye out for both Craig and the professor. If we have them in our sights, then they can't be committing murder."

"Get somebody to find Andrew Peterson, just in case my first instincts are wrong," Mark said as he got into his car.

"I'll take care of it," Richard replied. When the two men had disconnected, Mark started his engine and the resulting roar of the engine mirrored the roar of terror that shot through his heart.

Dora was the next victim. She would be found somewhere with a note card placed on her body that read Failure. He had to stop it. He couldn't let this happen.

He pulled to the curb in front of Amanda's apartment building and parked with a screech of tires. He was out of the car like a flash.

Somehow he felt Amanda was his only hope. He believed the young woman knew a lot more than she'd told anyone. Mark needed any and all information she had about Melinda. Dora's life hung in the balance and he'd do whatever necessary to get some answers out of Amanda. He didn't care that she was afraid—it was time for her to step up before another murder occurred.

When he reached her door he banged on it with both fists, the terror inside him just barely contained. He didn't even want to consider what his next move would be if Amanda wasn't home.

He was about to pound on the door a second time when it opened. "Mark!" Amanda said with a startled look on her face. She was clad in jeans and a sweatshirt that read Gladiators across the front.

"I need to talk to you," Mark replied, striding past her and into the small apartment. As she closed the door behind him he turned to look at her.

"Dora has gone missing. I need you to tell me everything you can about Melinda and if I think you aren't telling me everything you know I'll arrest you for obstruction of justice."

He should feel bad, threatening a young woman, but he was beyond compassion, caught up in a race for Dora's very life.

"Dora's missing?" she echoed. She walked on wooden legs to the sofa and sank down. Tears filled her eyes as she stared up at Mark. "I think Melinda and Ben concocted the whole kidnapping scheme."

"What makes you think that?"

"Just stuff I've heard between the two of them, little snippets of conversations. They never said anything directly to me about it, but sometimes I overheard them talking. I heard Ben tell Melinda that she should be glad he only broke her arm, that if he'd broken her leg it would have been difficult for her to get around campus."

"You left the note on my car."

Amanda nodded. "I was starting to believe that Melinda and Ben had killed those men, and then I heard your name mentioned between them. I wanted to let you know that Troy Young was innocent and I needed to warn you that you might be in danger."

She raised a trembling hand to swipe away several tears that had escaped her eyes. "I wanted to believe I was wrong in my suspicions. I wanted to believe that Melinda was a brilliant, wonderful woman who would never be involved in any criminal activity. But truthfully, she scares me and she has Ben completely wrapped around her finger."

Mark's cell phone rang and he held up a finger to Amanda as he answered. "Agent Flynn."

"We've checked both Ben's apartment and Melinda's place and nobody is home at either place," Richard said. "The police department has stationed a man on each address to see if either of them turns up."

Mark fought against a new wave of fear as he thanked Richard and then disconnected the call. If Dora wasn't at either of those places then where could she be? Was she already dead and buried in a shallow grave? His brain rebelled at the very thought.

"Do you know if Melinda has another place besides the one where she lives? Does she own a getaway cabin or anything like that?"

Amanda frowned. "Not that I know of."

"Neither Melinda nor Ben are home. Do you have any idea where they might be right now?"

"I imagine they're already out at the bonfire site." Amanda jumped up from the sofa. "Maybe there's some information about Melinda owning another house or something in the paperwork she left with me on the day after she was supposedly released from her kidnappers."

Mark stared at her, his heart thumping. "Papers?"

Amanda walked over to the closet, opened it and then withdrew a tin lockbox from the top shelf. "Melinda brought this to me for safekeeping," Amanda explained. "At the time she told me she was afraid of what might happen to her next and that this was all the paperwork anyone would need if something bad happened to her." She held the tin box toward Mark, who grasped it eagerly.

"Get me a sharp knife or a screwdriver," he said as he carried the box to the small table. The box was locked, but it was cheap, and if Mark couldn't pick the lock, his adrenaline would give him enough strength to tear it apart.

He was vaguely surprised when Amanda pulled a pink case from under her sofa and opened it to display a small tool kit, complete with hammer, screwdrivers and pliers.

Aware of time ticking by, time that could possibly be measured by Dora's last gasps, he grabbed the Phillips-head screwdriver and attacked the lock.

After several agonizing minutes, he threw the screwdriver aside with frustration and picked up the hammer. He attacked the box as if it were the person who had taken Dora, and by the time he'd struck the lock several times the lock sprang and the lid unlatched.

Inside were three items and a digital camera. Mark stared at the three things: a gold-plated cigar lighter, a thick rope gold chain and a tie tack bearing the initials of JM.

JM.

"John Merris," he muttered to himself. Souvenirs. This was a box of souvenirs from the murders. He was vaguely aware of Amanda moving to stand next to him.

Sheriff Burris was a cigar smoker and David Reed's ex-wife, Eliza, had mentioned that David always wore a chain around his neck, a chain that hadn't been found on the body.

Mark's heart thumped in his chest as he picked up the camera and turned it on. The first photo displayed was a picture of Senator John Merris, obviously dead and resting in the shallow pit that had been prepared for his body.

"Oh, my God," Amanda exclaimed, and whirled away from the table.

Mark hit the button to go to the next photo…and the next…and the next. *Prove it or disprove it.* The words rang in his head.

With fingers that trembled, Mark pulled out his cell phone and called Richard. "You need to get over to Amanda Burns's apartment. She has in her possession everything we need to nail Melinda Grayson and Ben Craig for the murders."

He disconnected the call and then turned to Amanda, who had huddled into a small ball in the corner of the sofa. "Stay here," he commanded. "An FBI agent will be here to collect the box and its contents. Tell him everything you told me."

"Where are you going?" she asked, her voice small and fearful.

"To the bonfire. I've got to find Dora before those two monsters make her their next victim." He left the apartment at a run, forgoing his car for the swiftness of his feet as he raced toward the campus.

Night had fallen and a raucous noise drifted on the air from the bonfire site. Laughter and screams and cheers mingled together to form the sound of a rioting, drunken crowd.

He checked his watch. It would soon be nine and the

fire would be lit, kicking off the homecoming festivities. The air smelled of popcorn, apples and madness.

Wild. The night was filled with wildness and it whipped through him as he ran, praying he wasn't already too late.

Chapter 17

Dora regained consciousness in agonizing increments of sensation. Her head ached with a nauseating intensity that kept her eyes closed for several long moments.

She became aware of an ache in her arms, an unnatural position of her legs and a general heaviness in her body. What had happened? What was wrong with her?

She tried to open her mouth, to ask for help, and it was only when she realized she couldn't open her mouth that full consciousness claimed her, along with a sense of panic that nearly stopped her heart.

Ben. She now remembered Ben coming to her door and the cloth that had been pressed against her nose and mouth and the plunge into darkness.

She needed to run. She had to escape, and yet she couldn't move. Her eyes finally flickered open and she couldn't make sense of anything.

Her brain felt wrapped in cotton, unclear and foggy.

It was an effort to keep her half-slitted eyes open. She remembered this horrible feeling from the days when she'd drunk herself into a stupor.

Was that what she had done? No, it had been Ben. He'd done something to her. He'd drugged her and slapped duct tape over her mouth so she couldn't scream for help.

She hovered above a crowd of people, her brain trying to make sense of things. Was this was it was like to die? Was she having an out-of-body experience and watching the people left behind as her soul ascended to heaven?

That didn't make sense. She was certain that when a soul left the world, it didn't go with duct tape across the mouth. Her head felt heavy and she suddenly realized there was something on it, a helmet.

She lowered her gaze and saw that she wore a blue football jersey and long blue pants. Who had dressed her like this? And why? She fought against the drowsiness that threatened to pull her into darkness.

As the layer of cotton that wrapped her brain parted a little bit, horror shot an arctic wind through her and she frantically tried to move. But Ben had done a good job. Her arms were outstretched to either side, tied in several places along the pole that made a cross, and whatever drug he'd given her made it difficult for her to even attempt to get free.

She was lashed to a tall pole by her arms, around her chest and waist, at her knees and feet. Below her the crowd awaited the traditional lighting of the bonfire. The noise was so loud that even if she could scream for help nobody would be able to discern her cry for help among the revelers.

She was in the center of the bonfire pit.

Oh, God, as all the pieces finally fell into place she screamed beneath the duct tape.

They were going to light the fire to burn the effigy of the opposing team player.

She was the effigy.

The crowd was huge. People jostled against Mark, drunken alumni and students falling into him, clapping him on the back in good-old-boy fashion as he tried to find Ben or Melinda in the throng of people.

Too many people, he thought frantically. He weaved his way around a table where several kegs of beer were set up to be sold by the glassful along with hot dogs and marshmallows.

The effigy was already in place above the crowd and it wouldn't be long before the fire would be set. So, where were Ben and Melinda? They had to be here someplace. And where on earth was Dora?

Mark wanted to weep in despair. He wanted to run to the bench where he'd first encountered Dora after class and sit there and wait for her to emerge from the building, safe and sound and so achingly beautiful to him.

He needed to have her in his arms right now, her heart beating against the frantic beat of his own. Melinda might have deemed her sister a failure, but Mark knew the strength that flowed through Dora's veins, the determination that would see her through the rest of her life. She wasn't a failure and he had to find her now.

In the distance he saw the flash of an FBI windbreaker and Joseph Garcia's dark hair. He worked his way toward the fellow agent and when he reached him he saw that Joseph's eyes were as dark as Mark felt his heart had become.

"No sighting of either suspect yet," Joseph said. "I've had a kid vomit on my feet, a hot dog shoved in my face and an inebriated woman flash her boobs at me, but I haven't been able to find anyone who knows where Ben or Melinda might be."

Mark knew the only way to find Dora was to find the two murderers. Otherwise, he had no idea where to search, where she might be stashed…or already buried.

"Some of the deputies checked out the area where the other three murder victims were found," Joseph continued, "and there were no signs that anything had been disturbed or a new grave had been added."

Mark found little relief in the information. "There's no way Ben and Melinda can know we're on to them. There's no way for them to know about the evidence found in the box at Amanda's apartment. So, they should be in business-as-usual mode."

Joseph frowned. "This isn't a night of business as usual for anyone."

The two men parted to continue the search. Despite the ever-growing throng of people and the increasing noise level, Mark could hear the stutter of his heartbeat inside his head.

We have to find her.

We have to find her.

It was a mantra that ticked to the beat of his heart.

Mark stepped beneath a tree to catch his breath, his gaze sweeping the people, seeking a sleek-haired, tall and beautiful woman. Melinda had to be here some-place. She would thrive on the chaos, the primal elements that whirled in the air.

He leaned back against the tree trunk and closed his eyes. The sound of the crowd faded as he went deep inside his head, as he attempted to access the minds of the killers.

He dismissed Ben, for he knew the grad student was nothing more than Melinda's inferior partner. Melinda would be the mastermind of everything. She was the Sociopath in Society.

She'd probably seduced the three dead men at some point in time and it had been easy for her to call them to the place where they met their death. She would revel in the power of the kill. She would find pleasure in knowing that she was smarter than everyone else, that she not only had managed to provide herself an alibi, but also had enjoyed labeling the men as a species substandard to herself.

Liar. Cheater. Thief. And failure.

The first three murders had been shocking. He frowned, trying to crawl deeper inside her mind. There was no way she'd go off someplace quietly to kill Dora. She would want shocking drama, horrifying theater, and tonight she had a huge audience to play to.

His eyes snapped open and he stared up and straight ahead to the effigy. Melinda would need more than what she'd gotten when she'd killed those men. Her thrill level would need to be raised. She would want... She would need to make a big statement with Dora's death.

Was it possible? From this distance the effigy looked

like what it was supposed to be, a straw-stuffed football player from the opposing team. But he was too far away to be sure.

With his heart renewing a beat of frantic fear, he started forward, needing to get closer to the fire pit, closer to the figure hanging on the cross like a witch ready to be burned at the stake.

Surely it wasn't possible. His brain attempted to deny the thought that tried to take hold. It would be the height of madness. It would be a horrific crime that would haunt the campus for decades to come. And Melinda would like that, a little voice whispered.

Moving quicker now, he shoved people aside, unmindful of anything but getting closer. The crowd was thicker the closer he got to the pit, and frustration gnawed him as he struggled to make forward progress.

He had to be wrong, he told himself as he advanced closer and closer. He finally reached the edge of the pit and peered up. It was virtually impossible to see what might be under the helmet from his vantage point.

He scanned the body, seeking some clue that the effigy might be something other than what it was supposed to be. Straw hung out of the end of the long-sleeved blue jersey that covered the torso and in the midst of the straw Mark spied the pale white skin of a hand…a human hand.

Dora! Her name screamed inside his head as he threw himself into the pit. At that moment Melinda and Ben appeared on the side, a lit torch held in Melinda's hand.

Everything happened simultaneously. Mark ran for the pole that held Dora, the crowd quieted and Ben lifted a megaphone to his mouth. "Let the fun begin," he shouted at the same time that Melinda touched the torch to the dry tinder at the base of the pit, and flames instantly licked upward, eager to devour whatever might be in their path.

The cheers turned to screams as people became aware of Mark in the center of the flames that were quickly building. Heat surrounded him along with the sting of smoke in his eyes.

The smoke rose like a killing column up the sides of the pole that held Dora. Mark gasped. He finally reached her feet and frantically tugged at the ropes that bound her. Too tight. The ropes were thick and tied in knot after knot. It would take him hours to unravel them to get her free and he didn't have hours. He had only minutes before the fire consumed them both.

"Mark! Hey, Mark?"

Mark tore his gaze from the rope to peer beyond the flames that inched steadily closer and higher. He saw Joseph standing at the very edge. Joseph held up an ax and as Mark watched he threw it into the pit near Mark's feet. Mark didn't stop to wonder who in the crowd might have provided the ax; he grabbed it and began to chop at the ropes that held Dora captive.

The fire burned the bottoms of his feet through the soles of his shoes as he choked and gasped in the smoke. When he had freed her feet he reached up to chop at the next rope.

He had no idea if she was dead or not. He only knew she did nothing to aid him. He was vaguely aware of people screaming, not in revelry but in horror.

He was never going to get her down in time. The

hungry flames now licked at the back of his legs, the intense heat searing through him. He paused long enough to reach down and slap his pants where flames had jumped to greedily consume the material.

Realizing he didn't have the time to chop at all the ropes that held her upright, knowing he couldn't reach her upper body without a ladder, he began to push on the pole, needing it to fall and praying that somehow, if she was still alive, the fall wouldn't kill her.

He didn't know if it was the smoke or the agony of his heart that shot tears streaming down his face; he only knew that he was the failure. He wasn't going to be able to save her from the flames.

And then Joseph was next to him, helping him push against the pole, and Lori stepped into the fray, manning a handheld fire extinguisher that cleared the area around the base of the pole.

Mark cried out with effort as he and Joseph shoved on the pole and felt it teetering, ready to fall. The crowd of people behind the pole began chanting and Mark realized they intended to break the fall, to catch Dora.

The tears that now raced down his face were a mixture of emotions. She wasn't going to be burned alive... but was she already dead? She hadn't given any indication of consciousness since he'd begun working to get her down.

As the pole fell backward, several men caught it and eased it to the ground. Mark and Joseph jumped out of the fire. He had no thoughts other than those for Dora. As he pulled the helmet off her head, Joseph worked the last of the ropes that held her to the pole.

"Please...please..." Mark repeated over and over

again, pulling the silver tape from her mouth and checking the pulse in her neck. He nearly sagged into a puddle as he felt the beat against his fingers. "She's alive," he yelled to nobody and everyone.

"An ambulance is on the way," Lori said as she squatted down next to Mark and Dora. Mark nodded absently, his focus solely on the woman he now held in his arms.

"You have to be okay," he whispered to her, unmindful of the people gathering around. "Dora, hang on. Help is coming." As if summoned by his words, the sound of a siren filled the air.

It was only when Dora was loaded into the back of an ambulance and driven away that the rage took hold of Mark. He looked around at the crowd, his heart beating the thunder of anger. The flames from the fire pit burned bright, torching red and yellow colors on the faces of the spectators.

What had happened to Ben and Melinda? He'd been so intent on making sure he got Dora down that he didn't know what the rest of the team and the local law enforcement had been doing in the meantime.

He spied Richard standing at the edge of the people and beside him was a handcuffed Melinda. He fisted his hands at his sides as he stalked toward the woman who had nearly taken away Dora's life.

"I thought you might like to have a word with her," Richard said as Mark approached.

"Where's Ben?"

"On his way to the sheriff's office in matching bracelets."

"It was Ben's fault," Melinda said, tears streaking

mascara down her cheeks. "He killed those men. He put Dora on the stake. I didn't know anything about it all. He's crazy."

Mark raised his hands and clapped them together three times. "Stunning performance, Melinda. You should have majored in drama," he said.

"You have to believe me. I had nothing to do with any of this," she exclaimed.

"I've got your tin box."

Her eyes narrowed and glinted with a hard stare that reminded him of his nightmares of her. "I don't know what you're talking about."

"The photos on the camera speak for themselves," Mark replied. "Maybe you can teach some classes from the prison cell where you'll spend the rest of your life." He looked at Richard. "I'm done with her," he said with obvious disgust. "She's a complete failure."

As he walked away he heard Melinda raging behind him, telling him that Dora was the failure and calling him a loser. The last thing he cared about was what a sociopathic killer thought of him and Dora.

All he wanted to do now was get to the hospital as quickly as possible and be there when Dora opened her eyes. He needed to assure himself that she was going to pull through and that the nightmare that had struck the small town of Vengeance, Texas, and her was finally over.

Dora awoke in a hospital bed alone in the room. The ache in her muscles competed with the pounding of her head. But she was safe. She was alive.

She turned her head slightly toward the window in

the room, noticing by the sun that it was apparently afternoon. She'd been unconscious for the entire night and most of the day.

Flashes of memories of the night before played in her mind, the heaviness of the helmet on her head, the horror of finding herself on a stake in the center of the fire pit. Flames licking closer and the smoke choking and Mark appearing like an avenging wraith in the dark, it was all like a dream.

But it hadn't been a dream. It had been a nightmare orchestrated by the sister she'd admired and her assistant. Melinda had not only taught courses about sociopaths, she was one.

Mark. Dora jerked up, a hand on the side of her pounding head as she searched for a button that would summon the nurse. Was Mark okay? He had been instrumental in saving her, but at what cost to himself? Was he here in this same hospital burned half to death by his heroic efforts?

Before she could find the button to summon a nurse, a tall older man walked into the room and introduced himself as Special Agent Richard Sinclair. Dora knew he was not only Mark's superior but also his friend.

"Mark?" she asked before he could say anything else. "Is he okay?"

"He's fine." Richard pulled up a chair next to her bed as she slumped back against the pillows. "He was here with you all night and I finally pulled him out of here and sent him back to Dallas to debrief and file his reports. I'm sure he'll be in touch with you when he finishes up there."

Dora nodded, although she had a feeling she wouldn't

be hearing from Mark again. He was back in his space now, the place where he belonged. She remembered that he'd planned time for his daughter the next day and by then he'd recognize that there was nothing for him here in Vengeance.

"If you're feeling up to it, I've got some follow-up questions to ask you about what happened to you last night," Richard said.

She nodded and for the next half hour she and Richard went over everything she could remember from the moment Ben had stepped into her house the day before until she'd opened her eyes just before Richard had arrived.

Their conversation was interrupted once by a doctor who stepped in to check on her and confirmed that she had been drugged with a heavy dose of tranquilizers administered through a needle. The doctor proclaimed her ready for release and Richard offered to take her home.

An hour later Dora sat in Richard's passenger seat as he drove her from the hospital to her house. Although the doctor had assured Dora that she'd slept off the effects of the drugs, a bone weariness made her want nothing more than to crawl into bed and sleep for hours…for days.

Her sister had tried to kill her and Mark was gone. She looked at Richard and still tried to make sense of everything that had happened. "Melinda killed those three men?"

Richard nodded. "Along with Ben's help."

"But why?" Somehow she needed to make sense of this.

Richard didn't reply until he'd parked at her curb. He shut off the engine and turned to look at her, a hint of compassion in his eyes. "I believe she orchestrated her own kidnapping and then the murders because she could and for little other reason. She got a kick out of watching all of us scramble around like headless ants, unable to figure out the pieces to put the puzzle together."

"How did Mark know I was in the fire pit? That I was going to be burned to death?"

A smile curved Richard's lips. "Because he's a special man and somehow he managed to get into Melinda's head and anticipate what her next move might be."

Dora shifted her gaze out the front window. "She and Ben left cards on the other victims. Was there a card for me?" She turned back to look at Richard, who frowned. "There was, wasn't there. What did it say?"

"Melinda had a card in her pocket that said 'failure.' We believe she intended to place it on you sometime after the fire went out and before anyone realized that the effigy was a murder victim."

Failure. She waited for the word to find purchase in her heart, for her to embrace what her sister had apparently believed about her. She waited for the fracture of self-confidence to occur, and when it didn't, she knew that she had truly moved away from her past.

"Thank you, Agent Sinclair," she said as she opened the passenger car door.

"Dora, you've been very brave through all of this. You should be proud of yourself," Richard said.

She got out of the car and leaned down to smile at him. "I am," she replied.

Richard had told her that her house had been locked up by officers who had been there to process the scene for evidence. She had been taken from the house without her purse or keys but had told Richard she had a key hidden outside that she could use to get back in.

As she approached her front door, she tried to blank her mind. Monday morning, life would return to whatever the new normal would be. All she had to do was get through the rest of today and tomorrow and then it would be back to business as usual.

While digging into the bottom of a planter on her porch for her spare key, she wondered who would be teaching Melinda's courses. Would they bring somebody in from another college to cover for the professor killer?

Her sister, the killer.

As she stepped into her house, the silence surrounded her, threatened to consume her. Her thoughts continued to play in her head.

Samuel and Melinda had obviously been cut from the same cloth, choosing to walk the path of monsters while Dora and Micah had made the decision to navigate through the murky waters of life with a conscience.

She thought about calling Micah to tell him everything that had happened, but instead she sank down on her sofa with memories of Mark filling her head. She hated that she hadn't had an opportunity to thank him for being smart enough, special enough to save her life. She hated that she hadn't had a chance to tell him goodbye.

He was a special man who deserved a special woman, and she wasn't that woman. Yes, he was back in Dallas where he belonged, hopefully being a father to his little girl, and where he would eventually find the woman who could keep the darkness away from him, who could be his safe place to fall.

Wearily she closed her eyes and fell asleep and dreamed of a life with Mark, and when she finally awoke it was with the trace of tears on her face.

Sunday might have been a long day if not for the surprising support that came from faculty and students for Dora. Her doorbell rang at a steady pace as people stopped by to bring her casseroles and flowers.

She hadn't realized how many lives she had touched working in the bookstore and attending classes; she hadn't realized how many friends she'd made on campus.

By the time five o'clock came she was tired, but it was an exhaustion brought on by pleasant conversation and interaction with sympathetic and supportive people.

Just after five her doorbell rang again and she looked out her window to see Amanda Burns standing on her porch. Dora opened the door and Amanda nearly fell into her arms, crying about how sorry she was for what Dora had suffered.

Dora led the weeping young woman to the sofa where they sat down side by side. "I'm sorry. I'm so sorry I didn't tell somebody my suspicions earlier," Amanda said as she grabbed hold of Dora's hands. "I should have told Mark everything I felt, everything I feared before he came to me last night and you were in trouble, but I was so afraid."

Dora squeezed her hands to comfort her. "It's okay, Amanda. I know what it's like to be afraid." She thought of those days when she'd believed she was being stalked, although Mark had assumed the stalker had been his. Dora realized now it had been Ben who had been watching her, checking her schedule and assessing when she would be vulnerable.

She released Amanda's hands and sat back against the cushion. "At least you gave Mark the information you did in time for him to help me."

"I just admire you so much," Amanda said, the words surprising Dora.

"Admire me? Why?"

"Because you're such a nice person and you're so smart. I admire that you're obviously here to better yourself, to better your life by getting a degree." Amanda frowned. "I thought I wanted to be just like Melinda, so powerful and so in control. But I'd much rather be like you."

A lump formed in Dora's throat. "You'll never know how much that means to me," she replied. "You know, I admired her, too. I wanted to be just like her…smart and cool and able to command respect from others. But we're okay, Amanda. You're a smart woman who has her whole future ahead of her and you don't have to look up to anyone. Just look inside."

As Dora spoke the words, she realized that she had reached a place of peace inside herself. She didn't have to prove a thing to anyone. She had become the woman she was meant to be…strong enough to survive a horrible attack by her sister, the loss of a man she loved, and smart enough to continue her path to her own great future.

Minutes after Amanda left, Dora had just made it back to the sofa when a knock fell on the door. She assumed Amanda had forgotten something. She pulled open the door and her breath caught in her chest.

There he stood, with that darned sexy smile curling his lips and a simmer of something magic in his eyes. "Mark," she said, half-breathless. "You were the last person I expected to see this evening."

"And why is that?" He swept past her, his clean male scent eddying in the air around her. She quickly closed the door and hurried after him.

He sat down on the sofa and stretched an arm across the back, looking as if he belonged there. "I just assumed your work was done here," she said, trying to halt the desperate stuttering of her heart.

"Dora, my work here is far from done," he replied, and patted the sofa next to him.

She didn't want to sit next to him. She didn't want to feel his warmth and smell his familiar scent and know that when he'd tied up all his loose ends he'd be gone. Yet, despite her reluctance, her feet moved her across the room and she sank down on the sofa next to him.

Instantly he leaned toward her and placed his hands on each of her cheeks. He held her gaze with the crazy intensity that made her feel like he was looking inside her very soul.

"Did you really believe I would just leave without seeing you again? Without assuring myself that you were really and truly okay? Did you really believe I would just go and not tell you goodbye?"

Before she realized what he intended, he took her lips with his and she could do nothing but respond to the kiss that fired a thousand emotions inside her.

When he'd finished kissing her soundly, he leaned back slightly, but still held his hands on the sides of her face. "Did you really believe I was just going to leave without a plan for our future together?"

"Future together?" Her heart began to beat like the wings of a hummingbird, fast and frantic to keep her hovering in the air.

He finally dropped his hands from her face and instead grabbed her hands with his, entwining their fingers as if to keep her captive. "You know we belong together, Dora. I love you and I can't imagine going forward with my life without you in it."

An automatic protest rose to Dora's lips and she started to voice it and then stopped. She saw the light shining from Mark's eyes, a light that didn't lie. He loved her and she deserved to be loved.

"I love you, Mark." She said the words tremulously. "But, I don't know how we go forward from here."

He stood and pulled her up and into an embrace. "One day at a time. You finish your schooling and I go back to work in Dallas. That's only a short drive away and every spare minute that we have we can spend together, building something amazing, something that will last forever."

She believed him. She knew that if they wanted it badly enough they could make it work, and she wanted it…him…badly. "When I graduate I could probably find a job in Dallas," she said as she gazed up into his beautiful eyes.

He tightened his arms around her. "I'm counting on it, and you can count on me, Dora. If you give me your heart, I vow that I will take good care of it."

"I never doubted it," she said just before he claimed her lips once again in a kiss that stole her breath and replaced it with hopes and dreams she'd never thought possible.

She knew that Mark would take good care of her heart, because he was a special man...and because she was his special woman.

Epilogue

Dora checked the Christmas tree lights to make sure every single one sparkled brightly and then raced into the kitchen to pull the gingerbread cookies out of the oven.

It was late Christmas day and she had special guests due any minute. Her heart sang with joy as she removed the cookies from the baking sheet and placed them on a red-and-green platter with racing reindeers around the rim.

The past two months had been beyond her wildest imaginings. She had her days in class and at the bookstore and her nights whenever possible with Mark. Their relationship had grown stronger with every day that passed.

She'd known love broken and abused; she'd known the despair of wasted time; and now she knew the beauty of healthy, nurturing love.

Mark's daughter, Grace, had been a charming addition to her life. She'd met the little girl at Thanksgiving and it had been an instant mutual love. She'd also met Mark's ex-wife, Sarah, for coffee one afternoon. She'd found Sarah a warm woman who only wanted happiness for Mark. Dora suspected Sarah had wanted to check her out, knowing that it was possible Dora would be a part of Grace's life.

Melinda and Ben were in jail awaiting their trials for multiple crimes including the murder of the three men. Life in Vengeance had returned to normal, with students scurrying from class to class, and most days nobody even mentioned the horror of the homecoming bonfire. Melinda would hate that with each day that passed people were forgetting all about her.

The knock on the door sent Dora's heart racing with happiness. She opened the door and Grace marched in first, her cheeks pink and her smile bright. She held a bright red-wrapped package in her arms and paused to give Dora a kiss before she ran over and placed it beneath the tree.

"Do you like pretty pink scarves?" Grace asked as her father entered through the front door.

As always, Dora's heart leaped at the sight of him. "I love scarves," Dora said with a laugh to Grace. She smiled at Mark, who kissed her on the cheek. "And do you like gingerbread cookies? Because I just made some especially for you," she said to Grace.

Grace threw her arms around Dora's legs and smiled up at her. "I love gingerbread cookies!" she exclaimed.

"Then shall we go have some cookies and milk before we open presents?" Dora suggested.

"Sounds like a plan to me," Mark replied as he grabbed Grace and tossed her up on his back piggy fashion to head to the kitchen.

As they ate the still-warm cookies, Grace told Dora everything that Santa had brought her that morning and Mark alternated adoring looks from his child to Dora.

Dora wanted to capture this moment of father and daughter and Christmas cookies and milk mustaches and burn it into her heart forever.

Once they were finished with their treat, they moved back into the living room for the exchange of gifts. "Daddy bought you a ring," Grace said as she settled into a sitting position at the foot of the tree.

"Grace!" Mark gave his daughter a mock stern look. "That was supposed to be our secret."

"I wanted to share our secret with Dora because I love her," Grace replied.

Dora's heart pumped wildly. A ring? She looked at Mark. Mark smiled, the slow, sexy grin that had been Dora's undoing since the moment she'd met him.

"I love her, too, Grace." He never took his eyes off Dora as he pulled a velvet ring box from his pocket.

"I get to be the flower girl," Grace said.

"The flower girl?" Dora continued to look at Mark as he opened the jewelry box to display a princess-cut diamond engagement ring.

"Will you marry me, Dora?" Mark asked.

"Will you marry us," Grace corrected her daddy.

"After you graduate in May. That will give us five months to plan the kind of wedding you want and to find a place for us all to live in Dallas. Marry me, Dora, and make me the happiest man on earth."

"Yes, oh, yes," she said, and held her breath as Mark removed the ring from the case and slid it on her finger. The gold was warm and welcoming, as was Mark's smile as he leaned in to kiss her gently.

"Okay," Grace said impatiently. "It's time to open the presents."

Dora laughed as Mark stepped away from her and they all settled on the floor in front of the sparkling tree. She'd already received her present. The day Mark had entered her life he'd been the gift she'd dreamed about, the wonderful present she hadn't thought possible.

Her future with him was as bright as the lights on the tree, as sweet as the scent of gingerbread that hung in the air and as exciting as Grace's laughter when Dora handed her a present to open.

It had all come together for the little girl from Horn's Gulf. She'd found a man who didn't care where she'd come from, a man who only cared that at the end of the days, at the end of their lives, she was with him.

That was more than enough.

"Samuel." Melinda spoke into the phone.

"Ah, Melinda, I was wondering if I'd ever hear from you again." Samuel's smooth voice slid over the phone line. "Sounds like you got yourself in a little trouble in Vengeance."

"I beat you at your game, Samuel. You created a cult, but what I managed to accomplish will go down in the true-crime record books as something amazing."

Samuel laughed. "And yet there you sit in a jail cell

awaiting trial. I'd say you didn't do anything so amazing."

Melinda tamped down the irritation to reach through the phone and stab Samuel's eyes out. How dare he diminish what she'd pulled off. "Maybe I'm not finished yet," she said in a voice low enough that the guard on the other side of the room couldn't hear her.

"What are you talking about?" Samuel asked with obvious interest in his voice.

Melinda cast a glance at the big, buff guard and gave him a bright, beautiful smile. His cheeks reddened and he fidgeted from one foot to the other as he returned the smile. He was besotted with her. In another week or two she'd own him, heart and soul, and with his help her plans would be achieved.

"Have you ever been to Lucerne, Switzerland, Samuel?" She didn't wait for his reply but continued. "They have a charming little hotel there called the Jailhotel."

"First one there buys the champagne?" Samuel suggested, his voice filled with the thrill of the challenge.

"I'll have it on ice when you arrive," she said, and then disconnected the call, a smile curving her lips as she contemplated her future.

* * * * *

REQUEST YOUR FREE BOOKS!
2 FREE NOVELS PLUS 2 FREE GIFTS!

ROMANTIC suspense

Sparked by danger, fueled by passion

YES! Please send me 2 FREE Harlequin® Romantic Suspense novels and my 2 FREE gifts (gifts are worth about $10). After receiving them, if I don't wish to receive any more books, I can return the shipping statement marked "cancel." If I don't cancel, I will receive 4 brand-new novels every month and be billed just $4.49 per book in the U.S. or $5.24 per book in Canada. That's a savings of at least 14% off the cover price! It's quite a bargain! Shipping and handling is just 50¢ per book in the U.S. and 75¢ per book in Canada.* I understand that accepting the 2 free books and gifts places me under no obligation to buy anything. I can always return a shipment and cancel at any time. Even if I never buy another book, the two free books and gifts are mine to keep forever.

240/340 HDN FVS7

Name	(PLEASE PRINT)

Address	Apt. #

City	State/Prov.	Zip/Postal Code

Signature (if under 18, a parent or guardian must sign)

Mail to the **Harlequin® Reader Service:**
IN U.S.A.: P.O. Box 1867, Buffalo, NY 14240-1867
IN CANADA: P.O. Box 609, Fort Erie, Ontario L2A 5X3

Want to try two free books from another line?
Call 1-800-873-8635 or visit www.ReaderService.com.

---

* Terms and prices subject to change without notice. Prices do not include applicable taxes. Sales tax applicable in N.Y. Canadian residents will be charged applicable taxes. Offer not valid in Quebec. This offer is limited to one order per household. Not valid for current subscribers to Harlequin Romantic Suspense books. All orders subject to credit approval. Credit or debit balances in a customer's account(s) may be offset by any other outstanding balance owed by or to the customer. Please allow 4 to 6 weeks for delivery. Offer available while quantities last.

Your Privacy—The Harlequin® Reader Service is committed to protecting your privacy. Our Privacy Policy is available online at www.ReaderService.com or upon request from the Harlequin Reader Service.

We make a portion of our mailing list available to reputable third parties that offer products we believe may interest you. If you prefer that we not exchange your name with third parties, or if you wish to clarify or modify your communication preferences, please visit us at www.ReaderService.com/consumerchoice or write to us at Harlequin Reader Service Preference Service, P.O. Box 9062, Buffalo, NY 14269. Include your complete name and address.

Angry faces and moving bodies whizzed above her. Rebecca
braced both palms on the hot pavement and tried to stand
up, only to fall backward when someone bumped into her.
Someone else stepped on her foot, bringing a jolt of pain. Uh-
oh. This was bad. Her eyes couldn't seem to focus and shapes
were beginning to look blurry.

The fear finally hit her, clogging her throat and making her
heart pound.

She was going to get crushed in a stampede.

With a burst of adrenaline, she made another attempt to hurl
herself to her feet—and this time it worked. She was off the
ground and hovering over the crowd—wait, hovering *over* it?

Blinking a few times, Rebecca realized she *felt* as if she was
floating because she *was* floating. She was tucked tightly in a
man's arms, a man who'd taken it upon himself to carry her
away to safety, Kevin Costner style.

"Who are you?" she murmured, but the inquiry got lost in

e rioters' shouts and the rapid popping noises of the rubber
lllets being fired into the crowd.

She became aware of the most intoxicating scent, and she
haled deeply, filling her lungs with that spicy aroma. It was
m, she realized. God, he smelled good.

She glanced up to study the face of her rescuer, catching
impses of a strong, clean-shaven jaw. Sensual lips. A straight
ose. She wanted to see his eyes, but the angle was all wrong, so
e focused on his incredible chest instead. Jeez, the guy must
ork out. His torso was hard as a rock, rippled with muscles
at flexed at each purposeful step he took. And he was *tall*. At
ast six-one, and she felt downright tiny in his arms.

"You okay?"

The concerned male voice broke through her thoughts. She
oked up at her rescuer, finally getting a good look at those
usive eyes.

Boy, were they worth the wait. At first glance they were
own—until you looked closer and realized they were the
lor of warm honey with flecks of amber around the pupils.
nd they were so magnetic she felt hypnotized as she gazed
to them.

"Ms. Parker?"

She blinked, forcing herself back to reality. "Oh. I'm fine,"
e answered. "A little bruised, but I'll live. And you can call
e Rebecca. I think it's only fitting I be on a first-name basis
ith the man who saved my life."

His lips curved. "If you say so."

**Don't miss SPECIAL OPS EXCLUSIVE
by Elle Kennedy, available May 2013 from
Harlequin Romantic Suspense
wherever books are sold.**

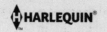

ROMANTIC suspense

CAVANAUGH ON DUTY

by *USA TODAY* bestselling author
Marie Ferrarella

Will the quest for justice lead to
unbridled passion?

When Esteban Fernandez suddenly found
himself pulled out of his undercover work and
partnered with unrequited love Kari Cavelli, he
thought his life was over. Little did he realize
that it was just the beginning.

Look for *CAVANAUGH ON DUTY*
by Marie Ferrarella next month from
Harlequin Romantic Suspense.

Available wherever books are sold.

Heart-racing romance, high-stakes suspense!

www.Harlequin.com

HRS278

HARLEQUIN®

ROMANTIC suspense

THE MILLIONAIRE COWBOY'S SECRET
by Karen Whiddon

Can a career-focused ATF agent and a bitter
cowboy set on vengeance find meaningful
ground in which they can lay to rest the ghosts
of their pasts? Skyler and Matt's combustible
chemistry makes for one tumultuous adventure.

Look for *THE MILLIONAIRE COWBOY'S SECRET*
by Karen Whiddon next month.

Available wherever books are sold.

Heart-racing romance, high-stakes suspense!

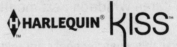